George Herman

TEARS OF THE

The Second Adventure of Leonardo da Vinci and Niccolo de Pavia

A Missing Necklace
A decadent court in Renaissance Italy
A reluctant detective

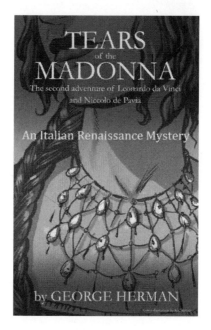

By
George Herman

DEDICATION

FOR ERIK

Striving artist, compassionate clown,
Dreamer and second son
whose gift of laughter
lightened my days.

REAL HISTORICAL FIGURES

(AS THEY APPEAR IN THE STORY)

Louis Valois, King of France

Cesare Borgia, Son of Pope Alexander VI

Isabella D'Este, wife of Gian'Francesco Gonzaga

Gian-Francesco Gonzaga, Captain General of the Venetian armies.

Cardinal Ippolito d"Este, Isabella's Brother

Cardinal d'Amboise

Cardinal Guiliano della Rovere, sworn enemy of Pope Alexander VI

Cardinal Albizzi, the "Griffin", assassin in "A Comedy of Murders"

Cecilia Gallerani, married to Count Bergamini

Guglielmo Gaetani

Ser Ottaviano Cristani,

Ser Johannes Vendramm,

Madonna Maddalena d'Oggiono,

Andrea Meneghina, Chamberlain to Isabella

Ser Agnolo Marinoni, Venetian banker,

Lucrezia Borgia, Daughter of Pope Alexander VI and sister to Cesare.

Madonna Laura Gonzaga, Spy for Lucrezia Borgia

3

Don Ramiro de Lorca, Cesare Borgia's
  majordomo
Niccolo Machiavelli, Florentine Emissary
Contessa Caterina Sforza
Elizabetta da Gonzaga
I Comici Buffoni, commedia dell'Arte troupe
  invited to the Mantuan Court.

Mantua dwarfs, Nanino and Lizette

Assistants to Leonardo, Giovanni Francisco
  Melzi and Giacomo Salai

Leonardo da Vinci,
as himself
Niccolo da Pavia,
Leonardo's confidant and friend

TEARS OF THE MADONNA

CHAPTERS

CHAPTER ONE

THE INCIDENT

Y*es.*

This is the man sent to kill me.

Cecco Pratolino was certain of this.

It was logical and inevitable, considering what he was transporting for the Cambio, but he was an experienced courier, and the realization did not especially alarm him. His horse had been bred for both speed and stamina, and upon leaving Mantua a day earlier, he felt reasonably confident he could put enough distance between himself and any pursuer. There had been similar instances and threats over his five years as courier for the bankers' guild, and he had always delivered his pouches and packets on schedule and without harm to either the materials or himself. These past successes and his calm deliberations and cunning were why he had been chosen for this delicate assignment.

The mission, as always, was conducted in the strictest secrecy. Gossip of false departures and several routes were circulated in advance. He traveled without armed escorts, because they would only draw attention. His specific route had been laid out in the smallest detail, sometimes incorporating a re-tracing of steps and maneuvering in a direction completely opposite to his final destination.

Like all couriers of the guild, he was never publicly

identified by name or family, thus preventing blackmail or reprisals, and he dressed simply, without ornamentation or *impresa,* to give the impression he could be nothing more than a traveler on a pilgrimage or perhaps a clerk carrying nothing more than tedious contracts between merchants and banks in Lombardy and the Dolomites.

He had no reason to suspect this assignment would be more perilous than any other despite the value of what the box contained.

He was confident upon departure all the planning and deceptions should bear fruit. Although winter threatened, there was still an autumnal warmth, and the roads proved clear.

Then, where the road forks above Legnano, where the towering trees created a quilt of alternating pools of dark shade and sudden sunlight, he became aware of the soft footfall of a horse behind him.

He then decided to break his journey at the Olive Tree tavern just outside Montagnana.

The Olive Tree was an unattractive inn in need of fresh paint, new lumber and clean air. It was small, untidy, usually quiet. He had frequented it before when necessary, and now it would provide him an opportunity for rest and - perhaps - enable him to formulate a plan to save both himself and the small black box inside his saddle bags.

He was, as usual, welcomed by the fat proprietor, Signore Pepoli, who always reeked of smoke and sweat and whose apron consistently was spattered with wine and grease.

He quickly and deliberately scanned the uncrowded

common room.

At a table near the entrance two friars in the dark brown robes of the Franciscans sat eating in silence and with appropriate detachment from everyone else. Three middle-aged men, presumably bargemen who were possibly operating ferries or hauling cargo on the Adige, were angrily attempting to divide the day's profits over large tankards of ale. A drunk farmer and an equally-intoxicated woman were bent over their table which was awash with spilled liquid and a few scraps of boiled mutton. He strode over the straw-littered floor, his saddle-bags slung over a shoulder, and eased himself onto a wooden stool. He gave an order for soup, black bread and mulled wine, knowing these were likely to be the most digestible and the least likely to prove sickening.

He was barely settled when a specter momentarily filled the doorway.

Wrapped head-to-toe in a black and hooded cloak the new arrival slowly but methodically surveyed everyone in the common room as Cecco had done. When he glimpsed the courier, there was a cold smile of recognition, but the veteran messenger could not remember ever meeting the man, and averted his eyes.

Cecco judged the new-comer to be in his mid-forties with the affectation of a single curl of his dark hair molded against his forehead. He wore a short, neatly-trimmed beard and mustache modeled after the current style favored by the nobility. There was a small scar above his nose which appeared now inflamed by the firelight. Thick brows shadowed his eyes. A soft cap with a single pheasant feather anchored on it drooped to one side of his head. He wore no spurs, and he moved fluidly despite his heavy, knee-high boots.

He crossed to a bench near the fire. When he raised his hands to undo the clasp of his cloak, the courier noticed a wide golden ring on the middle finger of the man's right hand, capped by a large emerald. Cecco had seen such rings before. He knew from experience the jewel concealed a hollow receptacle filled with a white and poisonous powder.

When the newcomer removed his cloak, Cecco could see he wore a burgundy velvet tunic and the striped hose of an aristocrat. His rigid posture suggested he was accustomed to authority and appropriate service and was fully aware of everything and everyone around him. A thick leather belt at his waist supported his sword. A dagger sheathed in a plain, black scabbard was evident in the small of his back and angled to the man's left.

A *main gauche.*

Cecco decided the man was right handed, and probably adept at fighting with both weapons simultaneously, the sword in the right hand and the dagger in his left. It was a style practiced by the Venetians, and the courier was well aware the Janus – the school and training ground for assassins – was in Venice.

Still, the courier reasoned, *swords and daggers are also common necessities for travelers on the Lombardy plains and not necessarily an indication of the man's profession.*

The possible assassin seemed to concentrate on the warmth of the fire, and Cecco's attention was drawn to a medallion suspended from the newcomer's shoulders by a chain of woven gold. He could not discern any heraldic crest or *impresa*, no badge of familial or political loyalty.

The man ordered, and the proprietor bowed with half-hearted courtesy as he backed away and slipped through the curtains into the scullery. He reappeared shortly with something which might pass for a *tournedo*, a small mound of undercooked veal and kidneys, and a tankard of lukewarm Muscadine.

This man has never eaten here before, Cecco thought. *This is unfamiliar territory for him, but without question, he is the one sent to kill me and take the black box.*

He pondered his options.

He glanced through the small window at the mist beginning to rise from the Adige river far below. It would be a moonless night, clouded, and the attack - when it came - would be quick and on some secluded section of the roadway, probably bordered by thick woods which sliced through the mountains. Although trained in combat, he knew to turn and fight the professional on a shadowy road could prove disastrous.

He was not afraid but cautious.

He puzzled over the identity of this new challenger. He had to assume the man by the fire – despite all precautions - knew his destination, the route he would probably take and what he carried.

Someone from Ferrara possibly blood kin to the rival family, or from Imola, considering the part that particular city played in the history of what he was transporting. Perhaps someone from one of the courts still in sympathy with the now-deposed Duke of Milan, Ludovico Sforza. The possible assassin could even be in service to the Vatican, to the Borgian pope who dipped his white-gloved fingers in many pies.

The list was endless.

The record of what rested in the velvet packet was so entangled with a history of intrigue, wealth, politics, assassination and the pursuit of power, it made further speculation useless.

He briefly considered leaving immediately and racing his opponent to Padua, three hours away, where he could be provided with a fresh horse and perhaps arrange for an armed escort to accompany him further. Word of his departure from Padua would surely precede him, and the Cambio would likely have their own mercenaries watching and waiting to see him and his burden safely into Venice.

No.

He certainly could not leave the inn without the man noticing or being immediately told of his departure by the proprietor. His opponent's horse may be equally well-trained and fast.

No.

His best chance was to stay at the inn overnight and attempt to sneak away before the assassin could be aware of his flight.

He knew the proprietor of the Olive Tree. He knew the man and his family huddled together in the lofts over the stables, so there was only one room at the top of the stairs to accommodate overnight guests. The assassin - should he also decide to stay - would have to sleep on the hard, short bench by the fire.

Cecco reasoned he would wait until the man was asleep, and depart through the window of his room, make it to the barn unseen, saddle his horse by lantern light, cut the cinches on the assassin's saddle and be away.

But the enemy might not choose to stay.

He might decide to ride on a little farther, perhaps to where the road forks toward Terme, and where there was a larger and more popular inn. The late autumn nights were not yet cold, and although the sky was clouding there was no indication of rain or snow. The killer could be there in three-quarters of an hour, just as the dark descended completely. There he could rest his horse, eat a good meal and prepare an ambush on the road to Padua.

Cecco loudly summoned the proprietor by name so the assassin would know he was familiar with this inn and perhaps with some or all of the guests.

"I will stay the night, Signore Pepoli," he announced. "Please see to it my horse is fed, brushed and provided with water and oats. I want us both rested before we resume our travels at mid-day tomorrow."

He knew the assassin would consider this a ruse.

Still it might raise questions about his real plans, and anything contributing to the killer's confusion had merit.

He rose and casually dropped four *soldi tornesi* on the table. They were coins of base copper and a little silver, but other currencies Cecco carried with him would only arouse suspicion. The amount represented twice the normal payment for the meal, and it was enough to cause the corpulent Signore Pepoli to smile broadly through his blackened and broken teeth. The proprietor bobbed his head in appreciation, seized a fat candle and led the young man toward the staircase and then to the second floor landing and the only available room.

The man by the fire gave no sign of recognition or interest as Cecco passed by him on his way to the staircase. The possible assassin continued to stare into the fire, but his right hand remained rested on the hilt of his sword. The other hand was occupied by the tankard of wine.

The few other occupants of the inn paid no attention to the courier or the proprietor as they brushed by them and mounted the stairs.

The room, which the proprietor described as "clean and comfortable", was dirty, drafty, narrow and tucked directly beneath the roof. There was a wash basin and a cracked pitcher of milky water resting on an unstable three-legged wooden stand by the solitary window which was paned with waxed paper. A table near the door supported a single lantern which the proprietor lit with the candle. He smiled as though he was proud of the accommodations, and Cecco quietly gave thanks he would not be required to inhabit the dung heap for very long.

Pepoli closed the panel of the lantern and bobbed with satisfaction at the additional coins Cecco deposited in his out-stretched hand and quickly left before the new tenant realized the extent of his generosity.

The courier immediately barred the door with a

heavy section of wood which apparently had been placed there precisely for that purpose. He threw his saddlebags on the bed which, to his surprise, was more than the expected pallet, but covered with a single, thread-bare woolen blanket and dingy and stained sheets. He noticed the floor was burdened with a light, frayed and ugly carpet – still an unusual luxury in such an inn.

He was weary and felt the need of sleep, but he knew he should not and probably could not. He had to think, to devise a plan, and he confessed to himself it was just such challenges as this one which made his work interesting. He planned to take the coiled rope always carried in one of his saddlebags, tie it to the bed leg, climb from the window, and slip away in the middle of the night.

He opened the window now and threw back the shutters to satisfy himself he could fit through the small opening,

Then he saw him!

The possible assassin, again mantled in his heavy black cloak, was striding toward the stables!

So!

Cecco decided with some relief, the would-be killer had decided to ride on to the more comfortable inn at the crossroads, spend the night in warmth and then prepare an ambush, just as the courier had anticipated!

A confrontation had been delayed!

This was the best Cecco could hope for at this point.

Now he could wait awhile, calmly walk to the stables, saddle his horse and head in the opposite direction. He could circle above this road and take a different route to Padua. It would mean a delay of several hours, but time was not a necessity in this assignment, and it was better than the alternative.

He sat on the edge of the bed which shuddered and groaned at the unexpected weight. He unlaced his blouse and opened his saddle bag to assure himself the velvet box was still intact. Then he wrapped the rough woolen blanket around himself and waited.

He sat huddled under the warming wool for some time, trying desperately not to sleep. He was not aware how much time had passed since the cloaked man rode away, but it did not seem very long.

Suddenly there was heavy thudding against the door of the inn and a rising cacophony of several voices shouting at one another!

The courier quickly slipped the saddlebags under the bed and blew out the flame from the lantern. In the dark he made his way across the carpeted floor to the solitary window. He did not open it immediately, but attempted to peer through the waxed panes. All he could discern were a number of lights moving rapidly through the deep darkness like fireflies. Frustrated, he cautiously and slowly opened the window and pushed back the shutters enough to see five or six horses being led into the stables by armed and armored men! The man in the dark cloak was arguing loudly and vehemently with a man in a military uniform. There were no *impresa* visible, but the courier recognized the green-and-gold of the Gonzaga garrison. The two brown-robed Franciscans who had apparently decided to spend the night and were granted permission to sleep among the horses were now being evicted at swords' point and forced along the road to Padua!

He immediately realized the cloaked assassin had *not* ridden on to the crossroads as he assumed! Apparently he had been summoned from somewhere and now returned with a small detachment of mercenaries to take what he was sent for!

This was unpredictable.

It was not the way a professional assassin would work, which surprised and puzzled the young courier.

Where had this detachment been waiting?

Who provided them?

Matters like this were customarily settled quickly and quietly, without witnesses, and usually made to look like an accident or a misjudgment or a sudden lack of attention on the part of the victim. This barbaric invasion was crude and - he thought - stupid.

It appeared now to be a matter of time. The assassin's need for whatever Cecco carried was apparently urgent. For some reason all the customary stealth and cunning of a trained assassin was being abandoned. What needed to be done must be done quickly and to hell with the ritualistic charades of sudden and silent murder!

This would be fast and inevitable!

He *would* be killed!

But he had his duty as a trusted and responsible courier for the bankers, and he calmly determined the killer and his mercenaries must still be deprived of their prize. He slipped on his boots and tunic, seized the saddlebags from the bed and glanced round the room.

Bed.
Floor.
Walls,
Roof.
Rafters.
Washstand.
Too late!

$$*$$

Downstairs in the common room, Signore Pepoli hurriedly shuffled in his bare feet to the barred door. The loud and persistent pounding had an urgency to it. Still, although he was only in nightdress and cap, he paused long enough to light a lantern.

"No room!" he called. "I have no rooms, signori, and the cooking fires are banked."

"Open the door immediately!"

The imperial command had the ring of authority and was followed at once by a resumption of the heavy pounding.

A cold hand gripped the heart of the fat proprietor. He quickly placed the lantern on a table and hastened to remove the stout timber which barred the door.

"Hurry!" The same voice thundered.

Pepoli no sooner removed the barrier before the door when it was flung open and the invaders poured into the inn, swords drawn and carrying torches. The man in the black cloak shoved the proprietor aside and studied the darkened interior.

No other patrons.

No witnesses.

That much - at least - was good.

The six mercenaries in the green-and-gold livery shoved past both men and began to probe the shadowed corners.

"I – I have no room available, signori! No food! No wine! No - !"

Another light illuminated portions of the common room as a heavy woman with a blanket thrown over her nightdress appeared with a second lantern. Behind her was a pretty, dark-haired and obviously frightened young girl. Wrapped in a blanket and wearing only a nightdress, she clutched her mother's arm and peered wide-eyed over her shoulder.

"If you want to see the dawn," the man in the cloak growled, "go back to bed!"

Signore Pepoli quickly crossed to the two women and herded them gently but firmly back into the scullery.

"It's alright," he said softly. "Just do as the gentleman says, please. Please."

One of the mercenaries forced the women out of the common room and drew the curtain which separated the two areas. Signore Pepoli fell back onto a bench as another mercenary seated himself facing him.

"Be silent," the mercenary whispered, "and you won't be harmed. My Captain knows his business."

The man in the dark cloak turned abruptly, went directly to the staircase and ascended it, two steps at a time. He was instantly followed by some of the intruders, and the proprietor could hear them kicking at the door to the only bed chamber. He heard the pounding and the pecking at the wood with swords continue until the leather hinges apparently broke away and the entire door collapsed with a thunderous roar.

There was a cacophony of breaking wood and glass, followed soon by a silence more frightening than the bedlam. Then a wild scream startled Pepoli who sat wringing his pudgy and trembling hands and moaning softly to himself.

The curtains to the proprietor's living quarters rustled, but one of the mercenaries commanded, "Go back to bed, ladies. This doesn't concern you."

Then the black-cloaked man stepped across the threshold of the ruined door, a bloodied blade in his gloved right hand, and the courier's saddlebags in his left. He immediately slid his sword back in the scabbard and quickly descended the staircase, followed almost at once by two mercenaries struggling under the weight of something wrapped in the stained rug.

The cloaked man went directly to the proprietor. "Nothing happened here tonight," the man calmly whispered to Pepoli. "Nothing. You understand? The gentleman who occupied the room upstairs stayed the night, drank too much, destroyed the room and departed at dawn. A few things were damaged by his carelessness, but this should more than compensate for them. You understand?"

He slammed something on the table before the proprietor.

It was a gold florin!

Gold!

Now the cloaked man stood erect, his voice louder

and even more demanding. "Speak of what happened here tonight to anyone – anyone - and I will return. I will make you watch as my men enjoy your wife and daughter and then cut all of you into little strips. Try to run away and I will find you."

He suddenly dropped the saddlebags, removed the glove from his left arm to reveal a tattoo between the thumb and the first finger.

"Do you see this?"

Pepoli drew closer and managed to focus on the mark: two faces looking in different directions and divided by a dagger shaped roughly like a cross.

"Yes," he managed to murmur.

"You know what it means?"

The proprietor's mouth was dry, and he could not voice the words, so he quickly nodded.

"Then you know I will keep my promises."

The assassin replaced the glove and shifted the saddlebags. He turned, strode across the room and out the door.

The mercenaries followed quickly.

Pepoli waited until he heard the drumming of the horses' hooves on the pressed earth grow softer and away. He struggled to his feet as his wife and daughter rushed back through the curtains and into his arms. He showed his wife the gold florin and pressed it into her hand. He turned and looked up at the ruined door, slowly ascended the staircase and worked his way past the shattered wood and entered the chamber.

It was destroyed.

The crimsoned mattress laid mutilated, bent against a wall as if for support. The sheets were shredded and goose feathers of the two pillows were a light snowfall over everything. The pitcher and the washbasin were shattered and the pieces scattered. Everywhere there was the stench of blood and urine.

The carpet was gone.

"Sweet mother," he muttered to himself. "Why would any man do this?"

*

It was not professional!

It was not the way I was trained!
It was not the way I planned it!
The way we agreed!

The assassin knew it was the obnoxious Toad who had changed things! Toad must have convinced the patron he could not do it alone. A captain and mercenaries had to be sent to "assist" him!

Assist?!

The assassin raced his gray stallion along the Corso del Popolo and continued to silently curse the interference which had made him resort to such barbarism. It was bad enough he was not trusted to do the job alone, but then the damned courier lived up to his reputation, and he was forced to kill the man!

Now he had left the mercenaries far behind as if to rid himself even momentarily of the memory of the "incident."

What was his patron thinking?
How could the family have so little trust in him?

He seemed to notice for the first time the flanks and chest of his horse were flecked with white, and his long

21

black cloak was now peppered with the threat of an early snowfall.

He raced across the narrow bridge over the Bacchiglione, slowed and nodded to the two passing Dominican monks and reined in his weary horse before the Capella Scrovegni. He loosely fastened the reins to the iron ring embedded in the wall which enabled the stallion to bend his head and drink from the trough. He patted the broad neck, took the saddlebags over one arm and entered the vestibule. He stomped his boots on the stone steps to dislodge some of the mud and dead leaves.

This caused an old woman praying in the back pew to turn and glare at him.

He smiled at her, put a finger to his lips to remind her she was in the house of God. He crossed to the silver metallic framework where tiers of candles burned before the Giotto fresco of Mary holding the Christ Child. With a sweep of his gloved hand he brushed aside some of the sand and burned tapers in the bottom tray of the candle-holder and extracted a small, folded piece of parchment. He read it and whispered still another curse.

A sudden change in meeting places!

Damn Toad!

Damn him to fourteen kinds of hell!

This is unforgivable, he ranted silently to himself: *I am not some servant to be ordered from place to place by a piece of shit like Toad!*

He angrily dipped the parchment in some of the hot wax of a candle and watched as it burst into flame. He dropped the burning document into the tray, brushed some of the sand to hide what little remained, wheeled and stormed from the chapel.

Once outside he stopped momentarily and thought: *Well, we'll teach them!*

He reached into the saddlebag, extracted the pouch which jingled and tucked it his tunic. He again draped the saddlebags over the saddle, silently apologized to the horse for having raced him away from the mercenaries, unfastened the reins, mounted and urged the still-weary animal to walk.

They went through the gardens which, he knew, once served the Romans as an arena. They turned down a narrow side street which took them past the university and into the marketplace before the Palazzo della Ragione. He continued to fan his rage as he went past the merchants and farmers hawking their vegetables, some late fruit, cheeses, milk and crusty bread. He ignored the butchers urging him to buy their slaughtered pigs and chickens, partridges, grouse and fat sausages, but the sight made him realize he had not eaten since the garbage served him at the Olive Tree, and now he was hungry.

He crossed the Piazza dei Signori, permitting his horse to work his own way past the wooden scaffolding, the sheets of lead roofing material, the baskets and barrows of mortar. He ignored the warning cries and curses of the sawyers and joiners as he passed their way, and he silently rained damnation on the construction guilds who had enough power to punish him for disturbing their craftsmens' work.

Finally he stopped before the Basilica of Sant'Antonio with its Byzantine domes and tall towers suggesting the minarets of mosques.

Blasphemous!

He again tied the horse to the hitching ring, gently patted the animal as if to promise some rest, lifted the saddlebags and entered.

Just inside the great doors, a junior officer in the now-familiar green-and-gold livery waited. "I apologize for all this," he replied quietly. "Toad insisted no one was to be trusted, so Captain d'Angeness – and our men - were ordered to – well – to help you."

"You mean to make certain I did what I was assigned to do by myself!"

"I am sorry," he repeated," Toad had the meeting place changed because he said the plans may have been compromised. I'm – I'm sorry."

"It's not your fault. Where is the little son-of-a-bitch?"

"The third confessional. I know all this is absurd and unprofessional, but what can I do? What can any of us do when Toad is given the authority? You know what would happen if we refused."

The assassin nodded, sighed, stalked down the dark interior to the third confessional, entered and knelt down.

Almost at once, the small wooden portal behind the screen slid open and a high-pitched voice croaked, "Well? Is it done, blockhead?!"

The assassin fought against the urge to push his fist through the screen and strangle the creature on the other side. He wanted to slice off his nose, his ears, his genitals – presuming he had any - but he knew if he so much as shook the man, his own life would be forfeit;

24

so he simply murmured, "It's done."

"You have it?"

"No."

The voice became shrill. *"No?!"*

"He wasn't carrying it."

"Imbecile! He hid it somewhere!"

"He didn't have it! I suspect he was sent as a decoy, and another courier carried it."

"You should have searched the room!"

"We did. Your men tore it apart! It wasn't anywhere in the room!"

"I knew you couldn't be trusted! I said so!"

"He *wasn't* carrying it!"

"He *was!* You're a liar!"

"Ask your Captain d'Angeness! He was with me all the time!"

"Did you torture the courier?"

"It was unnecessary! He didn't have it, I tell you! I killed him, and the body was removed."

"His head?"

"As ordered. It was taken by the Captain or one of your mercenaries."

"They were not *my* mercenaries."

"You commanded them! That much is obvious! It was a mess!"

The voice was glacial "You should learn respect! Obedience! Don't bite the hand that feeds you, you pig's behind! Use your head for once! Personally I am not surprised by your report. I always believed your kind was incapable of following orders unless they were tattooed on your prick!" When the assassin did not reply, the man behind the screen continued. "You'll be fortunate if you only lose your balls over this! Now go! Go! Get out of my sight! I will have to go now and report your failure!"

The Venetian scowled, said nothing, but spoke to himself:

He is an abomination!
He ruined everything!
I want to kill him!
He forced a smile.
I'll even offer a reasonable rate!

The assassin stood and strode quickly to the rear of the Basilica. He did not leave, but stepped back into the shadows with the junior officer – his rank marked only by the red ribbon twisted through his epaulets.

Then both watched and waited.

Toad rushed by them, robed as a Cardinal, complete to the scarlet cape, the wide-brimmed and tasseled hat, the soft slippers and the gloves. His eyes were green and heavy-lidded, and his mouth turned down at the corners in a constant mask of insolence and disdain. The dwarf stopped before the men, glared at them, snapped his fingers and gestured with a bob of his head at the Basilica doors.

The young officer opened them, and the miniature "Cardinal" passed through.

Immediately a black coach pulled up at the bottom of the staircase. A footman quickly dropped down from his perch to lower the coach step and open the door. He then closed the door behind his passenger.

The assassin noticed the family *impresa* was covered with a black cloth.

"It wasn't necessary," he said quietly. "We know

who sent you, Toad!"

They watched as the coach crossed the piazza and disappeared up a side passageway, and only then did the assassin whisper, "Now, my friend, I bear you no malice. You were only following instructions. So let us find a nice inn with a comfortable stable, oats and water for my horse, perhaps even two big-breasted women and some good food and wine, heh?"

"I cannot, signore," replied the officer. "Our agent in the court will be waiting for both of us."

A stiletto suddenly appeared in the assassin's hand, and it was immediately pressed against the officer's throat.

"Let them wait" he hissed. "Goddamn it! I've been paid well, and we need a drink!"

CHAPTER TWO

REUNIONS AND REFLECTIONS

The tall, full-bearded and mustached man was robed entirely in dark blue with a billowy, crushed-felt cap. His hair, now streaked here and there with silver, stretched beyond his shoulders and melded with his full lips which bowed downward at the corners as if in infinite anguish. His cheekbones were high and prominent. His brows were thick and shadowed both his dark eyes. There were pouches of age beneath those eyes which, according to both friends and enemies, observed all and penetrated to the heart of everything.

For nearly the past two decades the Castello Sforzesco had been the refuge of Maestro Leonardo di Ser Piero da Vinci. This had been the palazzo of his patron, Ludovico Sforza, Duke of Milan. The nobleman had often been caricatured as a Moor or referred to as "a blackberry" by his enemies. Now the Duke had been driven away by the invading armies of the French and their allies to seek asylum with the Emperor of Germany, and the Maestro had packed what he could of his books, his pigments and oils, some of the models of his inventions and shipped them ahead to the

28

ancestral home of his principal apprentice, Francesco Melzi.

Now he too sought to escape.

He was not afraid as he stumbled through the secret passageway revealed to him by his young friend, Niccolo da Pavia.

He had enjoyed the company of the short young man - sometimes considered a dwarf although he did not have the bent legs or the large head. For the past few years Leonardo had marveled at the remarkable gift Niccolo possessed: the ability to remember – in detail – everything he read or observed. The two friends had pretended to a mutual service. Leonardo had trained Niccolo in painting and perspective, and Niccolo had attempted to teach the Maestro Latin, the language of the European courts and the Church.

Leonardo had last seen the youth soaring from his workroom on his great "dragon wings" - an invention intended to enable a single passenger to fly and then descend without harm. Using the ropes attached to his wrists, the shape and contour of the wings could be altered, but in practice it made little difference. The occupant would really be *gliding*, not actually *flying*.

The best one could do was to become one with the wind and depend upon updrafts to raise him higher.

This was the device the two had decided Niccolo should use to escape both the invaders and the Moor's security men.

The Duke's mercenaries had been sent to seize Leonardo's "red book" which detailed all the intrigues, murders, tortures and political games played by the Moor and members of his court. The Maestro had recorded them - not as an indictment, but as protection against a possible turn-of-heart by the Duke who was given to sudden changes in loyalty and friendship. Leonardo kept several other volumes of notes, sketches and observations of everything he observed, but this particular book could be damning to the Duke if it fell into the hands of the German Emperor now offering the Moor sanctuary.

Niccolo had taken the book with him when he glided away on the wings of the dragon, and so the Maestro had only been threatened and then ignored when the Duke's agents realized the incriminating volume was no longer in the castello.

Now no one was left here to threaten or challenge him.

What he had to do now was escape the invaders.

He crossed immediately to the secret door in the bedchamber of Madonna Valentina, adjusted the medallion which worked the mechanism, and slowly worked his way down the worn and wooden staircase of the dark passage.

Soon he emerged in a piazza far beyond the fortress walls!

He momentarily leaned against the frame of the now-exposed doorway and struggled for breath. He attempted to focus on his surroundings and realized the day, like his mood, was darkening rapidly. Winter was fast approaching. He raised a hand to rub his eyes and noticed, as though for the first time, his fingers were stained with pigment. This did not disturb him for he regarded the discoloration as a badge of a life spent working with paint and plaster.

Suddenly he realized what was happening just a short distance before him!

The huge clay model for his equestrian statue of Francesco Sforza, the Moor's father, was under attack by jeering Gascon and Venetian invaders!

They went eagerly at the work with snaking ropes and long lances until the heroic figure trembled on the back of his steed. The horseman seemed to struggle to stay where he was, as if alarmed by the fury and venom of the vandals surrounding him. Then he tilted slightly and fell, slowly at first, and then with increasing speed until the hardened clay shattered against the cobbles of the piazza!

Leonardo watched this desecration of his work with bitter resignation and sighed.

It was simply one more personal tragedy among the many he had witnessed lately.

He already determined his "Last Supper" fresco at the refectory of Santa Maria della Grazie was doomed by his impatience with the traditional method of applying pigment directly to wet plaster. He had spent nearly two years walking between his workroom in the castello to his apartments in the city and then to the monastery to dab, revise and dab again with a new and untried method until he was at least partially satisfied with it and the painting.

No two apostles were alike and each told a different story, each expressed his own feelings. The room of the Last Supper appeared to be exactly the same width as the refectory itself and extended on to a landscape and a distant horizon in a startling demonstration of forced perspective.

But his new approach had failed!

The paint was already beginning to flake and fall away, and he knew the fresco was doomed.

He also knew his model city of Vigevano outside of Milan had been destroyed a week earlier by the invaders, so now he realized any remnant of his decades of service to the Moor was being wiped away as chalk beneath a wet cloth!

Wasted time and effort!

He could understand and forgive the rage against his former patron. Duke Ludovico had brought this once-prosperous city of northern Italy into war and destruction despite its lucrative armories and its salt monopoly. He had alienated some of the oldest and most respected families in Italy and even lost the credit of the European banks, especially his principal creditors, the Genoese Bank of St. George.

Now seeing his huge equestrian monument and his world crumble before him, Leonardo felt as if he, too, would collapse in the face of such unimaginable barbarianism and senseless rage. He watched this assassination of his masterwork, and momentarily wished to die with the day, to do away with the seemingly endless routine of working, sleeping in scattered fifteen-minute intervals, eating only to survive, and struggling with those in power who could not - or would not - understand what he dreamed and was attempting.

But summoning his courage and his last remnant of determination, he pulled the hood of his cloak up and forward to hide his face and slowly, carefully, worked his way through the crowded piazza to the point where he was told to expect a rescuer.

*

He had barely threaded his way through the crowded centerpiece of the city when trumpets from somewhere announced the arrival of the conquerors. He quickly stepped back into the shadows of a convenient doorway with the other massed and frightened people.

The triumphal procession appeared from the opposite side of the square, surrounded by cheering Milanese, either happy to be freed of Ludovico's yoke or pretending to for their own safety.

Leonardo assumed the majestic figure leading the invaders on the white horse was Louis, king of France and the Moor's principal enemy. The king's ermine-and-gold embroidered cloak trailed from his shoulders and fell gracefully over the flanks of his stallion. Close on the king's right Leonardo saw a slim, dark-haired gentleman dressed entirely in black with a velvet cap emblazoned with a huge diamond. The Maestro reasoned this had to be the king's chief ally, Cesare Borgia, bastard son of Pope Alexander VI and a man rumored to be of insatiable ambition and cunning. Behind him rode the enigma everyone knew to be Cesare's invaluable assassin, the shadowy killer known only as Michelotto.

On the king's right was Gian Francesco Gonzaga, captain-general of the armies of Venice, his breastplate emblazoned with the winged-lion emblem of that city. On his left rode a regal and bejeweled woman in

33

virtuous white velvet, her silk gown cut low on her shoulders and her sleeves gathered to below the elbow. Her long hair was braided and worn in a net of gold. Leonardo recognized her as Isabella d'Este, the Marquesa of Mantua, the wife of Gian Francesco and a woman who once commissioned him to paint her portrait, but later withdrew the contract when her sister, the Moor's wife, died abruptly.

It was rumored she blamed the deposed Duke for Beatrice's death.

Niccolo had once described her as "a flame encased in ice."

Behind the Marquesa rode her brother, Cardinal Ippolito d'Este, arrogant in scarlet and gold, and beside him was a grim-faced Cardinal Guiliano della Rovere, dreaming, as everyone imagined, of his gloved hand one day weighted with the Ring of the Fisherman.

Trailing behind them was the traitorous military commander, Galeazzo di Sanseverino, who had secretly and treacherously served Cesare Borgia and who used the romantic – if ridiculous - title of "The Griffin" as he plotted to assassinate Il Moro and set in motion what was described by a *commedia* actor as "comedy of murders."

Suddenly Leonardo was distracted by a sound behind him! He quickly wheeled, walked as rapidly as he could through the narrow passage and emerged in another, smaller piazza.

There, as promised, waited a large coach-and-four.

A dark-haired young man appeared at the window, smiled and called, "Hurry, Maestro! We have passes which should get us through the French and Venetian lines, and my father awaits us! Hurry! Winter is coming!"

Leonardo returned the smile of Francesco Melzi, and marveled at the contrast between him and his other apprentice, the yellow-haired, incorrigible thief and liar whom he had christened "Salai" - a servant to the devil. The Maestro had not seen Salai since he temporarily exiled him to live among the monks at the Santa Maria della Grazie for some malfeasance or another, but if any young man could survive this occupation by his cunning and total lack of conscience, it was Salai.

They would meet again, the Maestro was certain.

Apprentice Francesco, on the other hand, was generous, studious and gifted.

But not as beautiful.

Never as beautiful.

"To where, Francesco?"

"First, to the Certosa," replied Melzi. "The father abbot is expecting us. If we hurry we should be able to arrive there before nightfall. We can refresh ourselves there under the protection of the Church and then move on to my father's estate at Vaprio d'Adda in the spring."

The apprentice stepped down quickly and assisted the Maestro to climb into the coach. He then entered and slammed the door behind him.

The coach-and-four rattled rapidly through the piazza, under an archway, and was gone.

Leonardo could not bring himself to watch the looting of the city by the invaders as they raced through the piazza and down the Corso Porta Romana.

He nested among the cushions embroidered with the
Melzi coat-of-arms and suddenly realized the pocket of
his cloak contained Niccolo's copy of Epictetus. The
small book had been given to the young man to assist
in his character development. It had been a gift from
the father abbot of the Certosa to the foundling.

Leonardo turned to Francesco. "Did Niccolo
escape?"

Melzi nodded. "I personally saw him soar over the
castello walls on your dragon wings. I saw him land
near the wagons of that *commedia dell'arte* company
who were also running away from the castello –
probably with the silverware."

They laughed together.

"What was their name again?" Francesco asked.

"*I Comici Buffoni.*"

"Yes! Well, I trust they took pity on Niccolo and
carried him with them."

The Maestro smiled and took the Epictetus from his
pocket. He did not intend to read it, but a page was
marked with a ribbon, and he opened it to see what
had impressed Niccolo.

It read: "You have been given powers to endure all.
You have been given greatness of heart. Courage.
Fortitude. Should you not use these gifts to the end for
which you were given them - instead of moaning or
wailing over what has come to pass?"

Leonardo smiled, closed the book, thought of his
little friend and rocked by the rhythmic swaying of the
coach as it proceeded south, promptly fell asleep for a
quarter of an hour.

*

At that moment the subject of Leonardo's interest was taken up with the *commedia* players whose wagon was nearly struck when the young man descended following his flight on the Maestro's "dragon wings."

Now – two days later - he tried to smile at a ring of the players gathered around him in the shadow of the Torrazo. He was attempting to balance on the wooden staves lashed to his calves and ankles and hidden behind flame-red stockings and slashed pantaloons. Instantly Marco Turio, the tall and skeletal veteran actor who always played the role of the pompous Dottore Graziano, rushed forward to catch the young man as he began to pitch forward. As Niccolo fell into his arms, the chalky half-mask of the comic servant, Giangurcolo, slipped away and landed at the feet of Simone Corio, the chosen leader of the troupe.

Simone, proud wearer of the suit of diamond-shaped patches, said quietly, "It will take time, my young friend." He recovered the character mask and brushed away the dust. "But with continued practice you will eventually pass for a grown man."

"I *am* a grown man," snapped Niccolo.

Simone nodded. "But not as tall as you must be for the role of Giangurcolo. Remaking the traditional costume for a smaller man would cost us time, money and more effort than we can afford. Further it is non-traditional. Giangurcolo was of normal height, so we think it is easier to simply stretch you."

"You did well, Niccolo," said Rubini, the acrobatic Scapino as he danced over to the novice. "Take smaller steps and remember the stilts are attached only to your calves and ankles. Think of them merely as extensions of your own legs. If your body is not balanced correctly, if you cannot sense the center of gravity, you will fall – which would be amusing only if it is the *soggetto*."

"I thought you were excellent," said big-breasted Prudenza of Siena who portrayed the older and more cunning servant and sometimes the domineering, nagging wife to Pantalone. The wild-haired older woman gestured to Anna, the pert young woman who served as the songstress of the troupe, and together the two whipped away the young man's oversize pantaloons. "You did better than Rubini did on his first attempt at the taller stilts," said Prudenza.

The two actresses rolled and removed the long red stockings which stretched up to Niccolo's thighs and began to unfasten the two appendages lashed to his legs.

"I got distracted," he said.

"No, no, no!" Rubini assumed the role of a lecturing Dottore. "You mustn't let yourself be distracted! Not even for an instant! An actor cannot afford distraction. At any moment he must be aware of his character, his lines, the situation onstage, the mood of the audience and the degree of their laughter."

"Degree?"

"Oh yes! The laughter – or the lack of it – tells the actor a great deal. If it is weak and infrequent, it may mean the watcher spent his morning being harangued by his guild master or informed of some new tax being imposed upon him. Such a man did not come to think and will not laugh at our jests, but he will howl at the pratfall, because he imagines the victim to be his tormentor. So we improvise a little, add more pratfalls and throw in some fruit-in-the-face. If the laughter comes often and intensely, it is a sign the viewer possibly had a mid-morning fling with his beloved or got a fine price for his olives. He – or she – is in a festive mood and ready to be amused by anything."

"You see," Simone took up the narrative, "a *verbal* jest requires the listener to *think*, to get the joke and be able to follow the story line – such as it is - or to recognize the person being satirized. You, as an actor, must be able to read the mood of the audience and improvise around the *soggeto* to give them what they want."

"It sounds like work," said Niccolo as he donned his own trousers and boots.

"It *is* work!"

"And we better get back to it," Simone said quietly. He turned to the rest of the troupe gathered together behind their colorful wagons. "Let's continue with the rehearsal! Niccolo can grow a foot or two tomorrow."

Piero Tebaldeo, the cowardly but renowned Capitano, now strutted around with his sagging belly and absurdly long sword trailing behind him. Under his red half-mask which suggested the owner was both sanguine and perpetually in his cups, he resumed his customary arrogant posture and continued his boasting of his conquests in battles and bordellos.

"Behind my golden chariot," he proclaimed to the assembly, "I dragged the dead body of Achilles around the high walls of Pompeii!"

"I understood the body was Hector's," Isabella, the

39

beautiful ingenue of the company, laughed and corrected him. "And the city, my captain, was Troy."

The Capitano emitted a belch to rock the wall of the piazza. "It was the *Trojan sector* of Pompeii! I remember it distinctly! Dirty. Dilapidated. Foul. Like the sewers of Venice which they call *canali!* A virtual eyesore on the plains of Philippi!"

"Venice is nowhere near Philippi," smirked Isabella.

"*Now* it isn't!" The Capitano roared in defiance. "But in those days the world was much smaller, my girl! Hardly larger than a walnut! A thumbnail! Infinitesimal!" He began to mock-weep. "Ah, the good, the forgotten, old days! I weep at the memories! I weep! Why in those days I could leave Rome at matins and arrive in Constantinople in time for vespers!"

"Never!"

"Well – a day and a half at most!"

"More likely a month and a half."

"Well, yes," admitted the Capitano, "if you traveled by way of the Via Emilia during pilgrimage and perhaps stopped at Pavia for some of those delicious mussels in garlic sauce! But remember! I had the winged horse, Icarus!"

"Pegasus."

"It's true!"

"The horse's name was Pegasus."

"Who cares?! The point is the beast had wings! His back was as broad as the deck of a ship! His eyes lit the way before me! How many times we soared through the heavens as we circled over the Black Sea and looked down with wonder on the mighty pyramids!"

"The pyramids are in Egypt."

"Not *those* pyramids! Why, the Egyptian pyramids are mere dunghills compared to the pyramids of the Turks! The ninth wonder of the world!"

"Plato only mentioned seven."

"Well, yes," snapped the Capitano, "if you consider the Hanging Gardens of Ithaca as only *one* wonder! But the gardens were actually in *two* sections which Plato must have counted as *one!* There were the original Hanging Gardens, and then the one which merely sagged, and - !"

"The Hanging Gardens were in Babylon!"

The Capitano drew himself as tall as he could. "Did they move those damned things *again?!*"

Simone stepped between them. "A fair sequence," he judged, "but if the audience seems restless, Piero go into your strut, fall over things, get your sword entangled with Isabella's skirt and lift it a little."

"Like you did last Thursday between performances," said Prudenza.

Simone turned to Niccolo. "You keep practicing Niccolo," he said, "and we'll try working you into 'Pantalone's Last Day' when we get to Napoli."

The young man smiled and nodded. "I like the challenge. I really do. It reminds me of my days with Maestro Leonardo in the Castello Sforzesco. He always used me to test his inventions." His mood visibly shifted into a light melancholia. "I wonder," he said softly, "if he escaped the invaders?"

"You needn't worry about Maestro Leonardo," said Anna as she bit into an apple. "He is much more intelligent and cunning than the Moor's men. He'll winter somewhere."

41

"Maybe none of us will," said Isabella quietly as she stared beyond the circle of performers.

Simone and the others turned as eight armed and mounted men in tunics of chain mail under chasubles of blue-and-gray prodded their horses forward and encircled the troupe.

Always the first to fling himself into a situation, Simone looked at the man he took to be the commanding officer. "What is the meaning of this, general?! Do you know with whom you are dealing?"

Prudenza assumed her customary attitude toward authority. "What the hell do you want?!"

"If you want your money back," said Anna sweetly, "we give refunds only on Thursdays."

"Look us up next Thursday in Firenzi," added Francesco. "We'll be in Verona then."

Prudenza took the tip of the lance pointed at her with two fingers as if it were fine lace and delicately moved it aside. "I could teach you a few tricks with that thing," she smiled, "if you have the time and the balls."

Rubini and Mario quickly moved beside her, and the acrobat's hand muffled her mouth.

Simone resumed the more aristocratic attitude. "I hope I will not be forced to mention this unseemly interruption of our rehearsal to my revered father – which would mean either your instant death or imprisonment in the family dungeons from which no man has ever escaped."

One of the horsemen with a highly-polished breastplate over his chain mail prodded his horse forward and said, "Is one of you Niccolo da Pavia?"

Piero stepped forward. "I am Niccolo da Pavia!"

The officer glared at him. "I was told this Niccolo is a dwarf."

"Well, that was yesterday," Piero continued, smiling broadly. "I'm feeling much better today."

Instantly Francesco dropped to his knees. "I am Niccolo the dwarf!"

"No!" Turio yelled, falling on all fours. "Pay no attention to him! I am Niccolo the dwarf! This pretender likes to believe he's a dwarf, but he has none of my graces! No natural dignity! No inherited compulsion to bay at the full moon!"

"Don't listen to these idiots," snapped Anna as she pushed Turio aside. "*I'm* the one you want, but my name is not 'Niccol-*o*' but 'Niccol-*a*'. My mother had a terrible time with masculine endings. She was annulled four times because of it!"

During this exchange Marco had lifted Niccolo to his shoulders.

The officer urged his horse toward them. He pointed his sword. "Aren't *you* Niccolo the dwarf?"

"Do I look like a dwarf?" Niccolo frowned.

"You're sitting on that man's shoulders!"

Niccolo let his head drop in mock astonishment as he stared down at Mario. "A *man?!* Is *that* a man?" He looked at the officer. "Thank god! I thought I had a tumor!"

Simone smiled and said softly, "*Now* you have the idea, Giangurcolo."

The officer moved his mount closer to Niccolo and Mario. "If you don't come with us immediately, Signore Niccolo, my men will cut the legs off every member of this bastard assembly and render them *all* dwarfs!"

"What a concept!" Rubini grinned. "We'd be a sensation! We can open at the Venetian *carnivale* in three months and …!"

Niccolo indicated Mario should lower him to the ground, and the actor did.

"I must go with you?" Niccolo said quietly. "Go where?"

The officer leaned forward in his saddle to address the young man. "I was instructed not to tell you. My orders were merely to bring you to my lord."

"Your lord?" Rubini growled. "Why must all magistrates imagine themselves nobles?"

"My lord *is* a count," said the officer as he glared at the acrobat. "Imbecile!"

"Ah!" Mario roared. "Count Imbecile! I know him well! Why didn't you say so immediately!"

"Isn't he the bastard son of the Duke of Stupidity?" Isabella laughed.

"Probably French," said Francesco. "They have no decorum."

"True," said a frowning Anna, "They keep leaving their decorum all over the place!"

"Silence!"

The officer stood in his stirrups and again pointed his sword at Niccolo. "Now climb up behind me, Signore Niccolo." He glared at Simone. "If I wanted to be amused, I'd send for a trio of Neapolitan whores and not a band of grubby montebanks who perform only in the streets!"

Prudenza turned to Anna. "Neapolitan whores don't perform in the streets?"

"Bad for the back," said Anna, "and the damned

44

mounted officers just won't climb down from their horses!"

The patient Simone did not smile or laugh. "What is this young man accused of?"

"I didn't say he was accused of anything," said the officer as he helped Niccolo put a foot in the stirrups and swing to the horse's back. "The count said merely to bring him, and I follow my orders."

Prudenza snorted. "If your count asked you to bring your horse to a gallop and plunge off a cliff, would you do it?"

"Not after the last four times," frowned Isabella.

Simone crossed to Niccolo and put a hand on the young man's knee. "Don't worry, Niccolo," he said softly. "This is also part of being a player. Someone stole a cow? Look for the players! A lady is insulted? Search for the mummers! The magistrate will release you in a few hours, and we'll be waiting for you."

"Provided they don't fine you more than four *soldi*," Mario called as the horsemen moved slowly away with their passenger. "More than that, we'll either have to rob the poor box at the baptistery or move on. We'll wait for you in Arezzo on the Feast of the Nativity!"

Prudenza cupped her hands to her mouth and shouted after the departing mercenaries. "If you bastards come with him, bring your own wine!"

*

There was no discussion between Niccolo and the stiff-backed officer as the armed band crossed the piazza, moved slowly through two narrow

45

passageways, down a stone staircase just off the Via Palestro, across another piazza and under an archway into a courtyard of a palazzo.

Almost immediately two men in livery raced down the stone steps and helped Niccolo from the back of the officer's horse. As they led Niccolo inside, he had no time to study the arms carved in stone over the doorway. He wondered if he had been taken by someone allied to the defeated Moor since Cremona was a fief of Milan.

Did the Sforza want him?

Or was he a prisoner of someone attached to the invaders?

A French count perhaps?

A Swiss?

Surely not a Venetian! Any representative of the doge would be lodged in a much more impressive palazzo and be surrounded by guards.

Could it be someone after Maestro Leonardo's red book which he had carried away from the Castello Sforzesco, the book detailing the corruption and murders at the Moor's court?

He was led down a long corridor by the two servants who had to pace themselves so they would not get too far ahead. The walls of the corridor were lined with frescoes and large portraits of unfamiliar nobles in ceremonial dress standing erect in awkward and unnatural poses. He recognized a masterwork of Masacchio on one wall and another by della Francesca opposite.

And where have I seen Crivelli's "Annunciation" before?

Surely not in the Certosa, the monastery where I was abandoned as an infant and raised by the monks!

And he could not remember those works being in the collection of the Moor.

Then he saw something wonderful, and he smiled with relief!

Directly before him bathed in the soft light from a candelabra was a portrait by Maestro Leonardo depicting a beautiful young woman, her long and delicate fingers clutching a symbol of purity, an ermine. Her face was turned as if she was looking with a gentle love at someone standing beside the artist, perhaps the man who had commissioned the portrait and then given it to the lady when he had to inform her he was betrothed to another.

"Ah, my little master of intrigue and adventure," came the soft and familiar voice of Madonna Cecilia Gallerani, the Countess Bergamini. "Why did you take so long to come to me?"

The lady was radiant in a loose-fitting scarlet gown revealing her creamy neck and shoulders. Her hair was worn straight, bound around her forehead by a velvet band with a large ruby embedded in it. The third finger of her left hand supported the heavy ring with the Bergamini crest carved in ivory, and the forefinger on her right hand still displayed the diamond which Niccolo knew was a present from the Moor on the birth of their bastard son, Cesare. She turned and walked back into the antechamber, signaling Niccolo to follow her.

A servant closed the door behind them.

She seated herself on a chaise and gestured him to

sit beside her. "Aren't you pleased to see me?"

"And surprised," smiled Niccolo. "Shouldn't you be in Bologna with the Bentivoglio? That's where you said you and the count were going when the French came."

"A subterfuge," she sighed. "My lord and I had no intention of fleeing to his relatives in Bologna, but at the time the Palazzo del Verme was alive with spies for both the Moor *and* the invaders. We could not trust anyone, so I told you – quite loudly and clearly as I remember – we were running to the Bentivoglio. Actually we were always intending to come here, to Cremona, which is my husband's fief."

She paused and directed Niccolo's attention to a table beside the chaise laden with a carafe of wine, two glass goblets and a small platter containing small cuts of cheese, meats and pastries.

"Have a little something."

Niccolo chose one of the pastries and a goblet of wine. "How did you find me?"

"I never lost sight of you," she replied softly. "You were an agent of mine, weren't you? You served me as a spy in the castello, didn't you? I couldn't afford to have you just wander away knowing all you know about my activities during the Moor's last days. I remain – to some degree – his protector. He *is* the father of my son."

"I would never divulge anything to harm you or the Duke."

"I know," she smiled, "but we play a dangerous game. As it is, my friends informed me you escaped the castello on Maestro Leonardo's wings and were 'adopted' by *Il Comici Buffoni.* They had to get a permit from my husband to perform in our piazzi, so I waited for their arrival and arranged to have you brought to me."

"But – why?"

"Because I wanted to see you again," she said.

"But perhaps not as fervently as I wanted to see you."

The voice was also familiar, and Niccolo turned to see the Moor's servant girl with whom he became enamored during the final days of the invasion!

No longer in the scullery clothes she wore when he first met her, the girl was now radiant in satins and silks, her long blonde hair neatly combed and brushed and bound by a black ribbon!

"Ellie!"

As the girl ran to him, the Contessa growled, "Madonna Eleanora, please! Remember you are now a lady of my court - and have proven to be a delightful, clever and witty one." She smiled at the girl. "Pardon your blushes, Madonna."

The young courtier rose and permitted his lover to fall into his arms. The kiss was both passionate and promising.

"Now, children," the Contessa commanded. "Not in this chamber! The carpets were made in Constantinople and are worth a fortune. Besides," she added separating the couple and leading them to sit beside one another, hands clenched, "I have more happy news for you, Signore Niccolo. Your Maestro Leonardo escaped the castello too. He was whisked away by an apprentice." She paused, her brow drawn into a bow. "Oh - what was his name again?"

"Salai?"

"God forbid! No! The *decent* one!"

"Francesco Melzi?"

"Yes! I understand he was to take the Maestro to safety in the Certosa monastery. I believe they planned to seek asylum with Melzi's father on the family estates, but I offered both of them an alternative."

"Which is?"

"To come here of course!" She smiled, rose and crossed to the side table where she handed Eleanora the other goblet of wine. "I sent a courier with the invitation, making certain to mention I had his friend, Niccolo da Pavia, locked securely in my husband's palazzo until he could come for you. It will take a little time, but he will come."

"Thank you."

"I was happy to do it."

Niccolo beamed, his fingers still tightly entwined with Elenora's. "To see the Maestro again! I couldn't ask for anything more!"

The young girl frowned at him.

"Really?"

The persistent tolling of the monastery bells awakened Leonardo still bent over his small desk in his assigned cell at the Certosa. Accustomed to sleeping only in quarter-hour intervals throughout the day, he was not annoyed by the early morning summons to the monks. He and Francesco had been informed by the father abbot on arrival "the bells do not apply to you, signori. They call our brothers to milk the cows and goats, to prepare the ovens for baking and the chapel for matins."

He was pleased to see someone had invaded his tiny chamber sometime during his last brief sleep and refreshed the fire in the tiny fireplace. Winter had struck, and there was a penetrating chill in the air, so the Maestro removed the thread-bare woolen blanket from his hard bed and wrapped it around his shoulders. He felt a profound sympathy for the brothers who lived and worked under these conditions, offering their services and discomforts to the supreme deity as compensation for their sins and the abuses of the world.

His days here in the Certosa had proven both rewarding and difficult.

For one thing it was the Christmas period, and the monks spent a good portion of their time in prayer and ritual, but still attempted to provide the Maestro with a little cheer.

Very little.

On first greeting him, Father Abbot quietly warned "there are some of our brothers who consider you the devil's disciple, Maestro Leonardo. They question the morality of your dissection of bodies for what you maintain is anatomical study, and they believe you write in your journals in some language provided you by devils in order to hide your blasphemies."

Leonardo quietly explained his dissections were in no way meant to disrespect the dead, but to advance the knowledge of the human body. He insisted future physicians could use his notes to better solve the riddles of what harms humanity and how and why. He explained his journals were written in ordinary Italian and some Latin, but only in reverse, because being left-handed, he found it more convenient.

He did not mention his other purpose: to hide the information he had uncovered about the laws of nature which – in some cases – were contrary to what the Church taught and could possibly lead to a hearing before an ecclesiastical court.

He remembered with some bitterness when he and fellow apprentice-students were accused of sodomy before such a court who found them innocent only because one of the other defendants was a Medici.

His initial visit to the monastery's extensive library had been equally uncomfortable.

He knew this was where Niccolo da Pavia first manifested his remarkable memory and his all-encompassing power of detailed observation, but the young courtier had warned him of Brother Pax, the librarian, who firmly believed the Maestro held "blasphemous and heretical notions."

The aged monk was plainly annoyed and confused when Leonardo told him of reading Niccolo's volume of Epictetus and found it "comforting."

"I gave that book to Niccolo," replied the librarian on that occasion, "because Epictetus was a crippled slave, so his advice might prove of some value to a young foundling who was leaving the protection of the monastery for the worldly court of Duke Sforza. Epictetus had much to say about the importance of cultivating personal independence while subject to the will of a possibly decadent master. He, too, lived in an extravagant and blasphemous world. He stressed the necessity of searching for - and finding - happiness *within* oneself."

Leonardo had nodded and replied, "Those lessons are applicable to all of us, friar. In a sense, an artist is also something of a slave to his patron; and I agree it is important to cultivate an inner serenity among the decadence and intrigue of princely courts."

"Indeed?" The librarian had studied the face of the bearded artist for a quiet moment, and then added, "I would not suggest Epictetus for *your* reading, Maestro. I would probably recommend *The Meditations of Marcus Aurelius.*"

"Marcus Aurelius? Why?"

Brother Pax's smile had been both gentle and triumphant. "Because," he had said solemnly, "he was the last of the pagan moralists." Not waiting for Leonardo to respond, he had continued. "Of course he wrote in Greek. Do you read Greek, Maestro?"

Leonardo had felt a flush rise in his cheeks. A monk so well informed of his dissections and his workbooks must surely know he lacked a knowledge of classic languages, and Niccolo must have written about his "assignment" to teach him Latin; so he concluded the librarian was deliberately attempting to embarrass him.

"I regret I am *omo sanza lettere*, " he had said softly, "but I am surprised to find a monastic so well acquainted with the writings of a Greek; especially since the Greeks believed in the beauty of the nude human body and often depicted it in their texts."

It had been Leonardo's moment, and he had

pointedly given the wide-eyed monastic no opportunity to continue the debate.

"We are not of different worlds, Friar," he had said as he turned to leave. "We only perceive it differently."

And he had walked quickly away.

Leonardo's stay in the Certosa was not always so disturbing.

One day after the morning meal, two visiting Franciscans tucked their hands deep within the wide sleeves of their robes and appeared at the open door of his cell.

"Forgive us, Maestro," said the taller of the two. "When my companion, Fra Martino, and I heard you were in temporary residence, we asked Father Abbot's permission to meet with you and express our admiration for your *Adoration of the Magi*. We had the pleasure of seeing it in Florence at the San Donato a Scorpeto."

The smaller monk smiled. "Fra Angelo and I were there a year after the execution of Fra Savonarola."

"I am honored, friars," Leonardo said. "And how did you find matters in Florence following the burning of the monk? I consider the city my home, you know, and I have not returned for nearly two decades."

"Volatile, I'm afraid," said Fra Martino. "The place is in turmoil. Those who followed the dictates of the Dominican and attempted to establish his 'city of God' are still active and powerful. Their rival, Piero de Medici, seems content to waste both his time and his money in Rome. His followers in Florence are attempting to run the city from the Priorate."

"What were you doing in Florence?"

"We were – that is, we *are* - on pilgrimage," said the tall monk, "to the major shrines in Italy. We are petitioning God to move the hearts of the people and their rulers to mount a new crusade against the Turk. We pray to avenge the defeat of the Christian fleet at Sapienza."

"You are making a religious pilgrimage to advocate a war?"

The suggestion of a contradiction was lost on the friars.

Fra Angelo nodded. "We began at Assisi of course, then to Sant'Ubaldo in Gubbio for the Festival of the Candles."

"We have been welcomed and well-treated everywhere," said Fra Martino, "except for the unpleasantness at Montagnana."

"What happened at Montagnana?"

"We were on our way to the Santa Giustiana in Padua and stopped at a small inn ..."

"The Olive Tree," added Fra Angelo.

"Yes," Fra Martino nodded. "That was the name. The proprietor, an unhappy man, half-heartedly offered us some food and some accommodations in his stable, but near midnight we were shaken from sleep by a band of rude mercenaries who forced us from the stable and sent us upon the road. As we gathered our meager belongings we overheard an officer of the mercenaries arguing vehemently with a tall man in a dark cloak. We pleaded for compassion, because we were very weary and it was late autumn and cold, but they were armed and quite brutal."

"Although," Fra Angelo said softly, "one of them – I

heard one of the mercenaries refer to him as 'the captain' - whispered to me it would be best for us to leave immediately. He said we would not want to see what would happen there."

"What *did* happen there?"

Fra Martin shrugged. "We have no idea. We managed to find a relatively comfortable place to sleep in a small cave just further down the road, and sometime later we were both awakened by a man in a black cloak racing past us on the road to Padua. He rode a beautiful stallion. A little later the rest of the mercenaries galloped by us, and one – the one addressed as 'captain' - had a canvas bag attached to his saddle."

"It was bloody."

Leonardo frowned. "Did you see any *impresa*?"

"No."

"Curious," said the Maestro. "A nobleman and a detachment of mercenaries at a small inn on a remote road without an evident coat-of-arms of their service? It would seem they did not wish to be identified."

"Yes," said the taller monk. "We judged that to be the case."

"That *is* very - !"

They were interrupted by the sudden appearance of Francesco in the doorway.

"Oh, excuse me, good friars," he nodded to the monks. "I did not intend to disturb you, but a courier has just arrived with a message for us, Maestro." He smiled at Leonardo. "It is an invitation from Count Bergamini in Cremona."

The Franciscans smiled, nodded, decided the matter

was of a personal nature, turned away and slowly shuffled down the corridor.

"He and the Contessa wish us to visit them," Melzi bubbled excitedly as the monks disappeared around a corner. "The French now apparently consider them neutral. The Bergamini, in turn, can now extend their protection to us."

"The Contessa?" Leonardo beamed. "She escaped from Milan then! But what is she doing in Cremona? The last I heard from Madonna Cecilia, she and her husband the count were fleeing to Bologna! They were to be guests of the Bentivoglio!"

"Apparently it was a ruse to trick the Moor's spies. Ercole Bentivoglio had been appointed by Cesare Borgia as a commander of one of his armies, so it made the Bergamini appear to be allied with the invaders."

"But – well – we *were* going to your father's estate."

"I am still going there – with your indulgence of course. He worries for me at the moment. I assured him we both are well, safe and wintered in the Certosa monastery. As soon as the country roads are cleared of snow and my father's mercenaries come to escort me, I can visit the family and then return to study with you in Cremona. In the meantime the Contessa has sent a coach to take you to her."

Leonardo frowned. "I don't know. I appreciate the Contessa's invitation, but ... !"

"She offers an additional inducement."

"Really? What?

"Niccolo is there!"

The rest of the day Leonardo and Melzi packed what little possessions they brought with them after fleeing the castello, and the Maestro confided to his apprentice he was pleased to leave the monastery.

"I am grateful for Father Abbot's kindness, of course; but I suspect his welcome is wearing as thin as my patience. Half of the monks regard me as some sort of black magician and the other half are convinced I am simply a heretic. I have even heard some resurrect the charges against me as a sodomite. Father Abbot has gone so far as to outlaw any communication between me and the younger postulants. To allay some of their fears of my Satanic nature, I intentionally spent an inordinate amount of time in one of their side chapels."

"I know. Were you praying?"

"Studying Alberti's *Stations of the Cross*."

"I would think you enjoyed the monastery's notable library."

"Brother Pax is one of those who think I am Lucifer reincarnated," sighed Leonardo. "But I *did* have access to their excellent translation of Euclid's treatises on mathematics. The translation was in Latin from the original Greek, and I certainly could have used Niccolo's assistance in working my way through it."

"All the more reason to meet with the little courtier again."

"Indeed."

Not all the monks were grateful to see Leonardo the Heretic leave.

Brother Antonius, imperial overlord of the scullery, who resembled a rotund onion topped by an albino prune, silently mourned the Maestro's departure.

During Leonardo's stay the Father Abbot granted

Antonius permission to prepare special meals for their guests. Delighted to once again exercise his skills, he had soaked Leonardo's meat in wine and basted it with a sauce of quince and pear and orange. He had manufactured a delicate lace of brill and turbot, smothered seafood in a rich broth of garlic and mushrooms and decorated everything with small bouquets of parsley and basil. He had prepared such rarities as *trifoni,* a miniature masterpiece sculpted of sugar.

The artistic merits of the work were much admired, but the Maestro did not devour the delicacy with the enthusiasm Antonius hoped.

Leonardo had never demonstrated a preference for anything beyond simple fare. To the Florentine dining seemed to be something merely required for sustenance.

This was a great disappointment to Brother Antonius who believed an artist thrives upon recognition from other artists.

Now with the guests departing, the Maestro of the scullery would have to return to preparing black bread baked with poor-quality grain from the monastery fields and butter churned with asses' milk. Not that it mattered much to the others, because, like all religious houses, the Certosa meals were always accompanied by spiritual readings, so the attention of the diners should be focused on God and ignore the watery consistency of the stew.

Brother Pax was also a little annoyed to see "the devil's disciple" leave, because he had come to believe he had converted Leonardo from the barbaric practice of dissecting the dead. To reinforce the improvement, he tucked a text into the Maestro's luggage, *The Meditations of Marcus Aurelius.* He had marked a passage which read: "Consider this: you are an old man. Remember how often you have received an opportunity from the gods and did not take it. You must now perceive a limit of time is fixed upon you which, if you do not use it to clear sway the clouds from your mind, it will pass, and you will pass, and the opportunity will never return."

He was very pleased with himself.

Father Abbot, on the other hand, was relieved by the departure. He held no malice toward the Maestro, but he secretly wished the Florentine would be more like Fra Bartolomeo or Fra Angelico who understood art serves only to glorify the eternal. Informed the major guest was leaving, he seized one of the painter's huge hands, pumped it enthusiastically and then went straight to the chapel to offer four rosaries in thanksgiving.

On the day the Maestro departed in the coach sent for him, the wide sky above the Certosa was gray as ashes and accompanied by a cold rain, but it promised spring. Slightly uncomfortable with the realization he was about to impose himself upon the Bergamini, he opened Niccolo's copy of Epictetus at random and read a passage.

It read: "Behold me! I have neither city nor house nor possessions nor servants. I have no wife, no children, no shelter; but what do I lack? I am untouched by sorrow or fear, because I am free."

He was not consoled.

*

Niccolo and Eleanora, having reveled in their reunion and amorously celebrated it on several occasions, decided to look for another form of amusement since the spring promised freedom from the hard winter. The short young courtier remembered he had not had an opportunity to say goodbye to his saviors before the Contessa's men carried him away, and now *I Comici Buffoni* performed every afternoon before the 200-year-old Loggia dei Militi before preparing to head south.

The young couple made use of one of the Contessa's carriages to come to watch the performance in comfort among the gathering of peasants, shop workers, clerics and children. Earlier Niccolo had sent word to his friends he was safe and comfortable, but he still had to personally say farewell to his saviors, so he slipped behind the curtain to address the performers before their afternoon entertainment. He also brought with him a pouch of ducats which he knew would be more appreciated than any long speeches of thanksgiving.

"I genuinely enjoyed my time with you," he told them, "and I hope someday, somewhere, we will play together."

"I hope so too," said Simone as he juggled the purse. "It has been a profitable experience."

"I mean it," Niccolo insisted as the company laughed. "I hope to work with you again – before we die."

He was surprised when his emotional declaration was met with further laughter.

61

"I mean it!"

Simone slipped an arm around the young man's shoulders. "Don't be offended, my young friend. It is just – well – we believe old actors never die. We simply slip into the wings, change our makeup and costumes, and enter again, preferably up center, as the maid, the lover, the hero or the villain or – occasionally but rarely – as a God."

Niccolo returned to the carriage and Eleanora, and Simone slipped before the curtains in his ragged diamonds of many colors, a traditional uniform of an embittered soldier who had made a cloak of torn and tattered standards and flags in remembrance of the obscenity of war. He rapped three times with a staff, and this - the people knew - was the traditional warning a play was to begin.

The *sogetto* was typical *commedia dell'arte*, an absurd and disjointed plot allowing for a great deal of physical humor and improvisation.

Isabella and Francesco, attempting to keep the girl's father from preventing their elopement, attempted to convince Pantalone, the old man, he was pregnant. They insisted he should go into confinement immediately until the baby is born. Arlecchino, the cunning servant, and the would-be Dottore had assisted the young lovers with a verbal barrage of totally illogical "facts," but the old miser remained unconvinced.

"A man cannot have a baby!" Pantalone croaked.

"Yes he can," Arlecchino assured him. "History is filled with stories of men conceiving."

"Indeed yes," insisted Dottore. "It is called the

'Wandering Womb' disease."

"But it usually happens only to the most wealthy, signore," Arlecchino added, "because they are the only ones who can afford to support and raise a child in these trying times."

"Many of my male bankers are rich and have no children!"

"They do not have the time between foreclosures and lawsuits!" Arlecchino suggested.

"Still," Dottore exclaimed, "many male bankers have conceived children without assistance. You never see their brats of course, because they are regarded as liabilities until they are grown and can bring in more money. Until then they are kept locked in large cash boxes with other promissory notes."

Pantalone fumed and stormed around the platform-stage. "But – but – it takes two to make a baby! That's – that's *fundamental!* And I haven't slept with a woman since – well – it's been some time!"

"Centuries," offered Arlecchino.

"But in cases of the 'Wandering Womb'," said Dottore, "copulation is not only entirely unnecessary but also extremely tiring for a man your age. You did not *have* to copulate. The angels took care of that."

"Thank them for nothing!" Pantalone grumbled.

"The Church has never spoken against the disease," said Arlecchino, "because they maintain a child is a gift from God, and therefore can be bestowed on anyone, anywhere and at any time – if you're not careful."

"And your time has run its course," declared Dottore as he waved an enormous bottle of dark liquid at the dumbfounded old man. "Your urine sample reveals the delivery may come at any moment. You *must* go into confinement at once!"

"I never *give* anyone anything!" Pantalone thundered. "You have to pay for it!"

"We can no longer wait!" Dottore thundered. *"Now!"*

The comic women, Colombina and Lesbina, rushed in to assist the delivery. They forced the old man from his trousers as Dottore appeared to plunge the syringe into Pantalone's anus.

The audience roared with delight and surprise as Dottore produced "Pantalone's baby" from under his cloak – a fully-grown and black-masked Scapino who rocked the piazza with his wailing!

Immediately Arlecchino set to work picking lice from Scapino's hair, and Colombina rocked the "infant" at a rapidly-accelerating pace.

When everyone demanded Pantalone suckle his new-born, the sequence ended as most *commedia* scenes: with a mad chase over and around the sparse furniture, the two-bladed "slapstick" of the comic servants being noisily employed against backsides, and the Capitano's long sword occasionally lifting the women's skirts to their waists.

"It's silly," said Eleanora as the performance ended and the coach slowly and carefully maneuvered through the departing audience. "Imagine! A pregnant man!"

"Farce is not meant to be credible," argued Niccolo. "The absurdity is what makes it comic. You establish the situation quickly and then accelerate the action so the audience has no opportunity to think about it."

"Is that something the buffoons taught you?"

"Among other things, but what they are saying is true: much of life is absurd."

"Perhaps – but if all these clever and laughing male actors *really* had to endure a pregnancy and delivery, they wouldn't think it so absurd."

As the coach gathered speed and rambled through the narrow streets toward the palazzo, Niccolo found himself wondering: *Is she trying to tell me something?*

*

Maestro Leonardo had arrive safely and been greeted by the Contessa.

Now one sunny afternoon he sat comfortably in his rooms at the Bergamini court when he was treated to a sudden illusion. He tried not to laugh, but he was both amused and momentarily puzzled by the apparition staggering toward him. It certainly had Niccolo's face and voice, was well-dressed in a courtier's suitable attire, but he appeared to have grown until the young man's head was now on a level with the Maestro's own.

He was followed almost at once by the elevated scullery girl, now a lady-in-waiting to the Contessa, Madonna Eleanora.

"I see the Contessa has kept you well-fed, Niccolo," he smiled.

Niccolo beamed and attempted two more tentative steps toward Leonardo. "The very air up here is invigorating! It encourages growth!"

"What I see," Leonardo smiled, "is a somewhat awkward demonstration of balance."

Niccolo frowned. "What?"

"I presume you are balancing on some sort of extensions attached to your legs," the Maestro said softly. "It is a fine achievement, but I have often observed when a man balances on one foot, the shoulder of the opposite side is higher. Yours is not. I notice too the pit of the throat will be above the middle of the leg on which he rests. The navel, of course, must always lie on the central line of the weight above it, and ...!"

"I have often observed you have a talent for diminishing the fun in things," Niccolo grumbled. He carefully lowered himself and squatted on the edge of a table. He gestured to a laughing Eleanora who ran forward to help remove the stilts. "I expected applause rather than a commentary on the mathematical laws pertaining to balance."

Leonardo smiled at his friend. "I am sorry if I disappointed you, Niccolo, but as I repeatedly remind you, mathematics *is* truth. Two and two are four everywhere and at any time. Your walk was a fine attempt, a notable achievement, but surely you do not begrudge me the opportunity to apply what I observed of your newly-developed talent? As you know, I apply the laws of mathematics to everything, including my own attempts at invention. I am only trying to help you perfect the motion so your stride becomes natural and less - studied."

Eleanora rolled up the young man's pantaloons and unfastened the straps binding the stilts to his legs. "I think you did exceptionally well," she smiled at Niccolo.

"But what, in heaven's name, would compel you to

66

attempt such a thing?" Leonardo asked quietly. "Your own height is quite sufficient for your needs."

"I am consistently being mistaken for a dwarf!"

"Never by the knowledgeable," replied the Maestro. "Only by those poor specimens of humanity who feel it necessary to group individuals into classes, those who confuse intelligence with boredom, compassion with cowardice, and the poor with inferiority. I am ashamed of you, Niccolo! Such people are not worthy of your attention. Their ignorance is bred into them by their fathers and forefathers. Never doubt it. Some aspects of tradition can be comforting, but they can also blind you to the necessity for change. I assure you, my friend, stupidity and ignorance is passed on to future generations just as eye color, skin conditions and hair loss."

Niccolo shook his head. He smiled, knowing anything and everything could release the Maestro to deliver a dissertation, and usually he was not only correct but adamant. He slipped from the table's edge to stand erect on his own slippered feet.

"When I fled the Castello Sforzesco, I was befriended by the *commedia* players who had been performing for Sanseverino's festivities. They were preparing me to assume the role of Giangurcolo, and it required I should be of normal height."

"You *are* of normal height," Leonardo said. "For you."

As Eleanora took the stilts and the pantaloons and left the chamber, Niccolo approached and embraced the artist. "I *did* miss your lectures. Forgive me if I insulted you, Maestro. It's just – well – you observe a wealth of details, and you can never refuse an

67

opportunity to relate them. That can be overwhelming."

Leonardo smiled and nodded as Niccolo stepped back.

Yes, he thought to himself, *instruction can be boring. Ask any student.*

"Ah, young Niccolo," he finally murmured, "I apologize for attempting to make you brilliant. You have an incredible ability. One I wished I had. You observe and remember. I observe and note it in my codices. But the truth remains: whether in art or life, the truth is always in the details."

Niccolo nodded. "Wasn't my attempt to be taller at least amusing?"

The Maestro's mood became obviously darker. His voice lowered in pitch and volume and he said, "Amusing? Yes. I suppose so, but unhappily one man's amusement can be another's agony." He turned away so Niccolo could not see the tears gathering in his eyes or the trembling of his lips. "As I - as I was fleeing from Milan," he continued quietly, "I witnessed the invaders destroying my clay equestrian model, the one I had spent four years designing. They delighted in using it for target practice and then pulled the rider from the saddle with hooks and ropes. "He sighed. "They laughed as they did it. I imagine those who ravaged my model city of Vigevano were also - amused."

Niccolo put an arm around the Maestro as well as he could. "Aren't you the man who pointed out the blind cannot judge colors? What did you expect of barbarians but barbarity? But now, rejoice! You are here with me, with Eleanora and the Contessa! We are safe!"

"Yes," the Maestro replied softly, "but I had to abandon some of my equipment: easels, palettes, pigments, my collection of medicinal herbs and powders. I packed and shipped what I thought were most indispensable, but now and again, I discover I no longer have a favorite brush or the precise formula for mixing a particular blue. I have lost some of my small library, some models of my war machines, my tricks and games to amuse ..."

Niccolo raised both hands. "You have only lost what can be replaced in time and with a little peace."

"But the only work I have done here is a chalk study of the Madonna with St. Anne and the two children, the Christus and the Baptist."

"And it may well be enough alone to dazzle the future and make it remember you."

They walked together into the corridor and stopped before Leonardo's portrait of the Contessa.

"The ermine was inspired, Maestro," said Niccolo, "but it surprises me a little because I was told at the time you considered the lady as immoral, because she was the Moor's mistress. Yet you painted her holding an ermine, the symbol of chastity."

Leonardo nodded. "But I did not use the ermine as a symbol of chastity," he said smiling. "It is an amusement, a jest."

"A jest?"

"It is a play upon the lady's name at the time. It is Greek for 'ermine'." He turned to face the younger man. "I'm surprised you didn't know that, my young tutor of dead languages. Perhaps you should spend less time with Madonna Eleanora and more with your studies."

Niccolo grinned. "I spend my time studying Eleanora." He turned and began to walk away. "As for jests, that surprises me even more. I was not aware you were given to amusements in your work."

"When I was apprenticed to Maestro del Verrocchio," Leonardo said with pretended indignation. "I was considered quite amusing, and the games and puzzles I created for the Moor were declared delightful by every member of his court."

He stopped suddenly, and Niccolo stopped with him. "There are many times I feel compelled to laugh, Niccolo," he said softly. "Otherwise I would spend many of my days weeping."

Niccolo opened his mouth to speak, but the Maestro continued, "There are times I think perhaps I am one of God's little jests. I think He watches me, shakes His head and laughs."

"I assure you, Maestro," replied Niccolo, "no one, not even God himself, laughs at you!" They turned together and entered into the antechamber. "You are the consummate artist, Maestro. The Contessa's portrait stands in testimony to your greatness."

"But God created her beauty," Leonardo replied. "I only copied it. The lady is one of the few people I ever met who possessed perfect mathematical features."

Niccolo's grin stretched from ear to ear. "Indeed? And what are the perfect mathematical features of the face?"

"Well," the Maestro recited quietly, "for one thing the space between the mouth and the base of the nose is one-seventh of the entire face."

"Always?"

"It is an absolute," Leonardo nodded. "And the space from the mouth to beneath the chin is a quarter of the face, and the space between the chin and the base of the nose is one-third of the total. Furthermore," he rushed on without seeming to take a breath, "The space between the top of the nose to below the chin is normally one-half of the face; and the thickness of the neck one-and-three-quarters of the space from the eyebrows to the nape of the neck!"

Niccolo could only stare. Twice he attempted to open his mouth to say something, and each time he became stone, his mind refusing to pose a question.

"Furthermore, my young tutor," the Maestro continued, "the greatest width of the face at eye level should be equal to the area between the hairline at the top of the forehead and the mouth; whereas the width of the nose is half the length of the space between the tip of the nose and the start of the eyebrows!"

"Always?"

"Always! Unless you're deformed." He smiled. "It is mathematical, and it is recorded so in my workbooks!" He put a hand on Niccolo's shoulder. "There! Now don't you find *that* amusing?"

It seemed minutes before the young man managed to blurt out, "No! It scares me to death!"

CHAPTER THREE

INFORMATION AND INVITATIONS

Madonna Isabella d'Este, the celebrated Marquesa of Mantua, sat comfortably enthroned in the high-backed chair-of-state. Strands of lustrous pearls were woven among her blonde curls, and loops of gold paraded among the pile of her velvet gown. The milky whiteness of her throat was enhanced by a sable band supporting a large emerald. Always voluptuous since her early teens, her *camora* now exposed both shoulders and the shadowy canyon between her breasts.

She was pleased with her appearance.

But not with the assembly.

Her narrow eyes scanned the galleries of the great hall which was festooned with banners and heraldic shields proclaiming the importance and heritage of each of the hundred nobles and women now gorging themselves at the lady's expense. The less prestigious were seated at the several long tables placed diagonally before the Marquesa's own. She forced a smile as she surveyed the elegantly-dressed and chattering parasites feeding on her generosity and goodwill.

She instinctively reached across the damask cloth for the hand of her husband, Gian Francesco Gonzaga.

It was not there.

As usual.

Winter usually provided a relief from warring and normally the Marquis would spend the cold months in Mantua before resuming warfare in the spring; but after they had ridden together in triumph in Milan, Gian Francesco was immediately summoned to Venice by the doge and the Council of Ten - supposedly to render a general analysis of a new military and political situation, but the Marquesa also suspected she had a rival in the city of canals.

And she didn't care.

She *did* care she had been "instructed" to immediately return to Mantua.

She resented being "instructed" to do anything, and she despaired of ever understanding the complexities of Italian politics and the sudden shifts of policy. Still she managed to maintain a small garrison of her own, in addition to those of both potential friends and possible enemies, most of whom were now seated before her where she could keep an eye on them.

From under the golden canopy over her chair, she watched with a mixture of scorn and satisfaction as those ensembled celebrated the return of some sun and warmth to Mantua. She shook her head as she saw them finish off what remained of the great saddles of venison, the coveys of partridges and gaggles of geese, the lobster, trout and salmon. The platters of wild strawberries once nested in castles of citron were now sparse beds of crumbs and stems. The crystal carafes of the spiced Pauillac, the Malvesian, the Corsican and the Nerac wines held little now but a reminiscent scent.

She glanced down at her own empty, three-tiered platter of glazed majolica depicting Adam and Eve considering the apple, and she considered the worth of the golden utensils, including the relatively-new dining instrument, the fork.

"God made fingers before forks," her Cardinal-brother had warned her when they were first introduced at one of the courtly feasts.

The Marquesa smiled as she watched her court struggling with the new utensils. She was quietly amused at the sight of a courtier scooping up a piece of meat and gravy with his spoon, sipping the liquid and then harpooning the meat with his fork, stabbing it as one might attack an enemy, lifting it, and then removing the morsel from the tines and shoving it into his mouth with his fingers!

She despaired of converting the court to anything new.

Suddenly she was conscious of the tall, serious man in the silver tunic who had drawn closer to her chair and pretended to muffle a cough to draw her attention. He was bearded, over hollow cheeks with a narrow and hooked nose like a bird's beak. He had the wide, dark eyes of an owl, and he perched near the arm of her chair like a vulture prepared to steal a morsel from his lady's plate.

She did not like Andrea Meneghina, but her husband had chosen him as his chamberlain and "instructed" her to respect him – which she did – and to trust him – with she did not.

She sat back in her chair to enable him to whisper at her ear.

"I regret it has been verified, Excellency. There was nothing there," the bearded man said softly.

"Nothing?!"

"Captain d'Angeness was with the assassin and our mercenaries. He said they killed the courier, and some of his men took the body away. He – as instructed – kept and secured the courier's head so if the body is later found – it cannot be identified."

She nodded "Well at least one of the instructions were followed. Tell me about this alleged verification."

"We sent agents to verify what the Captain and Signore Cristani had reported to you after the – ah – the ' incident 'at Montagnana. Our agents said they returned to the inn, questioned everyone of importance, traced the route of the courier, returned and said everything verifies what had been reported: the Venetian and the mercenaries thoroughly searched and found nothing."

"I cannot believe it! I personally gave the courier the necklace – and in the presence of my husband! Now am I to believe it just vanished into thin air?"

"I cannot account for it, Excellency."

"Someone somewhere must know what happened to it!"

"Our agents also could *not* verify the report we received from the Toad – beg your pardon – Signore Nanino – concerning any incompetence on the part of Signore Cristani or the Venetian. It would appear, Excellency, Nanino simply took upon himself the authority to alter the original plan and assume command of the operation."

"Indeed?"

"Indeed. And the proprietor was questioned and some local people who saw the mercenaries arrive and argue with the Venetian, but they agree it was the Captain who paid the assassin who rode off immediately."

"What says Signore Ottaviano Cristani to this new report? I appointed *him* to oversee this operation for the court."

"He verifies his authority was also destroyed by Signore Nanino. He says the dwarf told him *you* had instructed *him* to take command of the operation, and from then on, he took charge."

"Nanino did that, did he?" She shook her head. "I wonder what the little devil had in mind? I indulge his whims when I can, but this – how did you put it – this 'incident' was of vital importance to myself and the Marquis. Well. Still – Nanino is infinitely more cunning than Ottaviano which could have proven an asset. Still, the Venetian had the confidence of our courtier and must have been furious when the plans were altered and our mercenaries were suddenly sent to join him."

"And Signore Cristani is definitely not happy."

"I must find a way to make it up to him."

"And the Toad - I mean - Signore Nanino? Surely he over-stepped his position."

The Marquesa frowned and emitted a sigh. "I'm certain he had good reasons to alter the plans, but I will take the matter up with him. The important thing is: our agents verify Captain d'Angeness' men searched thoroughly and there was no necklace?"

"Very thoroughly."

"And there was nothing to suggest deception?"

"Nothing."

She frowned and unconsciously toyed with her special fork which was shaped to suggest a Greek goddess emerging from a cocoon of grape vines. She wondered if everything occurred as reported to her, or had the chamberlain's incompetents missed the one vital indication she had been deceived. She did not enjoy intrigue, although she was a principal practitioner of the art, and she expected everyone else to be honest and totally trustworthy.

"Is it still possible the Captain is lying?"

"Perhaps, but my men report a junior officer who was with the mercenaries has been unusually agitated since their return to the court and has been drinking heavily. We may be able to extract more information from him, if you wish."

"Well," she replied, "it is always wise to eliminate anyone who knows too much about anything, isn't it?"

"Is that your will?"

She hesitated, not because there was a question in her mind as to the value of such an interrogation, but because the officer had probably served under her husband in the wars, and there is – as she knew - a somewhat mystical bond between men who faced death together. It would be difficult to explain his "disappearance" to the Marquis upon his return to Mantua.

The best thing was to make certain *she* was not involved in any of it.

Finally she sighed and murmured, "Well – decide for yourself, chancellor. Isn't that what you are here for?"

"Yes, Excellency." He nodded, drew even closer and

whispered. "One other matter. We have learned Maestro Leonardo da Vinci has escaped from the Castello Sforzesco, wintered in the Certosa and is now in residence in Cremona."

"In Cremona?"

"In the palazzo of the Count Bergamini."

"Contessa Cecilia? That bitch who was the Moor's whore? The tramp pushed aside when Ludovico married my sister? What is he doing with her? I thought the old fool preferred boys."

"We understand he is in sanctuary."

"How fortunate for him. But why is this of any importance to me?"

"My men were told he has in his possession a red notebook in which he recorded certain – indiscretions – which occurred over the years in the court of Duke Ludovico Sforza."

"I am not interested in the gossip of the 'blackberry's' court. I hold the Moor responsible for the death of my sister, and I hope he is damned for all eternity."

"I understand," said the chancellor, "but I am also given to understand if the contents of this book were made known to the Emperor Maximilian, he would immediately imprison the Moor whom he now shelters in Germany. He might also withdraw his support from those of our enemies who are preparing to usurp Ferrara."

Suddenly the lady was alert. She wrapped a fist around the half-naked goddess on her fork. "Indeed? And the Maestro keeps this book with him?"

"So I am given to believe." He paused and leaned

still closer. "I do not presume to advise you, Excellency, and perhaps the matter should wait for the Marquis' return, but I think it might prove advantageous for you to resurrect the commission once assigned to da Vinci to paint your portrait. Once he is here in Mantua, we could easily get the red book for you."

That's what I admire in you, Andrea, the Marquesa thought to herself. *You never bare your blade unless you are assured the victim could not possibly survive.*

There was a pause before she whispered, "See to it. Prepare an invitation and a commission. Gian Francesco most certainly could not object to having a portrait of me – even if he would probably use it for target practice. Make the amount sufficient to arouse the Maestro's interest, but not enough to arouse the fury of my frugal husband."

Andrea smiled and nodded which reminded the Marquesa of the movement of a cobra's head just before it strikes. "It is doubtful his Excellency would ever *have* to pay it," said the chancellor. "If he would impose a deadline for the portrait, and make clear the Maestro will receive nothing if the work is not completed *on time*, his investment would be safe. Maestro Leonardo is notorious for never completing a commission on schedule."

Isabella smiled.

Yes. Leonardo is known for never finishing a project in the time allotted him. The artist was also known to have whimsically refused a few profitable commissions for some reason known only to himself.

"Would he come here, do you think?"

"I believe he would," Andrea said softly. "He knows

79

you already have in your court Pietro Bembo, Baldassar Castiglione and Niccolo Panizatto. He enjoys conversation with men he respects. He also admires our court painter, Maestro Mantegna, whose *Dead Christ* he saw at the Brera in Milan and openly praised."

"Good."

The chancellor paused. "I – ah – I should also point out he travels with – well - a retinue."

"Mercenaries?"

"No. No. More like – well – servants. He has two apprentices, and ...."

"Oh yes. I remember the blonde one: the face of an angel and the soul of a demon."

"That would be the one he calls Salai. The other is Francesco Melzi, and I understand he has also now befriended a remarkable dwarf. They are together even now."

"A dwarf?!"

"This one gifted with a mind which remembers everything he sees or reads."

"Interesting – but I am surrounded by dwarves!" The Marquesa sighed, and the chamberlain immediately realized he had taken up far too much of his mistress' dinner time. "Should I invite them all?"

"See to it."

"I will," he whispered and discreetly backed away.

The hostess adjusted herself, sat erect in her chair and again picked up the heavy fork with the tines suggesting birds' bills. She repeatedly tapped the goblet of Murano glass before her. She was pleased with the resonate tones demanding attention. The glass, like many of the families of her court, was of quality.

Watching his lady, a courtier under the far arch instantly slammed his heavy wooden staff of authority against the floor with a resounding boom. Immediately the musicians and the two choirs in the side galleries who had been softly serenading the diners silenced their music and focused their attention on the hostess.

All conversations dissolved into whispers.

"My most illustrious lords and ladies," the Marquesa addressed them. "We are here tonight to welcome the spring and to honor some among you. First, may I introduce the noted and noble Signore Guglielmo Gaetani of Ferrara to whom we have granted our hospitality and our protection. His presence here may serve, I trust, as a warning: we of Mantua are defiantly opposed to any usurpation of Ferrara, the fief of our Gonzaga kinsman, the noble Duke Ercole d'Este. "On behalf of myself and my illustrious - but absent - lord, we welcome you, signore."

She turned and nodded to Gaetani who returned the salute. Some of the ladies loudly repeated the welcome and most of the men still capable of raising a goblet beat a tattoo of approval on the tables.

"Signore Gaetani," the Marquesa continued, "also brings us the news Cesare Borgia has been officially appointed Duke of Valentinois and is therefore, by God's merciful grace, no longer a Cardinal of Rome." There was a small ripple of laughter, and the Marquesa turned to smile at the scarlet-robed cleric sharing her table. "I trust, brother," she said, "you will not report this small jest to His Holiness, the bastard's father."

Again there was a brief, cautious wave of laughter.

The members of the court of Mantua were accustomed to the Marquesa's blunt speech and occasional use of profanity, but the open reference to Cesare Borgia's illegitimate birth was momentarily surprising.

Cardinal Ippolito d'Este, one arm around the waist of the lady beside him, smiled at his hostess. "I am no longer in the confidence of the Vicar of Christ, dear sister," he shouted. "And as for poor Cesare Borgia, I understand he is now searching for a titled wife to anchor his new position among the nobility." Again the diners laughed. "We are informed he has been defiantly refused by Princess Carlotta of Taranto, by Carlotta of Aragon and by the daughter of the king of Navarre."

"I would think," said the Marquesa, "the refusals from such noble women might give him pause and indicate to the Borgias how much Italy scorns these pretentious Spaniards."

The Cardinal laughed, turned and nuzzled his companion's neck. "I'm not certain Cesare is a rapid learner."

The Marquesa laughed with the assembly but silently reflected on the stories of the second son to the Pope.

Yes, she thought, *Cesare does not feel a need for intelligence and reflection. He confronts an obstacle and simply removes it.*

She lightly tapped the goblet again to restore order.

"We must also take this opportunity to thank our trusted and beloved Signore Ottaviano Cristani who – some time past – successfully performed a service of some delicacy for us." She nodded toward the chestnut-haired, middle-aged gentleman at the far left end of her table. "We sincerely thank you, Ottaviano."

The tall man who was singled out by the gesture, remained focused on his empty goblet, but loudly announced, "As always, my hand and heart are yours, Marquesa, although I regret the results of the project – which I understand have now been verified - were not entirely satisfactory to either of us."

How does he know of the verification?

Isabella's smile broadened. "*I* am not disappointed, signore, and as for your heart – at the moment it seems to be more entangled with Madonna Louisa's dark eyes which, as I can see, are gazing tenderly at you, and the only hand not lightly holding the lady's hand clutches an empty goblet."

Ottaviano flushed as the guests laughed. "Well, such as they are, Marquesa, empty or occupied, my heart and my hand are yours."

Some of the ensemble cheered and applauded.

The Marquesa thought: *they are all too far into their cups. They would probably cheer if I said the meal they just consumed had been poisoned.*

"In addition," she continued, "we welcome to our court for the first time Signore Johannes Vendramm, the young nephew of our friend and master of the Hanseatic League, the noble Bruno Vendramm. Young Johannes has been sent to us – as his uncle puts it – for 'seasoning'." There was another outburst of laughter, and the Marquesa smiled at the handsome and obviously embarrassed young man at the far end of the table. "I judge from your uncle's choice of words, signore, he mistakes you for a flank of mutton."

The Belgian flushed, smiled but managed to say, "It

is possibly because I come to your court, Marquesa, as innocent as a lamb and determined to be obedient and submissive to my beautiful and noble shepherdess."

This time the response drew louder applause and more cheers from the diners,

"Well-spoken, my young friend," Isabella smiled. "and your first obedience is to a ritual of this court. You are to prepare something for our Lenten Gifts. It is our custom to spend these long winter days preparing small benevolences: altar clothes, candles, laces. We then distribute them on the first day of Lent to all our abbeys, monasteries, convents and churches. As you are new to our traditions and may not understand what precisely is expected of you, I will assign someone to guide you." She scanned the room, and her eyes rested on a beautiful young woman with long red hair. "Yes. I think I will hand you to Madonna Maddalena d'Oggione. Is your damask altar cloth advanced enough, milady, to provide time for guiding our guest?"

"If it please you," the lady said, nodding from her chair.

"See to it," she smiled. Again she surveyed the room, and judging the appetites of her guests and courtiers had been satisfied, she proclaimed, "My illustrious lords and ladies, I now offer for your pleasure and delight our beloved master of amusements, the incredible, the irrepressible, the incomparable Nanino!"

Immediately a loud gong from somewhere beyond the archway alerted everyone to the procession of four dwarf maidens who half-danced half-shuffled into the great hall. They were dressed as nuns, although their

chins, mouths and noses were hidden under
diaphanous veils after the imagined fashion of the
Turks. The hems of their nuns' robes revealed bare
feet with toes painted scarlet, and their fingers danced
to the soft rhythms of tiny bells. Behind them came a
male dwarf wearing an obviously-false black beard and
seated on a throne which was carried by four other
small men.

Some of the guests immediately roared. "Nanino!
It's Nanino!"

Some sat in a stony silence.

Some laughed at the solemn demeanor of the mock
pontiff, robed head to toe in the immaculate white of
innocence and crowned with a triple-tiara too large for
his head. In each hand he carried a gold key which he
crossed upon his chest.

"My benevolent Marquesa, my illustrious Cardinals,
good lords and ladies, I come to confirm you in our
mutual faith as warriors of God," he declared loudly.
"This sacrament demands I must slap you as I assign
you a new name in Christ. Pray, do not take it
personally and slap me back!"

Again some of the guests roared with laughter.

The Marquesa turned to face her brother-Cardinal
and whispered, "I trust you are not offended by
Nanino's papal attire, Eminence."

Cardinal d'Este pretended a smile. "Not at all, sister
– provided the evening's amusement includes burning
your obnoxious Toad at the stake for heresy and
blasphemy."

"He does not like to be called 'Toad'."

"Begging your indulgence, sister, I do not give a

tinker's dam what Toad does or does not like."

The Marquesa quietly smiled and pushed herself deeper into her cushioned chair.

He is annoyed!

Some of my court is humiliated!

Most are intoxicated and will suffer tomorrow!

Rome and the Borgias have been ridiculed.

The evening is a success!

 The doors to Leonardo's chamber suddenly opened to admit the Contessa Bergamini, a vision of both majesty and gentility in a red silk chemise pulled into puffs at the shoulders and sleeves and topped with a fitted collar of lace. The sleeve points, allowed to drape rather than be tucked out of sight provided a nice touch of informality. The lady's head displayed a cap of pearl ropes which anchored a long braid of false hair which trailed down to her waist. In her right hand she carried a rolled parchment, the seal broken and the ribbons dangling.

Niccolo and Leonardo both saluted the lady with deep bows, their right arms placed diagonally across their breasts, their right legs extended before them.

"I thought I heard laughter," she said. "Have I interrupted something amusing?"

Leonardo stood erect. "I was just informing my young friend of the absolute proportions of the face, and he, in turn, has again been demonstrating his newly-acquired ability to appear taller, so he can become a *commedia* player."

86

"God forbid!" The Contessa crossed to the center of the chamber. "Is everything satisfactory?"

"Beyond all expectations, Excellency," said Leonardo.

"Then perhaps your expectations are set too low," she laughed. "But in any case, I am delighted to see you again after all these years. As I'm certain you have noticed, I keep your portrait of me in a place of honor."

"It was good to see it again," said the Maestro. "Perhaps while I am here, you will permit me to make some very minor changes in it?"

The Contessa laughed. "You will *not!* I know your methods, Maestro! You are never satisfied with what you accomplish! You are constantly altering and changing this thing or that! You paint over your own work! You have painted over complete portraits with different poses! Whatever are you after?"

"Perfection."

There was a moment of silence. "Ah," said the Contessa quietly. "Well, let us leave that to God, shall we?"

Eleanora reappeared carrying a silver tray with four goblets and a large glass carafe. As she placed them on the table beside the chaise, the Contessa shook her head.

"Whatever am I going to do with you, child? Please try to remember you are now a lady of my court, and you are not expected to lift and carry things. That is why we have servants. They will think you are trying to usurp their position and take the bread from their mouths. Now go, my dear. We have to speak about someone in terms which are not for tender ears."

Eleanora made a barely recognizable curtsy, winked

at Niccolo, and left the room.

The lady gestured the men to sit as she lowered herself into the comfortable, armed chair beside a table. She placed a parchment between the goblets and the carafe of wine, smoothed her skirt and looked at the duo.

"I have received an epistle from the Marquesa of Mantua requesting I send you both – and your apprentices - to the Gonzaga court. It appears Isabella has decided to reinstate her commission to you, Maestro, for a portrait. She offers quite a lot of money for your efforts. She wrote directly to me as if she needed my permission for you to come. Apparently the monster is under the impression I have you both under lock and key."

Leonardo smiled. "I have heard of the marvels of the Gonzaga court," he said. "I met the Marquesa and the Marquis once or twice in Milan. The Marquesa came to visit with her sister, the Duke's wife, Madonna Beatrice."

"I know the lady. Throughout Italy Isabella is noted for her intelligence and cleverness. She dresses elaborately and reads voraciously. Unfortunately for the lady, what she reads she fails to understand. She has a tendency to appoint courtiers to 'oversee' her projects, and then if they fail, the courtier is blamed. She can often be disarmingly charming and seduce owls to sing *tenebrae,* but her quick temper and her arrogant disregard for human life mar her character. Still - my analysis of the lady has nothing to do with the immediate question. Do you wish me to acknowledge her request and accept the commission for you?"

Leonardo stroked his beard. "Well, I cannot accept your generous hospitality forever, Contessa; and while I have been considering a return to my home city of Florence, I must recognize the fact I rely on commissions and subsidies in order to perfect my skills and feed myself and my apprentices. It is an unfortunate truth, but artists have always relied on patronage to simply survive. To the average man art is hardly a necessity. To the wealthy, portraits and frescoes are principally a way to preserve their victories and triumphs – however exaggerated."

"But surely patronage imposes restrictions? Is that not an impediment to the artist?"

"But not as severe as poverty and starvation."

"Surely it restricts your freedom? I mean, although the lady may have the face of a radish, you may not paint her that way."

"True." He smiled as the Contessa and gave a light laugh. "Fortunately a little liberty in shortening the nose of a general or disguising the facial hair on a lady's upper lip is part of honoring a commission. I must also consider the Mantua court has some attractions for me. Pietro Bembo is there, and so, too, are Baldasar Castiglione and Niccolo Panizatto, the young scholar of classical literature. These are men I admire and respect. I understand the Mantuan court also possesses an extensive library. I know they have copies of John Pecham's *Perspectiva Communis*, Pliny's *Historia Naturalis* and Sallust's *Bellum Ougurthinum* which are texts I have long wanted to explore."

The Contessa frowned. "The court also houses Isabella. She despised Ludovico and constantly referred to him as 'the Duke of Bari' instead of by his proper title. She has always denied Il Moro's legitimacy of succession and was furious when he rejected her as a possible wife. Only then did she arrange for her marriage to Gian Francesco, and Ludovico proceeded to marry her sister. Later she held the Duke responsible for the death of Beatrice. She was livid when told the Moor fell into the bed of the *puttana*, Madonna Crivelli, within a month of his wife's death."

"I am aware of her hatreds."

"The lady may want more from you than a portrait."

"What do you mean?"

"Well," smiled the Contessa, "despite your aversion to intrigue, you kept a record of all the – indiscretions - committed by Ludovico while you were in his court."

She passed a goblet to Leonardo.

"How do you know that?"

"I had more eyes and ears in the Castello Sforzeco than you can imagine," the lady said quietly. "It is a small notebook bound in red leather, unlike your other workbooks which are larger and bound in wood and dark leather."

Leonardo frowned. "I repeat: how did you know that?" He turned to Niccolo.

"No, no, no," snapped the Contessa as she crossed and presented a goblet to Niccolo. "Little Niccolo is your most trusted of friends – unlike one of your own assistants."

"Salai!"

The Contessa nodded. "The beautiful boy has an unfortunate tendency to reveal everything if the conditions are right – if he is gifted with an obliging wench and an ample supply of food, drink and the seductive 'clink-clink' of coins. I'm sorry to have to tell you this, Maestro, but it was obviously Salai who made the Duke's security men aware of the existence of your red book."

"I – I wanted them to know of it," said the Maestro softly, his attention focused on the wine. "I wanted the Duke to know I had it. It was for my own protection. As long as the Duke knew I had it, I was protected."

"I love you, Maestro," said the Contessa, "but you are an innocent in a corrupt world. You are simply making an excuse for Salai's treachery." She lifted the remaining goblet. "However, the point is moot. You kept a record. Isabella knows you kept it, and her invitation to paint her portrait may also provide her with an opportunity to get her hands on it. She knows it might be something she can show to the Duke's own remaining ally, the Emperor, and he may decide Ludovico would be better resting in his dungeon than in one of his bed chambers." She sighed. "But – well - if you wish to go, so be it. You can simply paint the Marquesa, and my dear Niccolo will probably peer into all the dark corners; possibly steal wine and pastries from the scullery and chase after the wenches." She smiled at Niccolo. "But god help you, my small friend, if your good lady Eleanora hears if it." She raised her goblet higher in salute. "Now! Go, merry gentlemen, and amuse yourselves!"

Leonardo and Niccolo exchanged glances – the Maestro suddenly feeling very tired and not especially relishing the thought of entering a bee hive where a single sting could prove fatal; and Niccolo visualizing himself with stilts, towering over assassins and deceivers, sword in his hand and fire in his belly.

They then, obediently, sipped their wine.

*

It was two nights later when Niccolo was aroused from sleep by a distant bell sounding the hour. He then became aware Eleanora was pounding on his shoulders. He turned over and realized she was beside his bed with two male servants carrying candelabra.

She barked at him, "Hurry! Dress and come to the Contessa's reception chamber! She has someone she wants you to meet!"

"At this hour?"

"Now!"

Eleanora and the servants escorted him down the corridor to the reception chamber. Eleanora pushed him in the room and then quickly withdrew and closed the doors behind him.

He was surprised to find the chamber in darkness save for a circle of light surrounding the Contessa and an aged and somber gentleman with white hair and a beard in a modest short gown of dark satin with a velvet collar. A cap of black velvet was perched to one side of his head, and his stockings were as black as his cap. The Contessa was dressed for sleep with a loose-fitting *turca* of white lace over a diaphanous chemise. She gestured to the man seated beside her.

"Niccolo, this is Signore Agnolo Marinoni, the grand master of the Cambio, the bankers' guild in Venice. He has just arrived to discuss some matters with my husband, and he confided something to me which I think you should know. I know it is very late, but Signore Agnolo must leave immediately to return to Venice, and I felt it imperative you hear this."

She gestured with a delicate hand to the gentleman. "Signore Agnolo?"

The elderly gentleman cleared his throat and began in a gravelly voice. "Signore Niccolo, I must insist what I have to tell you be kept secret."

"Niccolo is accustomed to intrigue, signore," said the Contessa. "He served me as a confidential agent in the Milan court. I will vouch for his integrity."

Agnolo nodded. "Of course. Well - some years ago Ludovico Sforza, then Duke of Milan, lavished an enormous dowry on his niece when she married the German Emperor. The Duke could ill afford it, but appearances must be maintained, you understand?"

Niccolo nodded.

"Later, faced with an invasion and his credit refused by the Bank of St. George in Genoa, he turned to the Cambio for a loan of fifty thousand ducats. Naturally, in light of the Duke's continued extravagances and the prospect of war - which always drains treasuries - our board required some sort of security in case the Duke should default on the loan. His wife, Beatrice d'Este, pleaded with her sister, Isabella, Marquesa of Mantua, for help. Devoted to her sister, the Marquesa offered as collateral a legendary necklace of great value. It was usually referred to as the Tears of the Madonna."

"Why?"

"Because of its design: three-strands of diamonds of different sizes but all identically cut and shaped like rain drops. They were bound together by gold wire twisted and shaped like thorns, suggesting the mock crown placed on the head of Jesus as he was led to the cross. The necklace was extremely valuable, and its' authenticity was verified by Dutch assessors, so we accepted the necklace as collateral and advanced the money to her sister and to the Duke of Milan. Of course when the Moor fled to Germany, he defaulted on the loan. The Cambio and the Venetian Council of Ten had no choice but to call for an impounding of the collateral. Isabella realized she *finally* would have to relinquish the Tears to us; if only to maintain the good credit of her husband. If she refused, we would have no choice but to cut off all credit to the Gonzaga, inform the other banks in Italy, demand the doge strip the Marquis of his position as general and imprison him in the doge's palazzo in Venice. If necessary, we would even provide Mantua's enemies with funds to war against them."

Niccolo said quietly, "You say this necklace was unique?"

"There is no other necklace in the world like it. It was the reason for the attack, I'm certain."

Niccolo leaned forward. "Attack? What attack?"

"Last autumn we sent one of our most trusted couriers to the Gonzaga court," continued Agnolo. "He was to take possession of the Tears, document its authenticity and transport both to us in Venice. We have reason to believe the Marquesa was reluctant to part with it, but her husband wisely insisted, and was present for the assessment and the transfer. We know the transfer *was* made, because the courier sent word by pigeon he had received both the necklace and the verification from the Marquesa. The courier reported he was returning to Venice in the morning with the Tears."

"So?"

"So Cecco - that was his name – never reached our way station at Padua where he was to change to another horse. After another two days passed with no further communication, we sent a second agent to find out what could have happened. This second agent traced the route of the courier and discovered Cecco had broken his journey to spend a night at a small inn at Montagnana."

Niccolo seemed newly engrossed in the banker's narrative.

"Where, signore?"

"Montagnana," replied the agent. "A miserable little inn called the Olive Tree. Our couriers usually spend a night - when necessary - at our licensed establishments, and the Olive Tree was not on that list, but the courier is in a better position to judge any potential threats and can stop wherever he must."

Niccolo clasped the palms of his hands together, placed the tips on his mouth, and murmured a quiet, "Fascinating."

The banker continued. "The proprietor of The Olive Tree told our investigation agents he showed the room to Cecco, but complained our courier was abusive, ordered an excess of mulled wine, became drunk and wrecked the room. He even suggested the Cambio should make restitution for the damage done to his pig-sty. The proprietor showed our agents the new

95

sections he had to replace in the room: some floor boards, holes gouged out of the wall, blood stains on the walls, a missing carpet."

"A missing carpet?!"

"Absurd isn't it, but the proprietor insisted Cecco took the carpet with him! He said he saw our courier ride away with the carpet on the road to Padua." He paused and his voice lowered. "The premise is blatantly ridiculous, but the basic fact is: somewhere between the inn and Padua, Cecco – and the Tears - simply disappeared."

"I understand."

"If the proprietor lied about his carpet, we can assume he lied about everything."

"What did the Marquesa say?"

"She suggested our courier, knowing the value of what he was carrying, simply ran off with it. We must accept this explanation, because we have no other evidence; and because the courier's last report was he had the necklace, verified it, and departed Mantua with it; so we have to consider the loan paid."

"Indeed?" Niccolo frowned. "That is curious."

"I beg your pardon?"

"The Maestro told me of an interesting encounter he had with two Franciscan monks while he was in the Certosa. They came to express their appreciation of one of his works, and they related quite a story. Apparently they stayed at that very inn on the night your courier disappeared."

"They did? You're sure?"

"They named the Olive Tree. They said the proprietor permitted them to sleep in the stable, because the only available bedroom was occupied by a traveler who paid for the lodging. That must have been your courier. The friars said they were grateful for the place to rest, because they were on a mission to various shrines and were exhausted, but suddenly – they judged the time to be about midnight - they were aroused from sleep and driven out into the dark at sword's point by a band of mercenaries."

Signore Agnolo was plainly interested. "Mercenaries? Whose mercenaries?"

"They could not be identified, but the monks said they witnessed the mercenary officer and a strange gentleman in a dark cloak vehemently arguing with one another before the friars were forced away."

"Ah," was all the banker said.

"Well," Niccolo continued, "the friars told the Maestro they were forced down the road to a cave where they were able to shelter for the rest of the night. They told him early the next morning they saw the man in the cloak race past them without the others."

Agnolo rose and crossed to Niccolo. "Who were these mercenaries? How many were there? Were they in livery?"

"I suggest you speak directly to the Maestro about it, but as far as I remember, the monks said there were no images on their breastplates and no visible *impresa*. Obviously they did not wish to be identified."

"Most certainly," said the banker as he turned back to face the Contessa, "because it confirms what we suspect. We think the Marquesa planned to recover the Tears before they reached us, because she was reluctant to part with them. What better way to have the debt discharged and still have the necklace than to send armed men to recover it and kill the courier? But we cannot say even *that* with certainty, because we have no body. *If* our courier was murdered and the Tears stolen, where is the unfortunate man's body? If – as the proprietor and the Marquesa would have us believe – he simply ran off with the Tears, where is he now? And where are the Tears? It is a unique necklace. If it were sold or passed to someone, they would likely store it away. They could not wear it or trade it, because we have a thousand eyes and ears, and we would make our claim to it."

"From your tone, signore, I suspect you believe it was the Marquesa who sent mercenaries to kill the courier and recover the Tears."

"It is possible, but we cannot press the matter, because we have no proof."

"Isn't it possible the men were sent by someone else?" Niccolo said quietly. "Couldn't it have been men sent by someone else of prominence less acquainted with the way things are usually done? Couldn't this someone have heard about the necklace and decided to snatch it for himself?"

"I suppose that is possible too," said the banker. "But this much is certain: Cecco was a trained, experienced and a totally honest man. He would never have ridden away with the necklace much less a carpet! It is not in his nature. We are reasonably certain he was murdered."

"But the whole thing is ridiculous," Niccolo smiled. "As you say, whoever has the necklace can never wear it publicly. If it is as unique as you say, Signore Agnolo, anyone seen wearing it or attempting to sell it would instantly be branded the thief and the killer of Signore Cecco. The Cambio could have the individual, man or woman, apprehended immediately and sent across the Bridge of Sighs to the doge's prison."

"Precisely, signore," replied the banker with a nod, "but we cannot wait for such a revelation. We loaned a great deal of money on that necklace and people saw our agent depart with it."

"But what value has it if it cannot be worn or displayed?"

"True. There is always the possibility whoever has the Tears may just lock them away, perhaps for generations. It may take years before they ever appear in public again, and in the meantime we cannot collect the monies due us, because the Marquesa maintains she gave the necklace to our courier, and that is corroborated both by the courier's initial message he had them and was returning - and by the Marquis himself who witnessed the transfer."

The Contessa rose suddenly to her feet and said, "Now to the interesting part! My clever Niccolo, on behalf of the Cambio, Signore Agnolo would like to enlist *your* assistance in uncovering the truth."

Niccolo frowned. "The truth?"

"Was it the Gonzaga who sent the mercenaries to attack one of our most experienced and trusted couriers," replied the banker impatiently, "and if so, where are the Tears!"

"I have already informed the Marquesa you and the Maestro have agreed to accept her invitation and commission. As the Maestro pointed out, he cannot refuse such a generous commission, and it will add to his stature. But if - while you are in residence - you come across the Tears, inform me, and I will send word to Signore Agnolo in Venice."

Niccolo emitted a mock-sigh and smiled at the Contessa. "You want me to be a spy again, is that it, Contessa? Haven't you had enough of intrigue and deception? Now you propose sending both myself *and* the Maestro into the very jaws of this notorious she-cat, knowing full well if we are discovered sending information to you, the Marquesa will not hesitate to lock us away in her dungeons and – like poor Signore Cecco – simply disappear!"

"We believe Signore Cecco did not 'simply disappear'!" Signor Agnolo said sharply. "We are convinced he was murdered! But we have no body! The proprietor said he rode away the following morning, but we cannot prove he was lying. The truth about what happened at the inn must be revealed and passed to all the courts of Italy! Not only to bring justice against his possible killers, but also to warn others the Cambio will not be cheated! If the word should spread our bank made a loan without collateral, it will be the loss of everything!"

"I understand."

"If the Tears appear in Mantua," Agnolo added quickly, "it will indicate it was the Gonzaga mercenaries who killed or abducted our courier. The bank can then take appropriate measures not only to recover the collateral but also punish the thieves." He leaned forward and smiled. "We will pay you for any information of value, of course – within reason - but absolute secrecy *must* be maintained."

The Contessa sat back in her chair. "You will be doing a great service to the Cambio, Niccolo, and as Signore Agnolo said, you will be rewarded for your diligence. It is a challenge which should appeal to you. You can travel with the Maestro as an emissary from my husband's court; so no one should be suspicious if you frequently send us messages; but be cautious. I personally believe the Marquesa has invited you, because she knows of the red book."

"How would she know of the red book?"

"Because she makes it her business to know *everything.* She probably knows if the contents of the book were revealed to the German Emperor, he would withdraw his protection of Ludovico and have him imprisoned. So I'm simply saying, be careful. You must realize if Isabella becomes suspicious, she would not hesitate to have both you and the red book 'disappear' – just as someone made the unfortunate courier and the Tears disappear."

"The Gonzaga court is particularly secretive and selective," added the banker. "They have connections with Rome and the Borgias. "

"And this should be of some interest to you," said the Contessa, "Isabella maintains an assembly of dwarves whom she treats as her personal playthings. They have their own quarters in a separate wing of the palazzo where everything is scaled to their size. She keeps them dressed in fine clothes and jewels. When they are not called upon to entertain or amuse her, she employs them as spies within the court and *one* – I am told – is an accomplished assassin. You must always be on guard. The Marquesa is a true virago, a woman who erupts with vulgar gutter language, and when angry she shows her claws." She smiled at the young man. "What do you think? Is this amusement to your taste?"

"When I left the Certosa," the young man replied grimly, "I thought I was leaving behind a world of severe conformity and discipline. I had no idea I was to trade it for a universe of intrigue, corruption and assassination."

Then the serious mask fell away, and Niccolo smiled.

Both he and the Contessa laughed.

"Fine," said the lady of the ermine, "now go and try to explain to Madonna Eleanora why you will be leaving her – again."

The day before the scheduled departure of Leonardo and Niccolo for Mantua, the Contessa again had a manservant summon the young courtier to a secluded chamber in her own wing of the palazzo. This time he found the lady seated at a small table and dressed informally in a chemise covered with an embroidered bodice to which was attached a red silk petticoat by ties and points. Her sleeves were separate and slashed with the chemise pulled through to form puffs. Her hair was unbound and crowned with an embroidered beret which was – according to Eleanora - currently the style in Venice.

As lovely as the lady appeared, Niccolo's attention was focused on the table filled with what he determined were platters of ham, pasties of pheasant, roe of mullet and sturgeon, a tureen of soup, and a small basket of pastries. Beside the platters of food was a carafe of wine and two of the silver-and-crystal goblets which Niccolo knew were only used on ceremonious occasions.

Next to the table and opposite the Contessa waited a single chair with a foot stool before it and a mound of pillows on the seat. The lady gestured to the chair with one hand and dismissed the manservant with a wave of the other.

Niccolo obediently climbed the foot-stool and nested himself on the pillows which to his surprise and delight elevated him to the relatively same height as the hostess.

"I thought we should have one last meal together," said the Contessa quietly as she poured wine into the two goblets, "and perhaps discuss your new assignment on behalf of the Cambio. I would have invited Maestro Leonardo too, but he is notorious for eating very little, at odd hours, and perhaps it is well he doesn't know too much about your commission. He has a dislike for intrigue, despite maintaining a record of the Moor's - 'indiscretions' – when he served Ludovico.'

"A fair analysis."

"So I thought it best to meet with you alone." She gestured to the platters. "I apologize for the poor menu, but I am fasting so a generous and loving God might assist you in your mission and bring it to a successful conclusion, but please partake of anything you see and enjoy the wine. It is from our own vineyards."

Niccolo smiled at the Contessa's concept of "fasting," but he proceeded to fork only small portions of the meat and fish on his own plate and garnished everything with the prugnoli mushrooms and the almond paste.

"Thank you, milady," he said.

"Now you must keep me informed of everything," she said as she heaped small mountains of ham and pheasant on her own plate. "Everything." She raised her goblet to her lips, took a deep swallow and brushed her mouth with her damask napkin. "How were your last days in the Castello Sforzeca?"

Niccolo brushed his own lips with his napkin and despite a mouthful of fish managed to murmur, "Well, it taught me the futility of vendettas. When we fled, the warring families among the staff and the mercenaries were slaughtering each other and their relatives. Sometimes at the rate of two a day! They seemed to be in competition for new and original ways to kill one another." He took a deep swallow of the wine and momentarily reveled in the subtle flavor of ripe fruit. "It was," he continued softly, "murder elevated to an absurdity, gross irrationality motivating revenge. I considered it a bestial madness, but Simone – he is the leader of the *commedia* troupe – he called it a 'comedy of murders', but I still don't quite understand why."

The Contessa shook her head and took another sip of the wine. "Yes, yes, yes. I know about the senseless killings, but I was referring to the conditions which brought the Moor to his downfall and his exile." She forked some of the ham in her mouth, chewed slowly and then almost whispered, "The Duke lost the war,

104

you know, because he never understood women."

"Women?"

She nodded. "For example, he saw his marriage to Beatrice d'Este as a profitable union of two prominent families which would reinforce his own ambitions and refurbish his treasury." She delicately sliced another portion of the ham to a suitable size and raised it to her mouth with her fork. She chewed in silence for awhile and then leaned toward Niccolo and said, "But any woman could have warned him against marrying the sister of a lady he had only recently rejected as a possible wife. It was like igniting the fuse of an explosive and then wondering why it erupted in flame and fury."

"Ah!"

"Then," the lady said, "the Duke compounded his stupidity by brazenly parading his mistress ..."

"His mistress?"

"Me! He appeared at court functions with *me* as a symbol of his virility and his power when actually any woman would see me more as a sign of *his* vulnerability! From that moment on every woman at court knew the Duke could be impaled on red-nailed fingers by any dark-eyed and willing lady. A woman's slender hand can reward the passion of a man and inflict more pain than a sword of any enemy."

"Ah," Niccolo said again.

"Naturally, Beatrice had to clear the court of beautiful women, not only to remove competition, but also to protect the Duke from himself." She took another swallow of wine. "Consequently I was the first to be eliminated. To Ludovico's credit he chose a husband for me who had wealth and prestige and was too old - he thought - to invite comparison. So he sent me and our son, Cesare, to the Bergamini."

Niccolo was confused as to whether he should say something to console the lady, who did not seemed to be in any particular need of consolation, or just continue to eat and listen.

He chose to eat.

Apparently it was the proper choice, because the Contessa emptied her goblet, poured more wine into it and said, "I tell you this, my young friend, because you are about to encounter one of the three most powerful women in Italy."

Niccolo swallowed the food without chewing which caused him to momentarily choke. He immediately hid his embarrassment by emptying his goblet which the Contessa filled again.

"These three women are of a distinct breed, Niccolo, "and they are all lethal. They are also beautiful, cultured, well-educated and experienced in the ways of the worldly and the exclusive. Like their male counterparts, they are devious and self-serving."

Still confused as to how he was expected to respond, the young man barely managed a weak, "Three you say?"

Again the lady nodded. "Much of the Romagna is actually controlled by Caterina Sforza, Countess of Forli and Imola, a licentious bastard daughter of the second Duke of Milan. This gives her connections to the house of Savoy, and her half-sister is married to the German Emperor which provides her with access to *their* powers. She also cleverly arranged to out-live three husbands."

Because of his experiences at the court and the warnings of the good monks of the Certosa who raised him, Niccolo's eyes widened and he barely managed to blurt out, "Poisoned?!"

"Oh no," the Contessa corrected him. "Although two *were* murdered. Caterina's first, a Riario, left her with a son when he was assassinated. She later avenged his death in a manner too cruel to mention – especially over a meal."

Niccolo listened with an open mouth, but he managed a nod, grateful to be spared the details.

"She then married the man who had been her lover throughout her first marriage, and then *he* too was murdered."

The young man could only murmur. "*He* was poisoned?"

"Niccolo!" the Contessa shook her head and laughed. "You really must get over your years with the Sforza. I assure you there are more assassinations in Italy by stiletto than by chemicals." She again forked a section of pheasant, transferred it to her plate and dissected it with a force which Niccolo found alarming. "Her third husband was a Medici. Giovanni. This aligned her with the ruling family of Florence – before *he* died." She smiled at him. "And no! Not by poison!" She chewed the meat, washed it down with wine, leaned across the table and almost whispered, "It is rumored he died of exhaustion attempting to satisfy Caterina's lusts."

Niccolo, stunned by this litany of the dead, could only manage a bob of his head and a murmured, "And the other two women?"

"The second is possibly the most dangerous and certainly the most interesting. She is Lucrezia Borgia, younger sister to Cesare, and bastard daughter to the present Pope. She is intoxicatingly beautiful, golden-haired, impetuous and totally devoid of any sense of morality. At eleven she was betrothed to a lord of Valencia and then to Don Gaspare of Naples. This resulted in nothing, and she was quickly married at thirteen to the Moor's brother, Giovanni di Pesaro Sforza. That marriage was conveniently annulled when the Pope forced Giovanni to confess to impotency, despite the fact Giovanni's first wife died in childbirth."

Niccolo managed a smile and again focused attention on the food.

"You have every reason to smile," said the Contessa, "and during the negotiations, Lucrezia was tucked away in the convent of San Sisto, and when she emerged she was pregnant by a Spanish chamberlain who occasionally visited his sister-nun there! She actually attended the signing of her husband's confession to impotency in her sixth month! Despite this fact a committee of Cardinals examined her and declared her *intacta!*" Then without even pausing for a breath the lady demanded. "Try a little of the roe. It's not too salty."

Obediently, Niccolo spooned a little of the fish eggs onto his plate.

The lady smiled with satisfaction. "It really was a case of immaculate deception." She erupted with a small laugh and then immediately continued. "Lucrezia then delivered a male child in the Vatican which was legitimatized by no less than a papal bull which declared Cesare the father by 'an unknown woman' and made the boy a ward of the Pope. Lucrezia was immediately wedded to Alfonso of Aragon, prince of Bisceglie, miscarried, and is now back in the Vatican which means, I suppose, Alfonso's days are numbered. Rumors persist the Pope has already chosen another husband for her, another Alfonso, heir to the duchy of Ferrara – which brings us to the third woman."

All that Niccolo could manage was a brief "Oh!" as he attempted to lick the salt from his lips.

"She is Alfonso's sister, Isabella d'Este, the woman whom you will soon encounter in Mantua, if you haven't already seen her in the Moor's court."

"I – I have," said Niccolo. "but I was never introduced or had an opportunity to talk to her."

"She, unlike the other two, is the legitimate daughter of a prince, Duke Ercole of Ferrara, and her mother was Eleanora of Aragon."

Niccolo beamed. "Another Eleanora!"

"And as unlike your precious lady as a hawk to a hummingbird," snapped the Contessa "She is also, of course, the wife of the Marquis of Mantua, general of the armies of Venice in the recent war. Consequently she is wife to the man who now controls northern Italy from the Milanese border in the west to Venice in the east. Her own heritage aligns her with the ruling house of Spain and the lord of Naples, so the lady is very, *very* powerful. You must realize, too, the Marquis permits her to administer his fief while he indulges himself with Italy's two favorite obsessions: war and women."

"The Marquis is unfaithful?"

"He is presently being treated for syphilis. That

much is certain."

"How do you know that?"

"Women," replied the Contessa. "That's my point. We have lines of communication which span empires. If fully understood, our warring husbands would die of embarrassment. For example, I suppose it is not widely known Isabella's brother - the young man now apparently in line to wed the Borgia daughter - is addicted to wandering naked through the streets of Ferrara after dark, and once let loose a bull in the cathedral, injuring scores of people, while he stood in the choir loft laughing."

"My god," was the best Niccolo could immediately respond, but after another long swallow of the wine he said," But – but what has all this to do with my assignment for the Cambio?'

"Because," said the Contessa softly, leaning slightly across the table to him, "I have been led to believe all three of these women have histories connected to the Tears of the Madonna, and any one of them might have the necklace *now*, because their histories are as woven among the diamonds as the gold wire which binds them together."

She reached across the table and took one of the small bowls of soup.

Niccolo, already confused, followed the Contessa's example and drew one of the bowls to him.

"Now try to follow, Niccolo," the lady said as she spooned some of the soup into her mouth and repeated the process of lightly tapping her lips with her napkin. "The origin of the Tears is somewhat clouded."

"No more than where I find myself at the moment," said Niccolo.

"Some say the necklace was designed by a Dominican saint, Vicente Ferrer, and crafted by monastic goldsmiths with diamonds acquired from the Moors after the fall of Jativa."

Suddenly Niccolo remembered reading testimonies of the battle among the manuscripts in the Certosa library, but he worked to keep his focus on the lady's narrative.

"Wherever it was crafted," the Contessa continued, "the Tears *first* appeared as part of the treasures of Senor Juan Domingo de Borja, a Spanish grandee and an ancestor of the present Pope."

Not knowing whether the lady expected a reaction, Niccolo nodded to show he was following the lecture, but his attention was centered at the moment on the exquisite scent of the broth which somehow managed to preserve the individual flavors of the carrots, potatoes and onions. The lady, having devoured her bowl of soup, placed it aside and poked around the pastries with a delicate finger. Finally she made a choice of a macaroon, broke it in half and bit into a portion of it.

Niccolo found himself in admiration of both the grace with which the Contessa conducted her search and her ability to apparently gorge herself on delicacies and still retain her slim silhouette.

"Juan's son brought the necklace from Spain to Naples," continued the Contessa. "This was Alonzo de Borja, bishop of Valencia and later Pope Calixtus the Third. Consequently the Borgias have always

111

considered the Tears to be a family heirloom, although
the pontiff gave it to King Alfonso of Naples who
supposedly gave it to his bride, Ippolita Sforza, on the
occasion of their wedding. It is also considered a family
keepsake by the Sforza." Taking another long swallow
of the wine, the lady continued. "At her death, Ippolita
willed the necklace to her niece, Caterina. She became
involved in a war with Cesare Borgia, and she needed
money. Duke Ludovico, had just come into possession
of Milan and offered her a loan which the lady accepted
and gave as collateral ..."

"Don't tell me!" Niccolo suddenly declared a little
loudly. "The Tears!"

"Precisely," replied the Contessa in a voice
calculated to diminish the volume. "And the Moor, of
course, gave it to *his* new wife, Beatrice d'Este."

"Ah," Niccolo responded, pleased with himself at
being able to finally see the matter more or less clearly,
"and Beatrice, for some reason, gave the Tears to *her*
sister, the Marquesa of Mantua!"

"Very good," smiled the Contessa. "Yes. To
commemorate the birth of Isabella's son! That is why,
you see, Isabella offered the necklace to the Cambio as
collateral on the bank's loan to the Moor. It was not to
help the Moor whom she despises to this day, but to
repay a debt to her sister who had given her the
necklace in the first place. So you see, the Borgias still
consider the necklace as a family heirloom. The Sforza
consider it *theirs*, because Beatrice only offered it as
collateral for her sister's loan, and the house of
Gonzaga consider it *theirs* for the same reason. It was
collateral. The Cambio, of course, consider it *their*

property, because the Moor defaulted on the loan!"

Niccolo finished the wine in his goblet and wiped his lips. "Why are you telling me all this?"

"Because it is relevant to where you are going and what is expected of you; and knowing your gifts, I know you will retain the information."

Niccolo shook his head. "What confusion! But I think you are convinced one of these three women ordered the courier killed in order to own the Tears."

"Yes."

"But which one? And Signore Agnolo said there is no proof the courier was even murdered. There was no body found."

The Contessa smiled. "Very good. So *if* the courier has *not* been murdered, where is he?"

"Are you saying the courier could have been bribed to turn the necklace over to an agent of one of the three women? That he did so *before* he was attacked at the Olive Tree."

Suddenly the Contessa was on her feet. "What a keen mind you have, my little Niccolo! Yes! That is what I am saying, and that is why I want you to pass any information directly to *me* first and not to the Cambio."

Presuming the meeting was drawing to a close, Niccolo slid off the pillows and descended the foot-stool. "But I don't understand! Why should I pass it to you first?"

The Contessa crossed to him, tucked a hand under his chin and raised his head so he was forced to concentrate on her face.

"Because," she said, "you will be dealing with a *woman,* and any information you receive may simply be interpreted as one thing or another. That's because you're a man, and that is how men reach conclusions. It takes another woman who understands the difference between what a woman *says* or *does* and what is *implied.*" She walked with him to the door. "For example, men value the Tears in terms of ducats or florins, but Isabella could sell her collection of artifacts and have enough wealth to sustain her family for generations. Madonna Lucrezia can siphon as much as *she* needs from the Vatican treasury, and Caterina may soon be completely out of the picture – unless she can get the Tears and use it to pay for men and arms against Cesare and his allies."

She stopped and looked down at the young man again.

"*That* is the true value of the Tears, Niccolo. *It symbolizes power.*"

"Are you saying the necklace is some sort of trophy? A symbol of a woman's stature over other women?"

The Contessa beamed. "Now you understand! And that is why any information should be brought directly to *me*. I can explain to the Cambio what it *really* means. Remember, my beloved Niccolo, women for centuries have said one thing to men and meant something completely opposite."

The young man sighed. "No wonder, we have wars!"

The departure of Niccolo and Leonardo the following day was a melancholic affair. Eleanora was torn between weeping and wanting to break something over Niccolo's head for leaving without her. The unfortunate young man was struggling to recall all the information about women and the history of the Tears and attempting to sort it into neat, little, mental files for future use.

Only the Maestro was in the present.

Using funds advanced by the count, he had purchased some pigments, oils and brushes he felt were needed immediately and which replaced those sacrificed when he fled Milan. His mind was on the commission, and he attempted to resurrect the facial features of a woman he had seen on few occasions and only twice in close proximity.

Count Bergamini, on the other hand, was pleased to advance Leonardo the funds for these items if the money would accelerate the departure of his guests. During their residency he had more or less sequestered himself in one wing of the palazzo with his foster child, young Cesare. The boy and the count had developed a warm and reciprocal devotion over the years. This was apart from the Contessa who, being a woman of some experience and still dedicated to worldly matters, had her days taken up principally with diplomats, messages and vital decisions. None of which concerned Cremona or the Bergamini. Life in Cremona was merely an extension of her days in Milan when her proximity to the Moor's court required a great deal of her time and attention.

The count was absolutely certain his wife and the Moor no longer entertained any romantic or personal relationship, and she was now completely faithful to him; but being of the privileged class, the unfortunate

115

overlord had been forced on too many occasions to "entertain" scholars and artists and diplomats and other equally-privileged "friends."

None of this was to his liking.

Suddenly discovering himself a father became a refuge from affairs of state. He was far more comfortable and happy helping young Cesare to build and float a wooden "ship" on the garden pond than in playing the role of a gracious host to even a celebrated artist and architect like Leonardo. Consequently the artifacts and décor of the palazzo were entirely the work of his wife. She managed the stables and stocked them with Arabian and thick-necked horses of the Bashkir strain. She presided at court presentations and established protocol while he taught Cesare some Latin by playing word games and saw to it the young boy would inherit the titles, wealth and problems of the Bergamini.

So now as the coach-and-four with Niccolo and Leonardo raced past the Palazzo del Commune, Count Bergamini breathed a sigh of relief - even as Madonna Eleanora dissolved in tears.

As an omen open to all interpretation, it began to rain.

The coach ride to Mantua from Cremona was brief and uneventful. The major road to the east took the occupants through only one reasonably large village, Bozzolo, and then across the Oglio river by ferry.

Niccolo spent some of the time reading Epictetus

and the rest watching the daily labors of the country people.

Leonardo continued to mentally run through a list of what he would need to paint the portrait and what he had lost in his flight from Milan. He knew Francesco would join him in Mantua and bring with him the materials he had shipped earlier to the Melzi villa at Vaprio d'Adda, but there were books which he treasured above all pigments, oils, potions and herbs and which had been left behind at the Castello Sforzesco.

On the positive side, he reasoned it would take some time to paint Isabella d'Este's portrait, and the Gonzaga court was famous for the scholars and artists in residence. He hoped to have conversations about something more than decorations for court festivals and the state of politics. It could be a relief after the severe environment of the Certosa and the preparations of the Bergamini court for war.

While still some distance from the city, the two travelers spied the spires of the twin churches of Sant'Andrea and San Sebastiano looming over the rooftops and challenging the crenellated towers of the Gonzaga palazzo beyond the city's walls.

Even the size and grandeur of the Sforza castello did not prepare Niccolo and Leonardo for the magnificence of the Gonzaga palazzo which occupied one complete side of the Piazza Sordello. Both fortress and castle, the structure proudly displayed banners of the winged lion, reminding everyone Gian Francesco was commanding-general of the Venetian armies. The *impresa* of the family itself – rearing lions and

117

alternating yellow-and-black stripes – was carved in stone over the archways.

Leonardo pondered why the nobility of every nation incorporated animals into their crests. Venice was obvious in its choice of the winged lion which was the symbol associated with its patron saint: the evangelist Mark; and the bull of the Borgias related to the national sport of Spain; but why the mythical figures of a unicorn and a griffin in the family crests of so many English? Why the red dragon and the white hound of the Tudors? And what is the significance of the Slavic symbol of the eagle with two heads, each head pointing in a different direction?

Does only one eat and the other think?

The coach slowed to a stop at the base of a wide staircase, and the newcomers were instantly and with great ceremony welcomed by Andrea Meneghina. In Niccolo's mind, he seemed to be performing a balletic *grande jete* as he literally flew down the steps.

As footmen in the Gonzaga livery opened the door and lowered the coach step, the chamberlain immediately began bowing and apologizing for the absence of "the master" who was "in Venice conferring with the doge on vital matters." Between bows he also begged Niccolo and Leonardo to "also "forgive the Marquesa" who "has pressing matters requiring her presence elsewhere, but be assured she will be with you soon. With the Marquis away so long at the wars, this is something of a world of women."

Niccolo remembered the last lecture by the Contessa.

As he led the two men into the reception area, Andrea continued his apologetic narrative, assuring the Maestro "the entire court was absolutely thrilled and honored" Leonardo had accepted the commission. He assured the newcomers "a more fitting and formal reception would be arranged very soon" and "in the meantime, I am privileged to show you to your quarters where you may refresh yourselves from the tiring journey and where little delicacies await your pleasure."

Leonardo wanted to inform the gentleman the journey was hardly "tiring" and consumed a little more than a day, but the effusive verbal barrage of compliments, reassurances and explanations rained down on the two guests and did not permit a response.

Meneghina was momentarily surprised at the scarcity of luggage, but quickly assumed there would be "more coming." He dismissed the small congregation waiting to carry a number of possessions, and again focused his attention on the new arrivals. He wondered if Niccolo would be "more comfortable" in the chambers assigned him next to the Maestro's or if he might prefer to be housed with Nanino and his "little friends" in their *appartamento* in a private wing.

Leonardo quickly drew the chamberlain's attention to the fact Niccolo was *not* a dwarf, being "perfectly proportioned without the bowed legs or the slightly larger head of a dwarf" and would therefore "perhaps cause some confusion and discomfort" to the little people if he were to be housed among them.

The distinction was lost on the chamberlain who merely shrugged and quickly nodded.

To reinforce the point both Niccolo and Leonardo assured the chamberlain the young man "should be happy to be in close proximity to the Maestro," because the young man was Leonardo's "tutor" and "his services may be required at any moment, night or day."

They both knew Meneghina would probably consider this a more personal and possibly sexual arrangement, considering the legends surrounding the Maestro's early trial on sodomy, but the chamberlain said nothing and led them down the corridor.

He escorted the two guests through several long corridors and past innumerable doors, each framed by armed men who stared directly in front of themselves, as rigid as stone. Some of the tall doors were paneled with bronze, some with ivory. Some depicted moments in the lives of the saints, another memorialized moments in the siege of Troy, and some romantically illustrated the Labors of Hercules.

"Appropriate," whispered Niccolo to Leonardo. "The Marquesa's father was named Ercole – Hercules – and from what I have heard, some of the gentleman's feats could also be considered legendary, especially among the ladies of the court."

Their journey took them through the massive *camera degli sposi,* the reception chamber which Meneghina foot-noted was "once a bridal chamber." He informed them "the walls were painted to fool the eye by suggesting a depth and dimension which does not exist." He smiled at the depth of his knowledge without realizing or referring to Leonardo's use of perspective technique in his "Last Supper."

The Maestro paused and scanned the walls and ceiling.

It was clearly the work of a man who had mastered the art. Two-dimensional archways led into non-existent gardens or long arcades. Columned decorations of illusionary cherubs and flowers were complete with folds and shadows. Shelves of imaginary books and varied musical and nautical instruments appeared ready to be employed. Masked courtiers and ladies stood in eternal conversations, and on one wall members of the Gonzaga family, complete with a dwarf woman in a formal gown, stared at the new visitors with no evident interest. Under a painted dome with an oval of blue sky beyond, groups of frozen courtiers and their ladies peered over imaginary balconies, smiled and appeared to gossip about the actual people below.

"Wonderful," said Leonardo, and then turned so only Niccolo could hear him and said, "Apparently in the Gonzaga court, nothing is what it appears to be."

"Apparently," Niccolo laughed quietly.

Absorbed in the illusions, Niccolo lost his balance, fell against a real wall with false flowers, and to his surprise, a panel moved inward revealing a small recess. The chamberlain quickly crossed, pushed against one of the flowers, and the panel dissolved back into the wall.

"My apologies," sniffed the annoyed Meneghina. "I should have warned you. There are a number of such doors in the palazzo. They lead to adjoining rooms."

Remembering the hidden passages in the Castello

Sforzesco, Niccolo smiled and noted the low height of the openings, acknowledged the chamberlain's warning the palazzo was also probably honeycombed with hidden passages and portals – and that many were sized exclusively for dwarfs.

The chambers assigned to Leonardo and Niccolo were spacious and well-furnished with chairs upholstered in red velvet, heavy tapestries, canopied beds and large fireplaces. To the east their latticed windows looked down on a small courtyard and a magnificent marble fountain depicting four satyrs holding up a bowl of overflowing water. To the west, a door opened into a larger room with floor-to-ceiling windows and was furnished with upholstered and pillowed chairs and stools, glass-doored armoires, walls of shelving with armies of books marching in quiet files, chandeliers with rings of candles among the crystal haloes and four newly-constructed and wooden work tables.

"The Marquesa thought this might serve as your workroom, Maestro," smiled Meneghina.

Leonardo, accustomed to bare walls and cradles of fat candles, seemed appropriately overwhelmed. He mentally positioned the primary easel near the windows where there would be an abundance of natural light. He pictured the Marquesa bathed in the light of the setting sun, a position he favored for portraiture. The large work tables would more than suffice for molding and modeling clay and for cutting and gluing inventions and machines to illustrate the laws of mechanics, but he wondered if the lady of the palazzo might also be suggesting he continue with dissections.

The Maestro said softly, "It – it is more than adequate. Please express my thanks to the Marquesa. I think the western light would be perfect for painting her portrait."

Meneghina drew himself erect. "These apartments are directly below the Marquesa's chambers - the Paradise rooms. It is her wish to be posed *there*."

Leonardo frowned. "The Paradise rooms?"

"It is her wish."

The Maestro sighed. "Then of course it will be in the Paradise rooms."

Niccolo had been examining the books. "These are treatises on physics and chemistry," he said.

"The complete library is in the north wing," responded the chamberlain. "You will, of course, have free access to it at any time. Simply go down the corridor and to your left. But if you require other texts, you need not trouble yourself with rummaging through the shelves. Simply inform one of the servants which book you wish, and it will be brought to you."

"Thank you," said Leonardo.

"You may rest now if you choose," said Meneghina. "I will come for you when it is time to dine. I regret to inform you neither the Marquis nor the Marquesa will be in attendance. However I am certain the other notables in residence will make themselves known to you. They were understandably delighted to hear of your coming." He paused and then frowned and added, "Of course if there are some you would rather *not* have hanging upon you, simply inform me, and I will see to it you are seated exclusively among those whom you admire."

Leonardo was disturbed by the implied arrogance in choosing only those whom he "admired" as fellow diners, but he forced a small smile, stroked his beard and replied again, "Thank you."

Meneghina performed another of his bows which Niccolo considered a sign of severe back trouble, walked backwards a few steps and then stood, turned and left, carefully and quietly closing the door behind him.

"Well," said the young man softly, "with Paradise above, where would you say we are now?"

Half-hidden in the shadows of an archway, Ottaviano Cristani watched as the chamberlain introduced the new arrivals to their chambers. He continued standing there when Meneghina left, and suddenly he felt his chest tighten and a shortness of breath. He coughed with such force and for such a long time he was forced to lean against the wall and muffle the sound with his handkerchief. Finally he replaced the linen in the cuff of his tunic, stepped into the light, tugged his dark cloak around his neck and shoulders, silently cursed the broken clasp, and made his way down the corridor.

*

That night Leonardo and Niccolo found themselves at the masters' table.

The chamberlain led Niccolo to a chair seated next to an obviously uncomfortable lady dressed inexplicably in black. On the opposite side of the young man was a gentleman with a black mourning band on his left arm who introduced himself as Signore Guglielmo Gaetani and who informed Niccolo he was a "fugitive from Ferrara." He did not explain, nor did Niccolo inquire about the mourning band.

The Maestro was seated beside a gentleman who introduced himself as a Belgian, Johannes Vendramm. To the left of this gentleman was Madonna Maddalena, a lovely but unsmiling young woman with long red hair cascading to her waist. The Maestro noted the lady's left palm rested on the gentleman's right hand.

On Leonardo's right was Cardinal Ippolito d'Este, and on the cardinal's right was another young woman with whom he spent most of the time in whispered conversation.

Accustomed to the excellent food and drink at the Bergamini palazzo, both new arrivals were surprised the dining at the Gonzaga was equal - and in some cases – superior. They admired the small ensemble in one gallery who played music for the first half of the meal, and the choir in the opposite gallery who then performed through the wine and fruit. Niccolo was amused when he realized the two central chairs, those of the Marquis and the Marquesa, were empty, but the servers bowed and offered platters to the missing host and hostess as though they were present.

Meneghina occupied a chair of some importance on the opposite side of the empty chairs, and Niccolo observed the chamberlain seemed less interested in the roast ham then in surveying everyone in the room.

Leonardo had been disappointed earlier to learn Signore Niccolo Panizatto, one of the men he admired, had "left the court, because the Marquesa is far too busy to continue her studies with him." Now the Belgian informed him another scholar, Signore Pietro Bembo, would be leaving, because the Marquis "chooses to no longer need his services."

The five dwarves of the Gonzaga Court, attired formally and elegantly, dined at a separate table erected on a dais at the opposite end of the room. Niccolo noted the glowering one seated in the center of that table and especially adorned in satins and silks. Beside him was an attractive young woman with midnight-black hair and a warm smile. Once she noticed Niccolo looking at her, and she lowered her eyes behind an ivory fan.

Situated as they are, thought Niccolo, *they might appear to be a miniature reflection of the host and hostess*

The fine meal was followed by a performance by a fool in a belled costume and cap who performed a remarkable toe-dance around a carpet of upturned blades. After him came fire-eaters and a bevy of young women in diaphanous gowns who twirled and whirled to a lively tune from the musicians in the gallery.

The chancellor's sudden pounding of his staff indicated the evening was at an end.

Niccolo noticed the dwarves departed first and quickly. He also observed Cardinal d'Este slip under an archway behind the masters' table with his beautiful dining partner.

As Niccolo rose to leave, he also noted a dark man in a burgundy tunic who paused in the center of the great hall and seemed to be focused on Leonardo. Suddenly he began to cough violently. He gasped for air and dabbed at his lips with a lace-edged handkerchief, recovered, turned and hastily swept from the room.

Several members of the court quickly descended on the masters' table to engage Leonardo in conversation, and among them was Baldasar Castiglione. Niccolo recognized the gentleman from a visit to the Castello Sforzesco where he delivered a lecture to the nobles on "genteel behavior" with frequent references to his own text on protocol. Deciding the Maestro could work his own way from the welcoming onslaught, the young courtier slipped away and attempted to find the corridor leading to their quarters.

Passing a shadowed archway, he was surprised to find the young female dwarf with the raven hair blocking his path. She was only slightly less tall than Niccolo with skin the color of ripe peaches and a small, delicate mouth. Her fingers, encased in satin gloves trimmed with a dark and elegant lace, were long and slender. Her nose was a button between cheeks glowing with the gentle blush of roses, and her hair gleamed under a thin veil sprinkled with spangles which glittered like stars against a cloudless sky.

"You were watching me, *m'sieur*," she said in a voice at once soft and demanding.

"My apologies, Madonna," Niccolo managed to murmur. "I assure you it was a compliment to your beauty."

She circled him. "You are not one of us, are you? We

127

are similar in height, but you are quite different, aren't you?"

"Well," replied Niccolo, "not precisely; but like you, I will grow no taller."

"*Bien,*" she smiled. "You are tall enough."

"For what?"

"Whatever you wish to accomplish," she said.

He remembered Leonardo had said the same thing.

"You are French," said Niccolo.

"How observant of you," she laughed. "*Oui, m'sieur.* I am French. My name is Lizette Fourget, and foregoing the customary ritual of introductions by friends, you are?

"Niccolo."

"That is it? Just 'Niccolo'? You assist Maestro da Vinci, do you not? The one who is to paint the Marquesa? The one who makes amusing toys and who has been given workrooms below the Paradise?"

"I hardly assist the Maestro. I sometimes tutor him in Latin."

"Yes? Well, m'sieur, are you so poor, you cannot afford a surname? Am I to address you as simply 'Niccolo'?"

"I am called Niccolo da Pavia, because I was left as a foundling at the Certosa monastery in Pavia. I – ah – I do not have a family."

Her laughter was high-pitched but not shrill. "A blessing! You are not burdened then with lies about the trials and triumphs of your ancestors."

Niccolo was about to respond when he noticed her attitude change dramatically. She became more erect, the ivory fan became a mask to hide her mouth. Her eyes - which a moment earlier were shining – now became those of a small, frightened animal. Something told the young man the threat was behind him, and he turned to face a scowling dwarf in an open doorway.

"I must go," Lizette whispered, but as she moved toward the other dwarf she suddenly said loudly and clearly. "Tomorrow after the noon meal, Signore Niccolo, I will visit your workrooms - if I may."

Without waiting for a reply, she quickly glided past the glaring dwarf and through the doorway. Then Nanino suddenly bit his thumb in an insult Niccolo immediately recognized, but instead of responding in kind, the young courtier snapped his heels together in a mock military salute, bowed smartly from the waist, wheeled and marched down the corridor.

He turned a corner, hopelessly lost, and nearly collided with the man who wore a black silk band of mourning.

"Ah, Signore Gaetani," Niccolo smiled. "How fortunate! I cannot seem to find my way back to my chambers."

The gentleman smiled and bobbed his head. "I will be happy to escort you, signore."

He started the opposite way, and Niccolo quickly fell in step beside him.

"I see you are in mourning, signore," the young man said.

"Yes. I am in mourning for - well – for my nephew."

"Your nephew?"

"I have received a report my favorite nephew was strangled in Sermoneta."

"Truly? Strangled? How? By whom?"

"By Cesare Borgia, that bastard son of the pontiff – either he or his hired assassin, Michelotto Corella. I also learned he lured my brother, Giacomo, to Rome where he had him thrown into prison."

At first Niccolo did not know how to respond to the man's story, but he finally managed to ask, "Thrown into prison? But – why?"

"Partly in response to my sanctuary here," murmured Gaetani. "It is the way the Borgia warn the Gonzaga they risk the enmity of the Vatican if they continue to shelter me."

"I – I don't understand," stammered Niccolo. "The Borgias are allies to the Venetians. Their general is a Gonzagan!"

"The winds of war blow in different directions after a victory – or defeat," said Gaetani as he continued to stride through an archway and down another corridor. "Old wars always breed new ones. The Borgias even now have an army marching south through the Romagna. They have laid siege to Imola which, I learned this morning, has not capitulated. I understand the Contessa, Caterina Sforza, remains defiant behind the high walls of her fortress of La Rocca."

He stopped abruptly. "And these are *your* quarters I believe, signore Niccolo." He gestured to the door.

"Thank you, signore," said Niccolo with a smile of gratitude. "I find it interesting a woman - Contessa Sforza - dares to stand against the Borgias, and you, also an enemy of the Borgias, are under the protection of yet another woman, the Marquesa of Mantua."

"Indeed," replied Gaetani with a nod of his head. "And as I understand it, both the pontiff and his bastard son are traveling with their army; so at the moment - and for the first time since the legendary Pope Joan – it is a woman, the pope's daughter Lucrezia, who administers the business of the Vatican."

Niccolo, momentarily stunned by the realization, could only reply, "Well, signore, if this conflict is principally between women, it would be a wise thing, would it not, for a man to hide himself until the blood has ceased to flow."

"That is precisely what I am doing."

Leonardo was apparently still involved with his admirers following the dinner, so alone in their chambers Niccolo considered all he had learned from the Contessa, the banker and now from Gaetani. He remembered an adage of the Maestro: "There is always another possibility."

Is it possible the courier was not carrying the Tears when he was, presumably, murdered? And if he was murdered, could the assassin - as the banker believes - have been sent by the Marquesa?

Or could it be possible the necklace was recovered by the assassin but never delivered to the one who sent him, but was given to someone else? If so, is it possible the courier delivered the Tears to either the Borgias or the Contessa Sforza first, both of whom believe they have a right to the necklace?

Is it even possible, without a body, the courier and the assassin together plotted to suggest he – the courier – had been murdered, but now both were living, protected and prosperous, after handing the Tears to one of the three women?

In the dark hours of the early morning, what he

called the "hoo-haa" time of nagging questions and profound confusions, regrets and remembrances, Niccolo was still awake.

CHAPTER FOUR

ROMANS AND RENEGADES

In Rome and in the Sala dei Pontifici Lucrezia Borgia, gowned in gold velvet, perched on the very edge of the papal throne. Attended by four women equally adorned in velvet and satin, she smiled at the brown-haired, delicate-appearing young man in silk who separated himself from two other men, stepped forward, bowed exquisitely and following proper protocol, kissed the offered hand of the lady.

"Signore Tebaldeo," said Lucrezia, "I am pleased to see you again. And how did you find matters at the Mantuan court?"

"Deplorable," sniffed the courtier. "I wasted my time correcting the Marquesa's awkward and incomprehensible rhymes, and writing sonnets to which she had the bad taste to affix her own name."

"Indeed?"

"Indeed, Madonna." He sighed. "I assure you! We – all the resident poets and artists – were crammed into small chambers no larger than an armoire, fed over-roasted meat and provided with the most vile wines possible. The Marquesa's hounds were treated with greater honor and respect. That is why I chose to enter service to Cardinal Ippolito d'Este, and why he graciously and immediately dispatched me here to Rome, the bastion of civilized behavior."

"Indeed?"

"I assure you, Madonna, compared to the Gonzaga court, the Vatican is paradise."

"Of course," Lucrezia laughed. "Where else would you find the Vicar of Christ?"

Wisely, the assembly joined the laughter.

"I am fascinated, signore, by your report," said the lady. "Pray, wait a moment. I want you to tell me everything you saw and experienced in Mantua, but first we have pressing matters to which I must devote some attention."

She gestured to the other two men who stood before her, carved momentarily into stone by both fear and wisdom.

"My illustrious majordomo and you, castellan of Sant'Angelo," the lady addressed the men in perfect Latin, "my father feels it is imperative we construct a new street between the Castel and the Vatican to accommodate the many pilgrims who will be coming to Rome for the jubilee celebrating the Holy Year. Further, he wishes the new avenue to be called the Via Alessandrina. Is that agreeable for you, Signore Martini?"

The fat and pontifical majordomo humbly robed in a brocade of browns and light green swallowed hard and nodded.

"And with you, Signore di Castro, as governor of the Castel?"

The dark-haired man in scarlet and gold, made an elaborate bow. "But of course, Madonna," he smiled, "but – well - usually when His Holiness proposes something in consistory a Cardinal is present to take down the details for the Vatican records; to make certain all terms are clear and completely understood. Should one be summoned?"

"Madonna Laura da Gonzaga here will later record what we have agreed to, signori," said Lucrezia. With a wave of one delicate hand she indicated a tall, chestnut-haired woman standing to her right. "She writes a lovely hand in both Latin and Greek, and she keeps a sharp pen in her chambers."

The Spaniard emitted a light laugh, acknowledging the play on the word *"penna"* with a second meaning of "penis." Bartolomeo Martini, being less gifted in languages, seemed confused by the laughter, and Madonna Laura covered her smile with her black fan.

Lucrezia pointed a condemning finger at di Castro. "You are wicked, signore," she said. "I assure you my lady's – necessary instruments – are kept in her chamber and away from lascivious eyes; but should she require a new quill now and again she has my authority to cut a fresh one from any male member of the court."

Recognizing the veiled threat, the Spaniard bowed and took a step back.

"Now," Lucrezia continued, "to the matter at hand. His Holiness estimates perhaps hundreds of thousands might kneel in reverence before the loggia of Santo Pietro to receive my father's blessings of *urbi et orbi*, and he feels we must prepare for such multitudes."

Both men nodded.

"Consider, too, the Duke of Sagan," she said, "is easily ninety and is traveling all the way from Silesia. Maestro Copernicus – on the other hand - will be coming from

135

the pontifical university, La Sapienza. Both gentlemen should be feasted and accorded honors upon arrival. A very special reception must also be arranged to welcome his majesty, Jean d'Albert, king of Navarre. Do you agree, Signore Martini?"

The majordomo nodded. "Of course, Madonna."

"And I think the bodies of the 18 criminals presently hanging on the Sant'Angelo bridge should be cut down, yes, Signore Juan? We do not wish to be considered barbarians."

"I shall see to it immediately, Madonna," said the Spaniard.

"And," the lady continued, "I think it might be wise if all Corsicans were expelled from papal territory during the Jubilee Year."

The Spaniard frowned. "*All* Corsicans, Madonna?!"

"The breed is acknowledged to be thieves and cut-purses, and we do not want our respected visitors and guests robbed or murdered, do we?"

Both men nodded in agreement.

"This will be a momentous occasion, signori," she said. She paused, rose to her feet and smiled. "Thank you for your attention and patience."

That evening when most of the Vatican was asleep or indulging in amusements, Madonna da Gonzaga, dipped her *penna* in the ink pod and inscribed a letter to her kinsman's wife. She wrote with a light touch, making small letters.

"Signore Tebaldeo was received with honor and

related blasphemous lies about the Mantuan court. Fresh from the bath, the lady later received an envoy dressed only in her Moorish peignoir. She also invited him to a buffet, provided gold utensils and porcelain plates, all decorated with the papal arms and embossed or engraved with '*Alexander Sextus Pontifex Maximus*'."

She paused to again dip her quill in the pod and resumed writing.

"Lucrezia then had her ladies unpack and clean her jewelry to wear during the Jubilee celebration. One was very familiar - especially the three strands of tear-shaped diamonds attached by wires of gold suggesting thorns."

*

In the encampment just outside of Imola Cesare Borgia brushed his dark hair and smiled at his majordomo, Don Ramiro de Lorca. "I am going to leave you here to serve as my vice-governor while I escort the Contessa to Rome for – appropriate punishment. I do not think you will have any problem with the people. Since I disciplined the troops who ravaged their city, the people look upon you as their benefactor."

Niccolo Machiavelli, the emaciated Florentine emissary surveyed himself in a small hand mirror and brushed a forefinger over his smooth-shaven chin.

"Of course," he said softly.

"The Contessa is incredible, isn't she?" Cesare responded as he quickly scrawled his signature on a parchment offered him by one of his subordinates. "Imagine! Riding out to greet me as if she were inviting me to tea, while secretly planning to lower the portcullis of her fortress after I entered and so take me prisoner! What audacity! By God, if I had a dozen officers with her courage and cunning, Niccolo, I'd have taken all the Romagna in two months!"

Machiavelli moved the hand mirror aside. "Your Excellency, I must be blunt and tell you: my superiors in Florence were appalled you forced the lady to sleep with you following her surrender. They feel this was improper behavior for a Duke of Valentinois. They consider it a gross insult to the lady and her family and violation of the rules of war."

Cesare smiled at the emissary. "Anyone who believes there are rules in war has obviously never been involved in one. And how did you respond to your superiors in Florence, Niccolo?"

Machiavelli grinned, exposing a line of even white teeth. "I told them it was an act of incredible '*virtu*' and '*terribilita*', the stuff of great princes and overlords, something every Italian male with balls would understand and appreciate. Then I added I have never known it to be necessary for you to use force to urge a woman to bed you."

Cesare gave a small laugh and adjusted his cloak around his shoulders. "A point well taken," he said "But perhaps I was a little hasty in 'inviting' Madonna Caterina into my embrace. I was curious. I wanted to personally experience a level of passion which – according to legend - actually killed a Medici before his time."

"And did you experience it?

Cesare placed the soft black cap on his dark curls and pinned a large diamond to the front of it. "As a gentleman, I cannot bring myself to defame the lady," he said. "But the point is moot since our illustrious French commander, Yves d'Alegre, took the lady away from me and placed her under his own command until now – when we ride together to Rome. He did not permit me near her." He pulled the black gauntlets on his hands. "I did not suspect the French of being so proper. After all, one doesn't acquire the French disease by eating bad fruit."

"The French call it the Neapolitan disease," Machiavelli replied with a laugh.

A junior officer entered the tent. "The command is ready, Excellency."

"Fine," Cesare responded. "I will be there presently." He turned back to Machiavelli who was adjusting his own cloak around his thin shoulders. "I have something else to discuss with you, as a Florentine. When I was in Milan, I had occasion to visit the workshops of Maestro Leonardo da Vinci. Incredible. War machines with sword blades affixed to the hubs of chariot wheels! Flying wings and devices for walking on water! I saw drawings of possible war coaches which could move rapidly under the power of men pedaling and be nearly impossible to stop! I had no idea the painter was so deeply interested in warfare. Indeed, I was told that he called war a 'bestial madness.'"

"Maestro Leonardo has often said one thing and then responded in precisely the opposite manner. He has spoken openly against war, but he came to Il Moro specifically to invent war machines to astound the world. He is an enigma, unreliable. He has accepted commissions and never completed them, because he became fascinated by some other aspect of life, perhaps a mathematical problem involving the response of structures to pressure exerted by water."

"Is he still in Mantua? Could you contact him for me? I would like to talk with him."

"He is still in Mantua, I believe," Machiavelli said, turning to leave the tent. "Painting a portrait of the Marquesa."

"Why inflict us with another study of virago arrogance?" Cesare groaned. "See if you can contact him. Tell him I want to meet with him. As a gesture of goodwill I am returning his collection of herbs and powders I found in his workrooms in the Castello Sforzesco,"

"If you really wish to impress the Maestro," said the diplomat, "I suggest you have the rest of his personal belongings - his books, his clothing and supplies which were not crated and sent to his apprentice's home – have them sent to him in Mantua. Send everything."

"To Mantua?"

"Yes," smiled Machiavelli, "or to his assistant, Francesco Melzi."

"Why Melzi?"

"To show deference and humility. Leonardo loves Francesco, and this would suggest you recognize the fact and appreciate it. It would also suggest you dare not address the Maestro directly."

"But I already enclosed a note of appreciation when I recently returned some of the other materials he left behind in Milan."

"Just do as I suggest, my friend," smiled Machiavelli. "You may know war and intrigue, but I know artists."

Cesare stepped into the bright sunlight. He glanced over the ranks and files of mounted knights stretching as far as he could see. He ignored the mounted officer in front and crossed to the gray jennet on which the Contessa Caterina Sforza sat sidesaddle, unsmiling but erect in black satin.

"Good morrow, Contessa," Cesare smiled. "Black satin?"

"I am in mourning," the lady replied softly.

"Surely not for your virtue," Cesare whispered.

"Nor yours," Caterina snapped. "I mourn for my poor people."

"Your 'poor people' are freed of your tyranny, Madonna, as all of the Romagna will soon be freed from the tyranny of the Sforza and the Varano and the Orsini."

The woman did not respond but turned her head. Cesare noticed the French commander glaring at him, so the Borgia stepped back from the lady's horse.

"Ah well," he sighed. "In any case you appear contented today."

Caterina frowned at him but did not speak. Instead she reached and opened her traveling cloak to reveal a necklace - a three-tiered necklace of diamonds suspended from three strands of woven gold wire! The diamonds were shaped like tears and capped with a pattern of gold filigree resembling pointed thorns.

She was pleased to see Cesare's smile vanish.

She leaned from the saddle and whispered to him.

"Diamonds are hard," she said. "Can't you just weep for them?"

∗

The letter from Laura da Gonzaga arrived at the Mantuan court by carrier pigeon at the same time a wooden barrel arrived from Rome for the Maestro.

The lady's message was taken from the small vial attached to the bird's leg, read, handed to Andrea Meneghina who then ignited the note by the flame of a candle.

The crate had been delivered to the Maestro's workroom while Niccolo was in the process of introducing Lizette Fourget to the various works in progress. She in turn, revealed the conditions under which the court dwarves flourished.

"We have everything," said the diminutive lady, "furniture, clothing, everything – scaled to our size. We eat and drink well, and very often we are called upon to entertain. This mostly consists of mocking rituals or customs and performing tricks, but the Marquesa sees to it we are treated with a modicum of respect while the Marquis merely tolerates us. Some of the mercenaries have formed 'alliances' with two of our women, and nothing occurs in the palazzo we do not hear of almost at once. Signore Nanino, of course, is the favorite of the Marquesa, and he rules the rest of us as if he were an emperor and we are his servants; so I *do* appreciate the opportunity you have afforded me to escape for a while and visit with you."

Niccolo assured her she would be welcome in the Maestro's workrooms whenever she chose to visit. He

142

explained to her how Leonardo prefers to work, the available source of natural light, some of the mirror writing in his workbooks. He described the process of making pigment, the grinding of the elements, the creation of a clay model of the head of the Marquesa so the Maestro can continue to sketch the lady when "she chooses not to pose."

They discussed their pasts: her birth in Lyons and the rejection by her parents when they discovered she was "deformed." She told of her time in a convent in Arles where she was sent and of the monotony and discipline enforced upon her, of the day the convent was visited by Ercole d'Este who 'purchased' her from the nuns and brought her to the court of Ferrara. She told of how the Duke later entrusted her to his sister, Isabella, who had just been betrothed to the Marquis of Mantua; and how that lady brought the girl here where she already had a small assembly of little people.

He in turn told her of his time in the Certosa, of the discovery of his ability to see, read and remember everything in detail; of his saving the life of the Moor from assassination, of meeting with the Maestro, and how they became friends.

He did not mention Eleanora, how they met, their experiences together or their present relationship.

He decided to change the subject.

"How old are you?"

"Twenty-and-five," she answered. "And you?"

"Barely twenty."

"You look older."

"It is a consequence of my – condition," he said quietly. "I read people of my small dimensions have a tendency to have old faces."

Suddenly she reached forward and touched his cheek with her gloved hand.

He felt as if he had been branded.

"I like your face," she said.

They were interrupted then by the arrival of Leonardo who had been told about the barrel addressed to him and now waiting in his workrooms. He smiled, nodded a welcome to Lizette and immediately focused his attention on the barrel. Niccolo quickly provided two crowbars, and the two set to work removing the lid.

To the surprise of both, tucked among the dry straw were dozens of jars and urns containing a variety of medical herbs and powders. There were brushes of several lengths with hairs of varying widths and textures. There were scrolls and texts and a small collection of razor-sharp knives and long-handled forceps for dissection. There were the Maestro's worn silver trays to hold blood and sinew. In short, here were many of the things Leonardo had been forced to abandon when he fled the Castello Sforzesco!

Tied to one of the jars was a sheet of parchment. The Maestro untied it and noticed at once it was embossed with a familiar *impresa*: a shield divided into two parts – one half depicting a bull in pasture and the other half with alternating horizontal stripes of black and yellow. Above the shield was the triple crown of the papacy trailing two long and swirling tassels and two crossed keys!

He broke the seal, unfolded the parchment and read. Then, without comment, he passed it to Niccolo.

It read: "My compliments, Maestro. Here are a few items I felt you may need or want and which you unfortunately had to leave behind. I regretted your loss, and with admiration and respect for you and your work, I decided to return these items to their proper owner. I remain your devoted admirer."

It was signed with a majestic scrawl: "Cesare Borgia, Duke of Valentinois."

*

The next day – and as far as Niccolo could tell - something definitely had happened!

There was marked hysteria on the part of the chamberlain; a marked increase in the comings and goings of envoys, and one or another of the nobles in the court inexplicably "disappeared" for a day or two.

It was only a matter of time before Lizette informed Niccolo "the Marquesa received a message from Laura da Gonzaga concerning a necklace which once belonged to the Marquesa - and *now* is apparently owned by Lucrezia Borgia. She has learned Caterina d'Este also had an identical necklace which was given over to Cesare Borgia as she surrendered her city to him. It is very confusing, and the Marquesa is furious."

Niccolo's response was startling and alarming for the young woman. He impulsively took both her tiny hands in his, kissed them, and then dashed from the room!

He pondered whether he should first inform the bankers of the appearance of two sets of Tears in Rome and Imola or should he, as expected, first inform the Contessa.

What did it mean?

Could the necklace which disappeared at Montagnana be the one in Rome, and did that mean the killers of the courier did *recover the Marquesa's Tears, but instead of returning them to the lady, they sold them to the Borgias?*

Or is it possible Lucrezia Borgia received the Tears directly from the Cambio courier prior to the raid by the Gonzaga mercenaries?

Why was the Cambio so certain it was the Marquesa who engineered the theft and the murder – if a murder even occurred? Especially now when the Tears seem to be appearing in Rome and Imola!

He remembered the Contessa Bergamini implying there were undercurrents concerning the Tears only she could recognize.

He wanted to talk to Leonardo about the matter, but he knew and understood the Maestro's aversion to court intrigues after his years with the Moor.

So he decided, being an agent for both the Cambio *and* the Contessa, to inform both.

But the Contessa first!

It was another week before the Marquesa suddenly appeared in the Maestro's workrooms, apologized for not "attending upon" him earlier, acknowledged and welcomed Niccolo, and said she had sent couriers to summon Leonardo's apprentices.

"I presume the terms and conditions of the commission are clear and agreeable to you?"

Leonardo nodded. "I am honored to be granted such a commission, Excellency."

The lady smiled, but Niccolo recognized it as a convenient and proper response without feeling or warmth. "I regret having to impose a time when the portrait must be finished," she said, "but I would like to present it to my husband on the anniversary of our marriage."

"I understand," said Leonardo.

"I wonder, Maestro," the lady said quietly, "if I may call upon you now and then to perform some little services for the members of my court who are now preparing their Lenten Gifts?"

She explained the custom of gifting the local convents, abbeys and churches with items made by the nobles and distributed at the beginning of – or during - Lent.

"It is intended to encourage the qualities of patience and humility among the members of the court at this somber time," she said.

Again Leonardo nodded. "I am at your service."

"I regret Maestro Andrea Mantegna is under commission in Padua to complete some frescoes and is not present to welcome you."

"I would certainly like to meet Maestro Mantegna. I admire his work."

"He may possibly return for the revelry of the Feast of Fools which is our way of celebrating the passage of Lenten restrictions," said the lady as she absent-mindedly toyed with an emerald ring on her right hand. "It is the time of gaiety and merry-making. We crown a mock king, and he chooses his queen. You

147

may find it amusing."

Leonardo smiled. "I am certain I will," he said. "It is a custom honored in many provinces. In Florence, where I was born and raised, it was not celebrated as much as in – oh – Milan."

For the first time the lady permitted a slight touch of boredom to creep into her tone.

"I believe I was told the English and the Celts created it."

"Quite possibly. They are renegades and notorious for creating ribald rituals."

She stiffened and lowered her voice. "If you find it convenient I would also like to commission you to design and perhaps construct amusing devices for our Festival of Fools. It involves the entire province: all the villages and townships under my husband's authority. It is a merry time and much relished by our people – although the Marquis does not share our enthusiasm."

"I will do whatever your Excellency wishes."

"Good. Now. Let us make some decisions about my portrait. For example: what should I wear?"

The Maestro shrugged and said softly, "It has been my conviction a model for a portrait should reflect the qualities he or she wishes to manifest, not only for today but for posterity. I would recommend something to suggest the type of woman you would want your children and your grandchildren to admire, something to suggest not only your wealth and power but also your generosity and amiability."

The lady visibly relaxed and smiled with a sincerity Niccolo had not seen before. She seemed to blossom, to become more stately, obviously pleased at Leonardo's suggestion.

"Indeed?" She took a step away and then turned and said, "Both my generosity *and* my power?

"It would seem appropriate."

"Jewelry?"

Leonardo nodded his approval and replied, "If your Excellency wishes. We can show the hands so rings or bracelets may be worn."

"A necklace?"

"If you wish."

"Diamonds?"

The Maestro seemed to reflect on the suggestion. Finally he asked, "Have you something in mind, Excellency?"

"Yes," she said quietly.

"Well – yes. Diamonds," Leonardo repeated, "if your Excellency wishes."

"Then it will be diamonds." She smiled again, turned toward the door and taking long strides, swept from the room.

*

When Leonardo told Niccolo what the Marquesa planned to wear for her portrait, the young Cambio spy was further confused. He was especially shaken when the Maestro turned to him and asked, "Could she be referring to the Tears of the Madonna?"

Stunned, the young courtier could only pretend ignorance.

"*What?* The *what?*"

"The Tears of the Madonna," repeated Leonardo. "It

is a very old necklace with a history going back at least four generations. I would think you would know of it – since the Cambio sent a representative to the Bergamini while we were there and made inquiries about it."

Niccolo stared at the Maestro in both amazement and confusion. "You – you *knew* about the Cambio representative and the Tears?"

Leonardo smiled and stroked his beard. "Do you know of a system of logic used by the Church in making judgments? The syllogism? A major declaration is made and another added. The result is a third statement which is considered true, because of the connection of the two facts previously stated. The prime example is always 'All men are mortal,' and then you add, 'I am a man," so the conclusion must be, 'I am mortal'."

Niccolo frowned. "Yes. Well. Fine. But – how did you learn of the visit by the Cambio banker and why it involved a necklace called the Tears of the Madonna?"

"I told you: logic." He smiled. "And if that happens not to work, keep your ears open when servants gather. They know and repeat everything to one another."

"What – do you know – about the Tears?"

"The truth is: their history is well known in the European courts." Leonardo sighed, turned away and concentrated his attention on the clay model of a head he was preparing. "And when I saw the banker come to the Bergamini, I suspected there was some intrigue concerning the matter. Knowing you as I do, my young friend, I knew if there was something involving

150

treachery and secrecy, *you* would be drawn into it."

Niccolo sighed. "Well, I am more confused than ever. A report from Rome said Lucrezia Borgia had the Tears, Caterina surrendered another necklace at Imola, and now it appears the Marquesa has them and wants to be painted wearing them!" He paused. "Could there be *three?* Could there be only one true one and the others replicas? And which is the true one? And if Lucretia Borgia had the actual necklace, before her brother arrived with Caterina's, how did she get it? "

"Interesting, no?"

The young man sighed, raised both hands in a mock surrender and snapped, "You – you *knew* all this? And you never mentioned it to me? Why?"

"Because," Leonardo smiled, "unlike you, I prefer not to be involved with matters concerning women." He looked up from his modeling. "They are like country moors. They may look beautiful by daylight, but they are actually bogs which will suck you down if you attempt to trod upon them."

He smoothed the clay with his thumbs.

"Now," he said quietly, "hand me that spatula."

The next few days were enlightened by the arrival of both Francesco Melzi and Salai. The apprentices were assigned a bed chamber together, and Francesco immediately set to work inventorying the materials sent from Rome by Cesare Borgia.

Salai, as usual, could seldom be found except at meals.

*

The Contessa Bergamini sat upright in her favorite chair placed within an alcove on the ground floor of the palazzo. Here she could bask in the warmth of the sun and pursue the activities of a quiet time while her husband walked through the gardens hand-in-hand with young Cesare. She marveled at her good fortune to be wedded to the count, an arrangement forced upon the Moor by his new wife, Beatrice. She mentally compared her amiable and obviously loving husband with the mates of the other noble ladies in Italy: Isabella d'Este's lord who was a notorious lecher and frequently away from his lady's bedchamber either by choice or warfare; the husbands of Caterina Sforza who were either assassinated or required the cunning and will of their lady to rescue them from oppressors; the hand-picked "husbands" of Lucrezia Borgia who maintained their position only as long as her father the Pope wished it.

Now she read again the reports from Niccolo in Mantua: a Gonzagan in the Vatican saw the Tears among the jewels of Lucrezia Borgia; there was another pair surrendered to Cesare Borgia at Imola, and the Marquesa d'Este had hinted she wishes to be portrayed wearing them!

How is this possible?

Could the Maestro have been mistaken when he interpreted the Marquesa's statement about "diamonds" to mean the Tears?

If the Marquesa or the Borgian daughter actually appeared wearing the necklace, it would immediately arouse the Cambio! They would most certainly send agents to both ladies and would also point a finger to one of the two as the agent responsible for the disappearance of their courier!

Would the ladies dare?

Suddenly the realization came to her, and she smiled. Then she laughed.

She would not inform the Cambio!

Yet.

And if Niccolo sent the same report to the bankers despite his promise to inform her first, she would simply say there was a misunderstanding. It - and all future messages from Niccolo - should be disregarded, because only the Contessa, as a woman, fully understands what is *really* happening and why.

No.

She will not yet pass on this information to the Cambio.

Because the game was just beginning!

Niccolo found himself invited to visit the dwarves' wing by no less than Nanino himself! He reasoned it was probably on orders from the Marquesa, but he said nothing and dutifully appeared at the time commanded.

He was fascinated by the scaled-down furnishings in the dwarves' wing. He didn't need a footstool to elevate himself to the height of a chair. Plates and utensils were his size and easily handled. He briefly sampled a bed and found he was cocooned in it instead of wallowing in a sea of sheets and blankets like a small ship caught in an ocean tempest. He did not have to stand on his toes to look through a window, and if he merely raised his hands over his head when he passed through a doorway, his fingers brushed the lintel. He was introduced to two male dwarfs, Pico and Grimaldi, and to another female dwarf, Louise. Although Nanino also formally introduced Niccolo to Lizette, the dwarf leader made it apparent he knew the two were acquainted and he disapproved. Lizette welcomed the visitor with a deep curtsy, and Niccolo, in turn, kissed the lady's hand, or rather the lace glove upon her hand which she always wore. He winked at her when the lady smiled at his attempt at courtly manners.

Nanino felt obligated to point out all of the Marquis' dwarves were richly dressed in satins, brocades and silks, in contrast to Niccolo's plain tunic and hose.

"Our wardrobe, you see, is indicative of our importance in the court," Nanino insisted. "The history of dwarves has always been associated with nobility. In ancient Egypt, I have been told, it was the court dwarves who were entrusted with keeping the accounts and maintaining the inventories." "That is true," Niccolo nodded, smiling at Lizette who now stood beside him. "And it was the same Egyptians who first dragged pygmy warriors into their courts where they were frequently attached to the thrones of the pharaohs with gold chains and jeweled collars." He glanced around at the others. "I see very little has changed, save for the removal of the gold chains.

He saw he had aroused the anger of Nanino.

"Better a jeweled collar," snapped the leader, "than the worn woolen neck piece of a common peasant pretending to be the equal of a noble - simply because he can read and write in Latin."

"Oh, I have no ambitions to be the equal of a noble," Niccolo replied quickly. "Why should I suppress my talents and intelligence to the level of a courtier whose principal concern every morning is whether to wear the red or the green slippers?" He sneaked a glance at Lizette who hid her smile behind the fan. "Besides," Niccolo continued, "your gold tunic looks a little threadbare itself, brother Nanino. If I am not mistaken, there is a snip of gold braid missing from the cuff of your left sleeve."

The embarrassed dwarf quickly examined the damage, and his face flushed. "It is of no consequence. If I so choose, I could wear a hundred different uniforms. I have the vestments of a bishop! Of a cardinal! Of a pope!"

"How fortunate for the Church vestments do not make the man," Niccolo smiled. "The Cardinalate is doubtless composed of several small-minded men, but small in stature . . . !"

It was too much for Lizette who laughed quite audibly, and in a moment Nanino, livid, tore the fan from her grasp. His right fist was raised, ready to strike the lady, but she did not recoil from the threat.

However Niccolo suddenly dropped into the crouched stance taught him by Rubini. In an instant his left leg swept in a wide circle, knocking both of Nanino's legs out from under him. The dwarf was sent sprawling.

"Did you feel that?" Niccolo cried, suddenly bending over the startled Nanino and offering him a hand. "Was that an earthquake?" He glanced quickly at Lizette who stood smiling. "Are *you* injured, Madonna?"

Nanino slapped Niccolo's hand to one side and scrambled to his feet. In a moment Pico and Grimaldi had assembled themselves behind Nanino, and Louise had crossed to Lizette's side.

"You dare strike *me?*" Nanino screeched. "The Marquesa shall hear of this!"

"Oh, I'm certain she will," Niccolo said quietly. "Pet dogs may attract fleas, urinate on the carpets and salivate at table, but they always count on the generosity and protection of their lords and masters."

To Niccolo's surprise, there were no immediate repercussions from the disagreeable confrontation. When he next met the dwarf lord in a corridor days later, Nanino nodded in stony salute as he passed and Niccolo responded in kind.

"It is rather strange," Niccolo told Leonardo that evening. "I would have expected some angry response from the Marquesa. She indulges Nanino. But no one has said a word. It is as if an overseer had snapped a whip and commanded the dogs to stop barking!"

"That is not unusual," said the Maestro as he dabbed with chalk at his study of the lady "What is unusual is the dogs apparently obeyed!"

"And I am still confused about the possibility of there being three necklaces!"

"Yes," smiled Leonardo. "Who would have suspected the Madonna had so many tears in her? Now," he insisted, "I insist you momentarily forget the whole thing and join me in the palazzo gardens to observe the trees, the grasses and the flowers." He took the young man by the arm. "Whatever exists in the universe, either potential or actual, can excite the imagination and place itself in the hands of the artist."

CHAPTER FIVE

DISCOVERIES AND DEADLINES

As Leonardo and Niccolo entered the gardens, Astorre, the aged head gardener, insisted on joining the two men in order "to learn something." Little more than a bent frame of wheezes and coughs mantled in earth-darkened rags, he had a respect for Leonardo which bordered on reverence. He suggested his assistant, Zecco, join them, but the younger gardener - in an apron wafting the perfume of fertilizer - pretended to be focused on trimming a hedge while secretly planning to slip into the tool shed and take a nap.

The trio trekked along the neatly-trimmed walkway between sculptured hedge and blossoming trees.

"Trees," Leonardo pointed out as they walked, "possess a wide assortment of green hues and shades. The bark of some lean toward the purple and some to almost total blackness."

"That's so, Maestro!" Astorre assured his companions. "Firs and pines and laurels, they tend to be dark!"

Leonardo smiled and nodded at this affirmation. "Thank you, Signore Astorre. Yes. While some tend to toward the yellow ..."

"True, Maestro!" The gardener, in turn, nodded his approval. "Like chestnuts and oaks!"

Niccolo stifled a laugh and whispered, "You have an enthusiastic pupil Maestro."

When Leonardo did not immediately respond, Niccolo paused and realized the Maestro had stopped and was focused on something to their right. He looked but saw nothing worthy of attention. Suddenly Leonardo bent and appeared to be studying a shrubbery. He ran his hand over the nearly-bare branches, stood erect, shielded his eyes with one hand and focused on the sun.

"What is it?" Niccolo asked.

"What is the matter, Maestro?" Astorre inquired earnestly.

"I was wondering," said Leonardo softly, "why this shrub was moved."

"Moved?" The gardener examined the shrub and asked, "Moved from where?"

The Maestro surveyed the garden, slowly turning in all directions before pointing to a hedge and saying, "From there!"

The gardener looked in the direction Leonardo pointed, frowned and said, "From where?"

Leonardo began to move beyond the low hedges bordering the walkway, and the other two men quickly followed.

"Surely you see," the Maestro lectured as he strode toward another row of hedge and another walkway, "the garden is symmetrical. Eight large polygons of grass and flowers bordered by these hedges and shrubs and all centered on the fountain."

Obviously bewildered, Astorre attempted to look in all directions simultaneously and dizzied, clamped an earth-stained hand on his forehead.

"Yes! Yes! It's true! It is! Everything in this area points to the fountain!"

"But look!" Leonardo commanded. "That border has been broken." He pointed back to the shrubbery he had examined. "That plant seems to be tucked on to that row, creating what appears to be a bulge on a straight line! If you had examined the poor thing as I did, you would have noticed from the moss and the stunted growth on one side it has been rotated. It is obvious it was not intended to be there. It upsets the symmetry."

Immediately the gardener paled and shouted, "Zecco! Zecco!"

The assistant gardener, about to enter the tool shed, stopped with one hand on the latch, sighed, turned and walked slowly toward the trio. "Yes. What now?

Astorre wheeled and cuffed the defenseless assistant. "What now?! *What now?!* Why has that shrub moved?!"

Annoyed and smarting from the blow, Zecco looked to where his superior was pointing.

"I don't know. I didn't move it."

"You didn't move it?!" Astorre erupted. "You didn't move it! What have we here? A garden of frolicking firs?! Of prancing pines?! Look! Look, you numbskull!" He forced the younger man's head to make him focus where he pointed. "This garden is sym ... sym ... *it has order!* Now are you going to tell me, you son of a rancid she-goat the damned thing just wandered over there and planted itself there?! Take it up! Pull it out!"

The harassed assistant half-stumbled to the hedge, lifting a trowel from his belt as he grumbled his way to it. He dropped to one knee, prodded at the earth beneath the brush and managed to rip it from the ground. He immediately slapped a hand to his nose and mouth. "My god!"

Instantly the three men were at his side, and just as quickly they covered their own noses and mouths.

"Mother of god," mumbled Astorre.

It was Leonardo who quickly dipped a gloved hand into the abyss and brought out what appeared to be a gelatinous mass crawling with worms.

"What is it?" Astorre asked, obviously afraid it was something he would be blamed for.

"A human head," said Leonardo quickly dropping the burden on the grass. "Apparently it has been there through the winter, but ..."

He leaned closer, now rubbing his hands on his cloak.

"Not much more than a skull with a few hairs remaining on it. Long hair." He stood erect and said quietly, "The color of autumn wheat."

Leonardo ordered Astorre to put the head in a canvas bag and take it to his workroom. He also swore the gardener to secrecy.

"I do not think it would be good for your reputation, my dear Astorre, if the Marquis found his gardener had to be shown a discrepancy in the shrubbery – much less the fact someone buried a head there."

Astorre paled. "Yes. Of course. Absolute secrecy.

161

Thank you, Maestro. Thank you!"
    Leonardo and Niccolo strode quickly to the palazzo.

Leonardo barred the doors to his workshop and posted a notice on the door saying no one should disturb him. He and Francesco brushed and scrubbed and bleached the skull until it was free of tissue. They then mounted the skull on a framework of metal rods on a turning wheel, and Leonardo set to work with calipers and compasses and called out a series of mathematical measurements to Niccolo who inscribed the numbers on a wax tablet. The young courtier then passed the figures to Francesco who converted them into equations and called out the final figures to Leonardo. The Maestro then cut varied lengths from a long wooden dowel and glued the pegs to certain points on the skull. He took thin strips of wet clay and laid them in narrow, criss-crossed patterns around the pegs until he achieved the depth hc wanted. Within hours the skull was slowly, slowly transformed into a semblance of a human face.
    Niccolo was then instructed to read and call out the final mathematical numbers again as Leonardo added some clay here, smoothed some away there.
    "The space between the slit of the mouth and the base of the nose is one-seventh the length of the entire face, "Leonardo recited as he worked. "The space from the mouth to below the chin is a quarter part of the face and similar to the actual length of the mouth."
    At first Niccolo thought the Maestro was again

instructing him until he noticed Francesco was checking these statistics against notations in one of the workbooks and now and again called out a correction.

The pattern of reconstruction continued for hours. "The space between the chin to below the base of the nose is precisely one-third the length of the face. The space between the mid-point of the nose to below the chin is exactly half the length of the face. The distance from above to below the chin should be one-sixth of the face and precisely one fifty-fourth of ..."

The forehead, cheeks and nose began to form as Leonardo pinched, smoothed, made adjustments until the ends of the pegs disappeared under a thin layer of clay.

The work continued throughout the long afternoon and into the night, broken at times as the Maestro rested his head in his arms and napped for intervals of a quarter-hour. Niccolo watched in amazement as a distinct face formed under Leonard's long fingers.

The litany continued. "The outer edges of the eyes to the ears is exactly half the width of ...!" "The width of the neck as seen from the side is approximately the same distance from the chin to the jawbone, and the thickness of the neck is exactly one-and-three-quarters of the distance from the eyebrows to the nape of the ...!"

Niccolo was stunned to see the face of a relatively young man slowly emerge from the wet clay. There were molded eyes and eyelids, eyebrows, cheeks, ears and a wide creased forehead. The chin was prominent, the neck relatively broad, the lips thin and unsmiling.

"I have no way of knowing," said the Maestro as he

worked, "whether the eyebrows were thick or thin, but the reconstruction of the mouth is relatively accurate. Consider, my young friends, these lips may be able to speak to us from the grave and perhaps even identify the person who beheaded him."

He stepped back to survey his work, sighed and wet the clay. He then covered it with a wet cloth.

"That is sufficient for the time," he said. "Francesco, go and bring us something to eat and drink. I'm certain Niccolo is famished. For a short man he has the appetite of a giant."

Niccolo slipped from his high stool and fell back into one of the two more comfortable chairs by the workshop windows. "Are we finished?"

"Not yet – but soon."

"What have we learned? Who is this poor soul?"

"I always knew whose skull this was," said Leonardo as he sprawled in the other cushioned chair. "Remember when we were in the Castello Sforzesco, and we were trying to determine who might be the father of Madonna Maria's child?"

"You said to count back nine months, and it coincided with the arrival of the mummers."

Leonardo nodded. "Good. Now from the appearance and what tissue remained on the skull, I would say it had been in the garden for four or five months. Count back and what do we find?"

Niccolo sat upright. "The disappearance of the Cambio courier!"

The Maestro nodded. "Yes. This is poor Cecco, and finally we have an answer to the first question. He did *not* run off with the Tears. He was murdered and beheaded, probably to prevent his body from being identified if it were found."

"So the head was brought here and buried in the Marquis' garden!"

"Yes."

"Then the killers were sent by the Marquesa!"

Leonardo sighed. "You have an unfortunate tendency to jump to conclusions, Niccolo. I keep telling you there is always another possibility. It could be one of the Marquesa's enemies – who are legion – committed the crime and bribed one of the Marquesa's servants to bury it here."

"The gardener?"

"Never." Leonardo shook his head. "He wouldn't have moved the bush. Discipline is his rule and order is his strength."

"Then," Niccolo frowned, "we learned nothing."

Leonardo sighed, pulled himself from the chair and returned to the work table. "Now I must make sketches of this structure, remove the clay and the pegs and then you must take it to one of the priests in the parish, say you found it and felt it should perhaps be buried in sanctified round, and swear him to secrecy."

"Why?"

"Because in a Catholic world, it is prudent to make concessions to Rome's rules."

"We won't be able to keep it secret for long."

"Certainly – and neither will Astorre. The word will get around, but we are in a position to see who reacts to it and perhaps clarify matters a little more."

He paused, smiled, and added, "or maybe not."

*

"I intended for the projects to be amusing as well as a tribute to the originality and generosity of my court," complained the Marquesa as she paced the floor of her private chamber. "The original proposals were promising, but it is the details which define the quality."

The chamberlain nodded.

"The Lenten Gifts," the lady continued as she moved behind the large mahogany desk, "are not to be considered mere activities meant to amuse! They are extensions of the superiority of this court and should reflect our dedication to the Church." She paused and picked up a parchment from the desk. "Look at this! Signore Girolamo has forged a pair of fire tongs! It undoubtedly has a useful purpose, but how does it reflect the grandeur of the Gonzaga? Perhaps if they were cast in bronze or gold with a suitable commentary from the Greek classics, but plain tongs?! Pitiful! And Madonna Francesca has spent four weeks working a *vestito* in shaved velvet! Now, I ask you, Signore Andrea, who will wear it? The Mother Superior of Santa Maria de Gaino? Imagine!" She glanced at the parchment. "And what is this? Signore Ottaviano is preparing *what*?!"

"Requiem candles, Excellency," said the chamberlain softly. "Black. With decorative figures and scenes from the Passion of Christ. He says he is waiting only for the return of Maestro Andrea to finish the designs on them, but the candles themselves are ready."

"Maestro Andrea, as you know, is presently preparing frescoes at the Emitani in Padua. Who

166

knows how long it will take him to finish his work?"
The lady slammed a hand on the parchment and the
desk. "What then? Will his Lenten Gift be simply black
candles?"

Meneghina sighed and said, "If I may make a
suggestion, Excellency: perhaps Maestro Leonardo
could finish the candles for Signore Ottaviano."

The Marquesa came around the desk to stand
defiantly before the court chamberlain. "He will be too
busy painting my portrait to work on requiem
candles!"

Meneghina pointedly cleared his throat. "That is
precisely the point, if you will excuse me, Excellency. It
may help to prevent him completing your portrait on
schedule and require - shall we say - some
renegotiation?"

The Marquesa studied the chamberlain for a
moment, then she smiled and said quietly. "Signore
Meneghina, you are *astuto*." She extended a hand, and
Meneghina ceremoniously bent to kiss it, but before
his lips were even close to her jeweled rings, the lady
quickly withdrew her hand and walked away,
gesturing for the chamberlain to follow. The
chamberlain smiled and pulled himself erect, arms
tight against his sides.

"One other matter of interest, Excellency," he said.
"Yes?"

"Our agent in Cremona reports the Contessa
Bergamini was visited some time past by the director
of the Cambio. He stayed only one night, and then
returned to Venice."

The Marquesa rested back against the pillow on the

chair. "Indeed?" She put one slim, elegant finger to her lips as if in thought. "That *is* of interest." She paused and studied the chancellor. "I have also heard - rumors - the Maestro found a human skull in our gardens."

"I have heard the rumor as well."

"Are they true?

"I am attempting to verify the reports."

"You realize if it is true, it will most certainly point to Signore Cristani's little project on my behalf. There will be further – possibly embarassing - inquiries."

"I understand," said the chancellor. "I have – taken steps."

He smiled.

Following his audience with the Marquesa, the dark-bearded chamberlain to the Gonzaga, still elaborately adorned in a morning attire of scarlet velvet trimmed in gold, strutted rapidly down the long corridor. As he passed a window he glanced down at the Piazza Sordello and saw the peasants unloading wagons and carts filled with gatherings of flower and colorful, seasonal fruit and vegetables. He frowned, remembering the collecting and sorting of the Lenten Gifts alone would demand valuable hours of his time, and although he knew the Marquis might return from Venice only briefly before he resumed the war, he silently wished for his return, because the Marquis did not hold with "religious nonsense."

He hurried past the wing housing the dwarves' apartments and threw open the great doors to the *camera degli sposi.* He expected to find an assistant there, but instead he found the reception chamber empty, so he crossed quickly into the smaller room adjoining it.

Here he discovered Nanino posturing before a life-size portrait of Federico Gonzaga, the Marquis' father. The little man appeared to be attempting to mimic the heroic pose and manner of the man in the portrait. He was dressed in identical tunic and hose, high boots and a short cape. A miniature copy of the ring on Federico's forefinger graced the same finger on the dwarf.

"Amusing yourself, Toad?" The chamberlain growled. "Trying to imagine yourself a man?"

Nanino did not seem annoyed at the insult. He merely broke the pose, shuffled toward Meneghina, smiled and said, "Who comes here? Ah! It is the chancellor who sees everything and knows nothing?" He came closer and mock-whispered, "I know something you do not, cabbage-head!"

The chancellor suddenly drew his stiletto from its scabbard, and the dwarf quickly backed away in surprise; but Meneghina simply crossed slowly to a credenza and speared an apple from a bowl. "It may not be prudent to know *too* much in this court, you obnoxious little maggot!"

"Oh no! Knowledge is power everywhere and under all conditions," Nanino grinned as he advanced quickly and snatched the apple from the stiletto's point. "Didn't anyone teach you that, you diseased dog?"

Meneghina wanted to reach out and choke the dwarf to death, but both he and Nanino knew such an act would only bring the Marquesa's wrath down upon her chancellor.

"You're fortunate the Marquesa indulges your perversions, Toad," said Meneghina as he sheathed his blade and took a bunch of grapes from the bowl. "You amuse her now, but your influence may soon vanish like the autumnal sun.

"So?"

"So Leonardo brought with him a dwarf of genuine achievement and nobility, a little man with a remarkable memory, a broad intelligence and a penetrating wit. In *your* circle, amusement is a fart ignited by a flame. Your concept of culture is illustrated pornography. If the Marquesa finds this newcomer more appealing, your days of favor may be drawing to a close, Toad."

Nanino hurled the apple at the chancellor, but Meneghina ducked and the fruit splattered against the wall.

"Stop calling me 'Toad'! You know I hate it!" The dwarf attempted to thunder at the chancellor. "And if I mention it to the Marquesa, you'll pay for it!"

Meneghina smiled at the dwarf's obvious frustration and anger. "Stay close to your protector and your army of tiny, twisted vermin," he said softly. "Stick to your talents for spying and assassination, but remember: the Marquis will return from Venice soon, and *I* have his ear!"

"But *I* have the *Marquesa's* heart," the dwarf grinned.

"That bond may have been broken a little after it was verified you usurped the authority of Signore Cristani concerning – *his* project."

"The man was a fool. He gave too much authority to

the Venetian assassin."

"Her Excellency punished you?"

"A brief deprivation of this or that - an annoyance –
nothing more." He seemed to calm, strutted toward the
chair of state, gave a coarse, vulgar laugh and said, "I
still say I know something *you* don't know."

"Doubtful," growled the chancellor as he popped a
grape into his mouth. "In your twisted substitute for a
brain, there can't be enough room among your vicious
obscenities, your blasphemous mockeries and the
perverse machinations for anything worth knowing."

"Words. Words. Words." The dwarf lifted himself into
the chair. "You want amusement? Untangle this riddle,
you pompous bag of pus! Beyond the walls, beneath
the moat, there is a ship which cannot float. There is a
nest, but the bird's abed - with a toasty fire at his feet
and head."

Meneghina's temper flared, but he dared not show
it. He was not annoyed so much by the dwarf's
arrogance as the fact he might actually possess
knowledge concerning the security of the court which
was the chancellor's province and responsibility. He
despaired when secret court matters became openly
discussed among the courtiers and the servants. He
knew the Gonzaga dwarves constantly spied
throughout the palazzo and maintained a pipeline of
supposedly confidential information, and to protect
himself and the Marquis, he had planted an agent of
his own among the community of little people. Like all
who are saddled with the responsibility of maintaining
security, he did not wish to stop the flow of
information but only to control and manipulate it.

171

"I haven't time for riddles, Toad," the chancellor snapped. "But if you are trying to tell me a junior officer of mercenaries is in my torture chambers beneath the moat, *I'm* the one who recently put him there, so be warned!"

"But *I* know what has been done to him," Nanino grinned. "You give commands, but you never know what happens after you give them! Did you know they fashioned an iron cage in the form of a boat, then chained their naked victim in it and swung it back and forth over a roaring fire until his screams almost deafened the torturers? Is *that* your concept of amusement, Meneghina?"

"I may yet have the privilege of roasting *you* on a spit, magpie, and how you will sing for me," smiled the chancellor.

"Is the young officer singing for you?" The dwarf dropped from the chair and stood on his bowed legs in defiance. "Is it a pretty song? Does he sing who has the Tears? Did your prisoner verify the Venetian assassin found no hiding place? Did he tell you it was true the Venetian ordered the place torn to pieces but found *nothing?* Is that what he said? Did he tell you what the Captain did with the bloody bag, eh?"

"I know everything there is to be known about the mission. You made it a mess from beginning to end, Toad! Signore Ottaviano was given the assignment to oversee the matter, because he – well – because he was the best possible overseer, and he had ties with the Venetian, but *you* did not think he could be trusted. Word of our plans must have reached the Cambio and they dispatched a number of couriers simultaneously.

Due to *your* misinformation, we chose the wrong one." Meneghina drew himself erect. "You'll pay for interfering!"

He marched away and slammed the door behind him.

Nanino scowled, wheeled, lowered his trousers, pointed his small backside in the direction of the departed chancellor, and shouted in the vulgar tongue.

"Cacapensieri!"

Within an hour, the Marquesa summoned Andrea to her chambers.

"Nanino tells me you now have a member of our garrison in your dungeons," she said.

Silently cursing the dwarf, Meneghina nodded and replied, "I - do, Excellency."

"Why?"

"I was informed he was one of the first ordered to search the room during Signore Cristani's – expedition. If the Venetian – or any of the others - lied about this as I now suspect, the young officer might know something and could be – compelled – to tell us the truth. If you remember, Excellency, I brought to your attention there was young mercenary officer involved with the- incident – who had been drinking heavily, and ...!"

"Yes! Yes! Yes! But Captain d'Angeness was in charge of our mercenaries, and *he* says the Venetian did not lie. On his return he reported to Ottaviano who served as our contact. The Captain swears they tore the courier's room apart, tortured the unfortunate, but there was no necklace."

The Marquesa frowned and swept back behind the desk, the train of her gown brushing the carpet. Annoyed, she swept the train around her ankles with one swift movement of her hand.

If it held a blade, the chamberlain thought to himself, *it would slice through the heavy folds of satin and cripple her.*

"It was presumptuous of you to order the young officer's torture" the Marquesa snapped. "However," she descended into the high-backed chair, "my husband and I know you are loyal and, as I said, *astuto*; so I suppose we must grant you freedom to pursue any course of action which serves our interests."

"Thank you, Excellency. May I then suggest you express your satisfaction with the garrison, inform them you do not intend to pursue the matter further, and perhaps arrange a special 'amusement' for those who took part? Wine - certainly. Women - perhaps."

"Why should I?"

"Because the mercenaries may be a little afraid. The Toad – that is, Signore Nanino - has spread the word about one of their own being in our dungeons. That may seem like a direct insult to Captain d'Angeness who was in command of the mercenaries. A sign of your gratitude may be appreciated, and wine may enable us to learn more than the brand and the rack."

The Marquesa smiled. "See to it."

Captain d'Angeness returned to his chambers

following the evening's amusements provided by the Marquesa. It had been a surprise, but he and his fellow mercenaries were informed the lady had been satisfied with their behavior during the past "incident" at the Olive Tree and so ordered the kegs of burgundy from the cellars of the Hospices de Beaune to be sent to them and granted permission for "visits" from selected women of the city.

It was even more of a surprise considering the recent and persistent rumors one of their own number had been taken to the dungeons and tortured without any of the garrison knowing why.

But Captain d'Angeness knew why.

He returned to his chambers now, a little agitated but more than satisfied with the wine and the women. He was pleased the matter was closed, and he could breathe again. He shuffled down the corridor, had to focus on the handle of the door to open it, and was not especially surprised to find the room illuminated only by the light of the moon spilling across the floor. It was his custom to leave a lamp burning on the mantel, but in his haste to answer the summons to the surprising amusements, he presumed he had forgotten. He picked his way carefully across the carpeted floor by the moonlight streaming through the balconied window. As he groped for the lamp, he thought he heard a sound as if someone in the shadows of the chamber had coughed or grunted. He managed to turn and start toward the source of the sound, but as he stepped into the pale light, he suddenly felt something encircle his neck and quickly tighten until he could not breathe. He raised his gloved hands to his throat in an attempt to

175

loosen the rope, but he could not find a way to work his fingers beneath the coiled garrote. He tried to scream or shout for help, but no sound emerged as the noose tightened even more. Suddenly he felt himself propelled forward, and as he struggled to maintain his balance - already unsteady from the wine - his momentum carried him through the open window and onto the balcony. He felt the pressure of the metal guard rail against his waist. He instinctively grasped it with one hand while the other twisted behind him to seize whoever was strangling him, but his fingers only seized folds of cloth. One swift move, and his legs were kicked from under him, and he felt himself catapulted over the railing and grasping only air. He felt himself falling, falling until he struck the hard surface of the courtyard.

The dead officer sprawled there in the cold, even as his assailant folded the dark cloak around himself, checked the broken clasp and became one with the shadows.

The body was discovered in the morning and quickly ruled a suicide by Cardinal d'Este which meant the victim could not receive the last rites or be buried in a Christian cemetery.

Ottaviano Cristani lost no time in taking advantage of the Maestro's help with the requiem candles which were to be his Lenten Gift. Early the day following the "suicide" he appeared in the workrooms, greeted Leonardo warmly, expressed his thanks and had his servants deposit on a table two wooden boxes of candles, nested carefully in straw.

Leonardo carefully removed one of the thick and heavy wax candles from its cradle, studied it, sniffed it, and said, "They are magnificent!" He passed it to Niccolo. "You made them yourself?"

"I did indeed," replied Cristani with a smile. "Every inch of them. The Marquesa requires everything of the Lenten Gifts to be made by the members of her court. It is only the fact I wanted them adorned which enables me to appeal for help from you."

"They are scented," added Niccolo.

"Lilies," said Ottaviano. He then broke into a series of gasping coughs and quickly removed a glove, slipped it under his arm and brought a linen handkerchief from the cuff of his coat to his mouth. After a moment of struggling for air, he took one of two deep breaths. "Your - pardon, signori. I - I am not altogether in the best of health."

"Indeed," said Leonardo approaching him and suddenly placing a hand to the gentleman's forehead. "Your brow is covered with perspiration, my friend. You have a fever."

"I - I cannot seem to rid myself of this coughing."

"Have you seen the court physician, Maestro Bernardo?"

"Frequently," replied Ottaviano with a surprising smile. "He supplies me with a powder to be mixed with water, but it does not appear to help." He again erupted with a series of deep, bronchial spasms.

"You're fortunate he did not suggest bleeding," said Niccolo who placed all physicians on the level with

Brother Pietro of the Certosa. "Among contemporary physicians it seems to be the universal cure. How long have you had these spasms?"

"They came on early last month," said the courtier as he dabbed at his lips with the linen.

"These coughing fits, are they consistent?" Leonardo asked. "I mean do they come and go? Do you ever have moments of relief?"

"Unfortunately they are – frequent."

"Do you have trouble sleeping? Do they keep you awake?"

"Yes."

Leonardo frowned, turned and crossed to his array of jars and urns. He chose three of the items, placed them in a pestle and began to grind them.

Still fingering the candle, Niccolo said, "These seem almost too beautiful to burn."

"Oh, Lenten Gifts are far too precious to be used," smiled Ottaviano. "More often they are stored in the vaults of the convents and monasteries or later sold. The Marquesa sees it as a demonstration of the affection of her court for the Church. It is nobility demonstrating its subservience to Rome and to the divinities."

He erupted once again with a short period of coughing, and again he attempted to muffle the sound with his handkerchief. Leonardo added a liquid to the powder in his pestle, ground everything together, poured the mixture through a patch of cloth and into a vial, corked it and brought it to Ottaviano.

"Take only a spoonful at bedtime," he said. "It will help you sleep and hopefully enable your lungs to rest

178

and heal. The body has remarkable recuperative powers."

"Thank you, Maestro. I am most grateful."

Leonardo took the candle from Niccolo. "Now," he said, "what designs would you like me to impress upon these?"

"I was thinking of scenes depicting the passion and death of our Lord."

"How many candles have you?"

"Six. I made more, Maestro," replied the gentleman, "in case some were damaged."

"A wise precaution," laughed Niccolo. "The Maestro will probably complete a set and then decide to revise his original designs. With a surplus he can experiment."

Leonardo replaced the candle in the box. "I'm afraid my young friend knows me too well, Signore Cristani, but I assure you I will keep the scenes simple. I will sketch the designs first, show them to you for approval, and then impress them on the wax."

Ottaviano bowed and replaced the glove he had removed when he first began to cough. "You are most generous, Maestro. If there is anything I can do to show my appreciation, please do not hesitate."

"Not at all," Leonardo smiled. "It is a challenge. When – and if – the candles are actually to burn down, the designs should erupt with color and perhaps scent. The choice of oils to mix with the paint will require a little experimentation. I'm grateful for the opportunity. I will send you the sketches in about four days."

The courtier managed a smile, turned and left the room.

179

"Interesting fellow," said Niccolo.

"Yes," the Maestro said as he again lifted one of the heavy black candles and carried it to a worktable.

"Did you observe the mark on his hand?" Niccolo asked.

"Mark?"

"In black," said the young man. "A stiletto separating two faces looking in opposite directions.."

"I didn't notice it," responded Leonardo. "What is it?"

"It is a mark I've seen only once," said Niccolo. He crossed to where the Maestro was studying the candle under a lens. "It is," he added softly, "the symbol of a brotherhood of assassins."

"And what significance do you attach to that?'

Once more the young courtier was surprised by one of Leonardo's questions, and once more he frowned, paused and finally murmured, "I – don't – know."

"Ah!" Leonardo smiled. "The beginning of wisdom!"

After a week of sketching and discussing the work with Ottaviano; Leonardo, Melzi and Niccolo completed two of the requiem candles employing a method called *spolverizzare* in which they abandoned the idea of painting the images and instead pricked holes in the sketches, dabbed the image on the candles using a bag of charcoal dust and finished with colored waxes blended together to create a dozen different shades.

Later they followed the procedure with the remaining candles.

Leonardo then presented them to the chamberlain as "the Lenten Gift of Signore Cristani."

Meneghina showed no enthusiasm, nodded, ran his wooden stylus through the wax tablet on which he had listed the members of the court and their gifts.

*

That same afternoon a surprisingly cheerful but pale Ottaviano appeared in the workrooms to "personally thank you, Maestro Leonardo, and Signori Niccolo and Francesco, for your kindnesses."

The declaration ended with yet another spasm of coughing.

"There is no improvement in your health, signore?" Leonardo asked.

"Oh – well – yes, I suppose," replied the courtier. "Your potion helped me sleep, but as for the cough – well - Maestro Bernardino tried one or two other remedies with no visible improvement."

Again a deep, rasping cough shook his entire body, and this time Niccolo noticed a touch of scarlet on the handkerchief used to muffle the sound.

"I – I came," Ottaviano continued after a moment and some deep swallows of air, "to inquire if my Lenten Gifts were delivered and where they may have been sent?"

Leonardo nodded. "I saw them loaded into the cart, and I believe the chamberlain said they were intended for San Zeno Maggiore. You know the church?"

"Yes," the courtier smiled. "It is a good place for them. Maestro Mantegna painted something there some years past."

"Yes," said Leonardo. "A Madonna. It stands above the main altar."

Ottaviano's mood seemed to lighten. "An excellent

181

place for them. I just wanted to make certain they were delivered. Thank you, Maestro. I cannot risk annoying the Marquesa."

"Very prudent," said Leonardo. "Now I suggest you return to your chambers and rest a little. I will try to think of something to relieve your persistent cough."

"It is really kind of you, but I think the problem will soon solve itself,"

Cristani murmured softly. He slowly turned and keeping one hand on the work tables, managed to carefully tread his way across the room and leave.

When the door closed behind him, Niccolo said, "I'll take the medicines to him."

The Maestro slowly shook his head from side to side. "You needn't bother," he said. "I have just seen death walking, and – well – he doesn't seem to care."

During the following month Signore Ottaviano visited the workshop twice to acquire more of the potion the Maestro had provided earlier. Although the courtier's mood and attitude seemed surprisingly cheerful, his health did not seem to be improving. The cough had diminished, that was plain, but the fever persisted, and he was growing visibly weaker.

Leonardo increased the potency of the herbal mixture. He compiled some herbs from two or three of his small containers and gave the mixture to the sick man.

Niccolo noted the Venetian made no effort to disguise the markings of an assassin on his right hand. "Do you really think Signore Cristani is dying?"

"I am almost certain of it.

"It is very curious," sighed the Maestro after his

patient had departed. "His cough has diminished as I thought it would, but there is something else. Maestro Bernardo, who has been treating him, says he does little but sleep. He has lost all appetite, and the fever persists." His voice lowered. "I think the man is dying. Furthermore I think he *knows* it, and can – or will not - do anything to prevent or reverse it. It is as if he is committing suicide."

During the days of Lent Leonardo concentrated most of his energies and attentions on preparing the bust of the Marquesa, and Niccolo was left to his own devices. He spent much of the time in the company of Lizette which caused some sleepless nights when he thought of Ellie waiting and sighing for him in Cremona. Eventually the lie that his association with Lizette was strictly business took precedence over his conscience. He successfully placed his attraction to the French dwarf in one bright corner of his mind and his promises to Ellie in the other - the temporarily-shaded corner.

The female dwarf provided him with volumes of information on the court and the residents. She opened doors to secret passages and explained why they existed and who made use of them. Despite this flood of information, Niccolo remained hopelessly confused as to how much he should send to the Contessa. Signore Agnolo had told him the necklace and the courier had disappeared. Then Lucrezia Borgia had appeared in Rome wearing the Tears, but the Marquesa had hinted *she* still had the necklace and intended to be painted with them on her breast; and to further confuse the situation, there were the reports from Imola the defeated lady had surrendered another 'Tears' to Cesare Borgia. If the genuine 'Tears' remained in the possession of the Marquesa, it would imply her agents were the ones who intercepted the courier and returned the necklace to her! Surely that was corroborated by the discovery of the courier's head in the garden. But he remembered the principle drummed into him by the Maestro: "There is always another possibility."

All he knew for a certainty was Lucrezia Borgia supposedly wore the necklace on a singular occasion according to one witness. Could the Borgian pontiff have sent agents to intercept the courier and then given the necklace to his daughter?

Or was the Marquesa's necklace authentic and Lucrezia's some sort of replica?

And what of the necklace surrendered in Imola?

If two were false who made the replicas?

And why?

The barrage of thought produced the usual response in Niccolo.

It made him hungry.

He could easily have summoned a servant and requested food, but old habits refuse to die. The young man reverted to his former reputation, the terror of the Certosa, the kitchen thief, the bandit of the scullery, slipping through the shadowed corridors to investigate the delights tucked away in cabinets and barrels. Even common bread, when stolen, seemed more delicious and nourishing than all the available loaves placed before him on a table.

He was returning through the *camera degli sposi* after his nocturnal raid with pastries of walnut and pecan and a dusty bottle of the local wine when he heard someone turning the handle of the door to the chamber. He quickly realized he could never retreat fast enough to reach the door in the opposite wall, but his momentary panic triggered a memory of something Lizette had told him, and he turned and scanned the painted walls.

Where was that panel?

Flowers!

Painted flowers on two dimensional columns!

There were several columns supporting flowered groups!

Which one?

Under the flickering light of the torches the painted figures, already life-like, seemed to move! The smiling courtiers looking down from the nonexistent dome appeared to mock him and laugh at his dilemma.

He quickly patted the various bouquets as he heard the door begin to open. Suddenly the hidden panel was revealed, and he quickly darted into the narrow passage as the small door clicked shut behind him.

He found himself between the walls. The panel before him provided a peephole into the camera, and he was surprised how clearly he could hear the conversation between the two approaching figures. He nibbled one of the pastries as he put his eye to the peephole and saw the Marquesa, mantled from throat to floor in a heavy, black velour robe, carrying a sheaf of papers. She was followed by a dull-eyed Meneghina, half-asleep, who carried a small receptacle containing a well for ink, a quill pen, and parchments.

Lizette had mentioned the Marquesa was known to walk and work late into the night and sometimes to the dawn's first light.

Now the lady moved with energy and grace, pausing only now and again under the light of a torch to study a page and then to bark instructions to the chamberlain.

"I want it made quite clear to Maestro Luca Lombieni I will not tolerate his inability to finish my commission in the time allotted! Either he presents the painting of my horse within four days or he is to return the monies allotted him! If neither, I will pass the matter into the hands of my kinsmen in Ferrara which will mean the termination of his career and possibly his life."

"You wish me to say that, Excellency? You may have him killed?"

"If I said it, Andrea, I meant it. Write it as I told you. These artists feel they have every right to take advantage of their patrons, and it is about time we enlightened them to the truth." She thumbed through some of the pages. "Prepare a letter for me to the Contessa Bergamini in Cremona."

Hearing the name of his friend and benefactor, Niccolo suddenly felt a cold wind brush against the back of his neck.

"To the Contessa?"

"Personally. Tell her I have commissioned Maestro Leonardo to render a portrait of me, and I remember he had performed this service for the Contessa when she was in the service of the Duke of Bari. Tell her I would like her to send me the portrait Leonardo did of her, so I can compare his previous work with the one in progress to determine if the Maestro is not rushing the assignment or doing inferior work."

"I understand."

"I doubt the lady will comply, because she is no longer the sweet-faced young thing who graced Il Moro's bed, but then again, she may. I imagine the portrait now serves to remind her time has etched its passage upon her innocent face."

"Innocent?"

"That is what the Maestro painted. The harlot beneath is not visible in the work as I remember it. The transformation was Leonardo's gift."

Again the Marquesa rifled through the pages in her hand, then she gave a deep sigh and said, "I was furious to learn Lucrezia Borgia was seen wearing a necklace identical to the Tears, but now with Madonna Lucrezia flaunting them in public everyone suspects it was the Vatican who sent mercenaries to steal the necklace, and the entire matter is now in the hands of the Cambio. We must encourage them in that belief."

Meneghina made another notation on his wax tablet. "Of course, Excellency."

"I cannot publicly declare what I think, because it is essential to maintain a good relationship with the Borgias, especially with Cesare taking Imola under siege and threatening Ferrara. In any case, mine are locked away for now. To appear with it would only serve to confuse Gian Francesco and prompt questions we do not wish to answer."

The chancellor nodded, used his stylus to inscribe something on the wax as he repeated, "Locked away."

"Fortunately Signore Johannes was able to provide me with a copy of the certificate of assessment, so Gian Francesco is convinced the necklace I gave to the courier was the authentic Tears. If Lucrezia wishes to parade around with it now, it will only draw the attention of the Venetian bankers, and the pope will have to answer for it." She lowered her voice. "But I think it is now quite clear what really happened at Montagnana, isn't it? Captain d'Angeness lied to me. The courier was killed, and the necklace taken."

"Yes, Excellency," Meneghina nodded. "But if he kept the Tears taken from the courier where are they now? We searched his room thoroughly before he - ."

"I suppose it is possible he gave them to the Borgias. They could be the Tears the Vatican bitch is waving about," said the Marquesa as she again referred to the papers in her hand. "Or vengeance. Nanino repeatedly said he could not be trusted, and – wisely as it turned out - he sent mercenaries to Montagnana. Nanino was right, but it angered the Captain and the assassin. The killer is a very proud man, a graduate of the Janus, and he felt he had been insulted." She looked up, "And that brings us to Signore Cristani. How is the gentleman?"

Meneghina smiled and placed the tablet and the stylus in a leather pouch suspended from his shoulder. "Maestro Bernardo says he believes it is only a matter of days before Signore Ottaviano will no longer be among us."

Ah! You see?" The Marquesa smiled. "My little

monkey is quite an accomplished assassin, no?! Of what apparent cause will Ottaviano die, according to our court physician?"

"Officially, a general malfunction or weakening of the lungs." The chamberlain echoed the Marquesa's smile. "Unofficially, Maestro Bernardo informs me he believes the man has been methodically poisoned, and the process has been ongoing for some time. He says the poison, which he cannot identify, has already damaged some internal organs. There is no remedy. The procedure is irreparable."

Niccolo could hear the satisfaction in the Marquesa's voice like the soft purring of a cat. "Isn't it too perfect? Aren't you impressed by my little monkey now? And whom does Maestro Bernardo suspect of poisoning Ottaviano?"

The chamberlain drew closer to the Marquesa, but from his hiding place in the wall of the Camera, Niccolo heard every whispered word.

"Maestro Leonardo."

"Of course," smiled the Marquesa.

The lady and the chamberlain no sooner departed the *camera degli sposi* when Niccolo pushed the small button in the opposite wall. This admitted him to the small adjoining chamber. He quickly and quietly made his way to the door leading to the arcade and found it empty and deep in shadow. With the bottle tucked under one arm he made a dash for the circular stairwell leading down to the workshop level, rounded the corner, and found himself face to face with Maestro Leonardo.

"Now, Niccolo," the tall painter said softly, "suppose you tell me everything you think I do not already know."

They walked together down the corridor to the Maestro's workrooms, and Niccolo began his long recitation of what he had overheard. They entered the workrooms and found them empty. Only a solitary candle on a small table near the window provided light and warmth, but soon Leonardo and Niccolo lit more and flooded the room with welcome illumination. Leonardo turned again to the clay model of the Marquesa's head, removed the damp cloth covering it, and picked up a spatula. Niccolo placed the pastries and the wine at the other end of the table and climbed upon the stool.

Leonardo set to work scraping at the clay. "You heard the chancellor say Maestro Bernardino believes I am poisoning Signore Ottaviano?"

Niccolo worked at removing the cork from the wine. "Yes."

"Why would I do that?"

"I don't know." The cork came away in Niccolo's hand, and knowing the Maestro is not given to nocturnal imbibing of stolen goods, he simply lifted the bottle to his face and swallowed directly from it.

"Well," sighed Leonardo. "In any case, there is nothing I can do about it. Should the young man die, and if the court physician attributes it to a malfunction of the lungs, it will not reflect on me; because ..."

The Maestro stopped suddenly and quickly crossed

to his shelf of jars and urns. He dipped the tip of his little finger in each and then touched it to the tip of his tongue. After his third experiment, the tall man sank dejectedly into a chair and murmured, "My god, *it's true!* It *is!* Someone laced *my* powders with poison! I cannot identify it, but it affects the taste of the herbs. I – I suspect there is probably not enough to kill instantly but over a matter of weeks or months …!" His voice dropped, and he seemed to sink deeper into the chair. "I thought I was helping the poor man, and I was actually assisting in his murder."

Niccolo wheeled on his stool to face Leonardo. "But he was already ill when he came to you."

"Yes. The poisoning must have begun earlier. That's what the Marquesa meant when she praised her 'little monkey'."

"Toad?"

"Probably." He sighed, pulled himself erect and returned the jars to their shelves. "The Marquesa may have sent him to poison Ottaviano, has been doing it, and when he came to me, he saw an opportunity to attach suspicion to me."

"I should have hurt him more than I did," Niccolo grumbled as he bit into one of the pecan pastries. "As it is, I can't understand why there hasn't been any repercussions about my knocking his legs out from under him."

Leonardo crossed again to the work table and returned to molding the clay. "I suspect you can thank the Marquis for that. He has no affection for the little people, but they came with his wife when he married her. According to what I have learned, she was the one

191

who demanded they have their own accommodations. Now she uses them as spies and assassins. If and when the Marquis returns, he will not want to hear anything about his wife's dwarves."

"Well, at least she uses Toad as her personal assassin. I doubt she uses any of the others in that regard."

"Especially Madonna Lizette?"

Niccolo lowered his head and said softly, "I – I can't see her hurting anyone."

Leonardo used his thumb to make a slight indentation in the clay. "Well, in any case it is apparent our uncovering of the courier's head in the garden started a ripple in the pond. First the young officer was tortured. Then the Captain was eliminated. Next on the list would be Signore Ottaviano – all the principals in the Olive Tree 'incident'."

"But - ."

"So I deduce Ottaviano had to move the Tears, because – after all – he was not the final link in the chain. He served someone else."

"He did?! Who?"

"I don't know." Leonardo wiped his hands on a damp cloth, dropped the cloth on the table and turned to another work table. "You heard the reason the Marquesa gave. It was either greed or vengeance. Remembering what happened during the last days at the Castello Sforzesco, I am inclined to believe it was revenge. You heard her say the assassin was a proud man and – what was it – 'a graduate of' – what?"

"The Janus."

"Yes. The Janus." He picked up a stick of charcoal

192

and began to draw on a section of parchment. "So too was Ottaviano. Remember? We saw the mark. In any case, it is possible the assassin, the Captain and Ottaviano were responsible for the courier's death, recovered the Tears, but reported the courier was not carrying them. When the young officer was being tortured, Ottaviano may have felt he would expose the Captain who would – in turn – expose *him*."

In any case Ottaviano had to get rid of the Tears – which he did."

"He did? How?"

"He hid them in one of the requiem candles, and they were passed to another Janus agent who took them from the church where they were assigned." He smiled at his young friend. "You are supposed to be capable of making judgments based on little – discrepancies. Surely you noticed one of the candles was far heavier than the others?"

"I – didn't."

"Ah. That much is certain. The Captain told the Marquesa the courier wasn't carrying the Tears. With the discovery of the head, she believed the courier *was* carrying them, and they were passed from the Captain to Ottaviano, perhaps because they were displeased at the interference of the Toad; so there was a mild panic among the guilty, and the chamberlain had the young officer tortured, the Captain murdered and Ottaviano is slowly being poisoned. And now the chamberlain sees the opportunity of pinning the poisoning to me. Signore Ottaviano must have told Maestro Bernardo I was treating him with my herbs. I was a fool not to be more cautious. I assumed our chambers were being searched in order to find and take the red book, but the assassin was actually *adding* something to my chemicals."

"Our rooms were searched?!"

"Of course. I would not have expected anything less."

"How do you know?!"

Niccolo climbed the stool and opened the first of the three books resting there: a text of Euclid. Then he thumbed through *The Meditations of Marcus Aurelius* and the Epictetus. "These books were moved?"

"Yes. *The Euclid,* which was in the middle, is now on top."

Niccolo quickly examined the books, leafing rapidly through their pages, and he shook his head. "Amazing," he said. "What do you suppose they were searching for?"

"A valid question," sighed the Maestro. "Nothing seems to be missing. It may have been curiosity." He suddenly looked up from his study of the stone. "You still have the red book in your possession?"

"I would never trust it to anyone else," Niccolo assured him.

"It's well hidden?"

"Absolutely."

"The book is the only thing we possess which could be of value to anyone. It could discredit Il Moro with his current benefactor, the emperor. At the same time it is *our* guarantee Il Moro will not send agents against *us.* Make certain it is safe."

Niccolo smiled. "It is safe, Maestro," he said. "That I promise you."

Leonardo smiled. "You are my rock," he said quietly. "If I threw you at someone I wonder if you might kill."

The young man was speechless.

Ottaviano Cristani died on the twenty-third day of April in the year of Our Lord fifteen hundred.

Warm winds blew across the Lombardy plains from the south and the west, and the warmth persisted throughout May and well into the pope's Jubilee Year. It became known as "the gift of the bull" in honor of the Borgian emblem.

Ottaviano's body was temporarily wrapped in white linen saturated with aloe and crated with layers of salt, because the delegation from the Cristani family would be arriving at the Mantuan court to take the body back for burial in Venice. A certificate of death was signed by Maestro Bernardo, and the cause of death was inscribed as "an inflammation of the lungs."

Nothing further was said to Leonardo or Niccolo concerning Bernardo's quiet opinion of slow poisoning caused by the absorption of herbs supplied by the Maestro.

Days later Leonardo and Niccolo watched from a courtyard loggia as two men in soft caps, wine-red tunics and hose and heavy black cloaks came for the body. With a quiet efficiency they loaded the wooden crate onto the cart and covered it with a canvas. The men seemed indifferent to their assignment, did not smile or speak, and the entire process took less than half an hour.

Leonardo noticed it was the Marquesa and not the Marquis who stood watching with Lizette and Nanino from the steps of the palazzo. Isabella was draped in black with no jewelry, and it occurred to the Maestro he had not seen her wearing the Tears of the Madonna. It was rumored the Marquis had taken the necklace from her and locked it away, but no reason was advanced for why he should do such a thing.

As the coffin was loaded and covered, he also noted no crest marked the coach or the cloaks of the men, but over the heart of each of the tunics was a symbol with which he was now familiar.

Two arcs broken by a single line.

The Venetian "family" came to Mantua to claim one of its own.

It was days later before Leonardo turned and looked at the young courtier and declared. "You know it is entirely possible the Tears the Marquesa handed to the courier were also false. And she had Ottaviano and the mercenaries intercept the courier, because she *knew* they were false, and the Cambio would be certain to recognize it and demand the *real* necklace."

Niccolo took another long swallow of the wine. "You're saying – you're saying the Tears the Marquesa gave the courier were *not* the real Tears? That there

196

were – there *are two* necklaces? The original and the Marquesas's copy?"

"That much is certain. The Captain told the Marquesa the courier wasn't carrying the Tears. She believed the courier *was* carrying them, and they were passed from the Captain to Ottaviano, perhaps because they were displeased at the interference of the Toad. In any case, she had to recover them or the fact they were false would disgrace her. Ottaviano had them. "

"You're certain the Tears taken from the courier were false."

"Certainly. Didn't we agree the Marquesa gave the courier false Tears? If they were the *true* Tears, would she agree to a slow poisoning of the man? No. She'd have him sent to the dungeons until he revealed the hiding place. It is far more likely the Tears Ottaviano received following the murder of the courier were false gems, so the Marquesa wanted them destroyed before they went to the assessors of the Cambio."

"Surely the courier would have examined the necklace when it was given to him? And being a trained courier, he would examine and test the necklace."

"He did, and *that* necklace *was* authentic. It was replaced by the false Tears *before* the courier returned to the Cambio; so she is just as happy they disappeared before the Cambio could discover the deception and demand the authentic necklace."

Niccolo scratched his head.

"I'm – I'm confused. The Cambio asked for the Tears to be returned when Il Moro failed to honor his loan. A courier was sent to get them, and the Marquesa gave him a false necklace with a certificate of assessment saying they were authentic! The courier disappeared. You say he was murdered. And then the necklace appeared on the breast of Lucrezia Borgia in public! Yet to the best of my knowledge the Cambio has not demanded them from the Vatican. So are you saying the Cambio knows there are *two* Tears of the Madonna, and they know Madonna Lucrezia's is not the real necklace?"

"That much is obvious," said the Maestro. "Madonna Borgia apparently has one, and the Marquesa has hinted she has another and what of the Tears surrendered to Cesare Borgia. Another false set of Tears were taken from the courier by the Captain and given to his superior – Cristani. But to whom did Cristani pass it by way of the requiem candles?"

CHAPTER SIX

FEASTS AND FESTIVALS

Elizabetta da Gonzaga, kinswoman to Gian Francesco, had been a former student with Isabella d'Este in the humanist school of da Feltre in Rome; but she had chosen to return anonymously for the Jubilee Year. She had traveled with a small entourage in order to avoid the roving gangs of bandits and *bravi* who preyed upon travelers who might appear to be carrying a little gold in their fat purses or elegant clothing and jewels packed on mules. She presumably came, as the thousands who thronged the city for the Jubilee Year, to receive the plenary indulgence attached to the pilgrimage, but she secretly came as a "silent emissary" of the Mantua overlord.

Now the stately Duchess of Urbino sat on a balcony overlooking the Via Alessandrina and watched the army of cardinals and civic functionaries inundate the Porta del Popolo to greet the return of Cesare Borgia. She was not interested in the parade of a hundred mules mantled in black which preceded the arrival of the Duke of Valentinois, but she joked with her attendant "the similarity between the hero and the burros is striking." She nodded politely as Cesare's younger brother, Jofre, saluted her; and she smiled to notice Lucrezia's new husband, Alfonso of Aragon, did

199

not ride beside his wife but behind her.

"Poor Alfonso," the attendant whispered into the Duchess' ear. "The bird has already flown and he has yet to notice the cage door is open."

Elizabetta stifled a laugh and then raised her eyes to heaven at the absurd allegory of the 11 chariots passing below her, each depicting an event in the life of the "other Caesar" - Julius.

The woman she had come to see, the Countess Caterina Sforza, was not included in the procession, although the Duchess knew Cesare would love to appear dragging the lady behind him in chains as did the ancient Roman victors. She assumed the lady's absence was due to the fact she was now in the hands of the French, having been taken in custody for her own safety following the outrageous and barbaric rape at the hands of the Borgian "hero."

"How frustrating it must be for the Duke of Valentinois not to be able to parade his feminine trophy," she whispered to the attendant. "He is so proud of his boudoir victories - given or forced."

"She is now in the deepest dungeon of the Castel Sant'Angelo," the attendant replied.

"What? Why?"

"The French imprisoned her in the Belvedere with two dozen guards assigned to watch her, but I heard she seduced the captain and managed to escape. When she was recaptured, Lucrezia took control and had her chained in a cell in the Castel."

"Two dozen guards and she managed to escape by seducing the captain?" The Duchess laughed. "I would expect no less of Caterina. She has no match for cunning and courage. Even Machiavelli had to concede the lady is remarkable. Imagine! Although in the later stages of pregnancy, she once rushed to Forli with her own forces to put down an uprising against her then husband and then dragged the ringleader through the streets by his hair! I swear if someone were to tell me the lady was dead, I would insist they wait a week before they buried her - just in case there was another resurrection!"

Elizabetta unhappily surrendered herself to the weeks of celebration which included an embarrassing race between Jews and old men strapped to the backs of donkeys and buffaloes. She attended and endured the bullfights in the Testaccio, and was amused only when two of the massive animals broke loose and wreacked havoc among the spectators. She dozed behind her fan at the Vatican ceremonies as – she put it later - "the fat, hook-nosed pontiff elevated his bastard son to the rank of captain-general and gonfalonier of the Church. He invested Cesare with the cloak and the crimson biretta and handed him, in one hand the standard bearing the Borgian arms and the crossed keys of St. Peter and in the other the baton of his new authority."

Finally, resigned to the fact Caterina would probably never be released or arrange still another escape, Elizabetta sat at the desk by the open window and wrote Gian Francesco.

"The rumor the Contessa appeared at Forli and then at Imola wearing the Tears of the Madonna was verified cousin, by the French commander and two of his officers."

201

She took a small cloth and cleaned the tip of the quill. She dipped it into the pod and resumed writing.

"If it is true, her Tears now repose in the Vatican treasury with the Tears belonging to Lucrezia, both of which – I assume – are imitations of the real Tears. The true diamonds are, I assume, still in the possession of your Marquesa. I know this may surprise you, my dear Gian Francesco, but it does seem to me the Tears of the Madonna are multiplying faster than Borgian bastards!"

Niccolo rested his head and said, "This is giving me a severe headache. Why – for example - was Ottaviano murdered?"

"I'm not certain," replied the Maestro calmly, "but I think everything happening at the court recently: the 'suicide' of the garrison captain, the secret invasion of our workrooms, and the slow execution of Ottaviano, all these are related to the matter of the Tears." He then made a movement with his spatula to "set" the hair on the clay model of the Marquesa's head. "Let us assume Ottaviano was the man to whom Captain d'Angeness delivered the Tears after the murder of the courier."

"Why?" .

"Because Ottaviano was in service to someone else."

"To whom?

"I don't know." Leonardo wiped his hands on a damp cloth, dropped the cloth on the table and turned to another work table. "You heard the reason the

Marquesa gave. It was either greed or vengeance. Remembering what happened during the last days at the Castello Sforzesco, I am inclined to believe it was revenge. You heard her say the assassin was a proud man and – what was it – 'a graduate of' – the Janus." He picked up a stick of charcoal and began to draw on a section of parchment. "So too was Ottaviano. Remember? We saw the mark. In any case, it is possible the assassin, the Captain and Ottaviano were responsible for the courier's death. They *did* recover the Tears, but reported the courier was not carrying them. As I explained earlier, when the young officer was being tortured, Ottaviano may have felt he would expose the Captain who would – in turn – expose *him*."

"So?"

"So he killed the Captain before the officer could expose him. He would then have had to get rid of the necklace as soon as possible and get it to the person he was really serving. But he was being watched."

"That's remarkable! You – you reached that conclusion from all the facts we shared, but I didn't see it!"

"But remember what I keep repeating to you: there is always another possibility. Perhaps he *didn't* lie. Perhaps the courier *didn't* have the Tears when he was at the Olive Tree. It is possible the courier had been bribed and had already turned the Tears over to someone else."

"The Borgias?"

"It is possible. The point is the Marquesa may also have concluded the Captain lied and kept the Tears, so she first had his rooms thoroughly searched for them.

When the Captain was eliminated the attention turned to Ottaviano. Then *his* rooms were searched."

"How do you know Ottaviano's rooms were searched?"

"It seems to be a common practice here in Mantua, doesn't it? I assume everyone, no matter how noble or how lowly, has been subjected to quiet searches. You realize of course it is also entirely possible the Tears the Marquesa handed to the courier were also false. And she had Ottaviano and the mercenaries intercept the courier, because *she* knew they were false, and the Cambio would be certain to recognize it and demand the *real* necklace."

Niccolo took another long swallow of the wine. "You're saying – you're saying the Tears the Marquesa gave the courier were *not* the real Tears? That there were – there *are two* necklaces? The original and the Marquesa's copy? But – they were tested by the courier and found to be genuine."

"Yes. Which raises another question." He looked up from his examination of an oddly-shaped stone he had found in the courtyard, "For your information, Niccolo, our rooms have been searched."

Niccolo climbed upon his stool. "They have? How do you know?"

Leonardo returned to his examination of the stone, tapping at it with a small hammer and picking at it with a curved metal instrument. "When I studied with Verrocchio, theft among the students was commonplace," he said. "Nothing of great value, you understand, because we had nothing of great value, but a new brush might be taken or a pot of freshly-ground pigment disappear. Subsequently I learned a few tricks. I would place a towel through the handles of two drawers so a certain small mark on the towel was visible. If the mark moved, it indicated someone had gone through my possessions. I also arranged brushes and books in a certain order. Any change in the location of these items indicated someone had gone through them, and a quick search soon determined what, if anything had been taken." Suddenly a wave of melancholy seemed to sweep over him. "None of this spared me the constant thievery of Salai, of course." He paused as if the memory caused him pain, but also brought him some pleasure. He gestured toward his brushes. "I noticed this morning my brushes have been moved, and our books rearranged."

"That much is certain. The Captain told the Marquesa the courier wasn't carrying the Tears. She believed the courier *was* carrying them, and they were passed from the Captain to Ottaviano, perhaps because they were displeased at the interference of the Toad. In any case, she had to recover them or the fact they were false would disgrace her. Ottaviano had them. "

"You're certain the Tears taken from the courier were false then."

"Certainly. Didn't we agree the Marquesa gave the courier false Tears? If they were the *true* Tears, would she agree to a slow poisoning of the man? No. She'd have him sent to the dungeons until he revealed the hiding place. It is far more likely the Tears Ottaviano received following the murder of the courier were false gems, so the Marquesa wanted them destroyed before they went to the assessors of the Cambio."

"Surely the courier would have examined the necklace when they were given to him? And being a trained courier, he would examine and test the necklace."

"He did, and *that* necklace *was* authentic. It was replaced by the false Tears *before* the courier returned to the Cambio; so she is just as happy they disappeared before the Cambio could discover the deception and demand the authentic necklace."

Niccolo scratched his head.

"I'm – I'm confused. The Cambio asked for the Tears to be returned when Il Moro failed to honor his loan. A courier was sent to get them, and the Marquesa gave him a false necklace with a certificate of assessment saying they were authentic! The courier disappeared. You say he was murdered. And then the necklace appeared on the breast of Lucrezia Borgia in public! Yet to the best of my knowledge the Cambio has not demanded them from the Vatican. So are you saying the Cambio knows there are *two* Tears of the Madonna, and they *know* Madonna Lucrezia's is not the real necklace?"

"I think so," said the Maestro. "Madonna Borgia apparently has one, and the Marquesa has hinted she has another. Another false set of Tears were taken from the courier by the Captain and given to his superior – Cristani."

"So the courier's Tears are still here in Mantua."

"No. Ottaviano had to get rid of them as quickly as he could. He hid them in one of the requiem candles, and they were passed to another Janus agent by theft or by the recipient."

Niccolo threw up his hands.

"I surrender!"

Leonardo managed a smile "Before the war has really started?"

*

That next afternoon Leonardo and Niccolo replaced the herbs which had been contaminated with poison.

"Whoever mixed the poison with my herbs was thoroughly acquainted with both the herbs themselves and the potency of the poison," the Maestro commented to Niccolo, "which was probably nightshade. The poison was mixed with the herbs they knew I would select to fight Ottaviano's fever and his cough, and in the exact proportions. No matter whether I increased or decreased the dosage, there would still be enough to kill the man. Further, the ground nightshade and the herbs I chose were of similar texture and coloring, which means the assassin was expert in poisons."

Niccolo checked the inventory as the Maestro opened jar after jar, examining the contents with finger and tongue and then replacing the receptacles on the long shelf.

"Was that Valerian root?" Niccolo asked.

"Yes," replied the Maestro, "and it is uncontaminated."

Niccolo made the appropriate notation in his book.

Leonardo then proceeded to test and replace the jars containing ginseng, ginger and the "happiness plant," borage. He pointed out to Niccolo the bark of the willow was a pain preventive. "I discovered the information in a book by Pedanius Dioscroides which was written more than thirteen hundred years ago. I owe it to the Certosa who possessed a Latin translation." He poured some crushed petals into the palm of his hand, brushed a finger through them, and then returned them to the jar. "Did you know stamen hairs of the spiderwort change color when exposed to 'unclean' air?"

"No," Niccolo conceded. "And I hope I shall never have cause to use the information."

"You would," Leonardo said grimly, "if you worked in mines or cesspits."

The Maestro then called out each ingredient as it was tested and replaced. Bloodroot, Goldenseal. Tansy. The saffron crocus, Thyme. Chervil. Nasturtioum. Chamomile. Angelica and woodruff. Foxglove and periwinkle. Larkspur and verbena.

"Yes," Leonardo sighed. "whoever poisoned poor Ottaviano knew precisely what he was about. That shortens the list of possible killers."

"How?" Niccolo asked as he rolled the inventory and placed it in its leather sheath.

"The killer had to be trained for such an assassination. He knew poisons and herbs. He was obviously a professional, someone who could kill and never be recognized as an assassin. He had been employed only to murder Ottaviano, but he cleverly saw an opportunity to incriminate me at the same time. I doubt he had any motive for placing me in jeopardy, other than to focus attention away from himself."

"But who could that be? Nanino?"

"I don't know," said the Maestro, "but I imagine – as I said before – when we open that door there will be no more little surprises!"

With the dispersal of the Lenten Gifts to the various convents, churches, abbeys and monasteries in the province, Leonardo, Niccolo and the court prepared for the festivities of the Feast of Fools, an attempt to lighten the mood after the austerities of Lent.

Men of the court were provided with the masks of animals and loose-fitting robes matching the color and shape of the beasts.

The Maestro was provided with a mask and a robe suggesting a fox.

Niccolo was assigned the mask and heavy hide of a bear.

The women of the court were provided with dominoes, half-masks covering the eyes, cheeks and nose. They were also issued gowns of rags, some exposing a single breast. Like the men they were to wear no shoes or hose.

Before the actual feasting could begin, the names of all male courtiers were inscribed on pieces of parchment and placed in a helmet. One of the ladies of the court then dipped a delicate hand into the helmet and withdrew one of the strips.

The name inscribed on it was Johannes Vendramm.

He would reign as *dominus festi* or Lord of Revels.

Niccolo's name had not been included in the drawing, nor had the names of Leonardo's two apprentices. They were considered, as the other artists-in-residence, as guests of the Marquis. Nevertheless Vendramm, the young Belgian scholar sent to Mantua to learn the traditions and procedures of the privileged, could certainly be considered a guest, but inexplicably he had his name included with the nobles.

Niccolo was relieved not to be a candidate, because he knew one of the traditional rituals of The Feast of Fools required the Lord of Revels to have his head shaved in a monk's tonsorial fringe.

This ceremony was carried out with mock solemnity by Nanino, assisted by the other dwarves of the court. Lizette, Niccolo noted, was assigned the job of holding the "barber's bowl," a metal helmet with a crescent cut into the brim so it could fit tightly against the victim's neck to catch the excess soapy water and the hair. Despite the obvious mess, the little lady persisted in wearing white gloves which stretched to her elbows. She and the other dwarves grinned as the "lord" was then publicly stripped of his doublet, blouse, cap and hose and invested with priestly vestments turned inside-out. The little people then "enthroned" him on an empty wine keg.

The Marquesa stepped down from the dais to bestow on Johannes the rod of authority, shaped like an erect penis.

This signal sent the members of the court first off to dine and then to designated chambers for "a continuance of the revels of love and ribaldry." Several couples, however, abandoned the great hall early and were involved in chasing one another down the corridors.

At the head table Cardinal Ippolito in the half-mask of a serpent and a gaudy cloak of gold and silver scales seemed engrossed in the festivities, pretending to hear elaborate and fictitious "confessions" from the ladies and proclaiming specific "penances" which usually required a male accomplice. One of the female confessors completed her "penance" by removing the mask of a courtier robed as a hyena and bestowing upon him a long and open-mouthed kiss as she fondled below his waist – to the delight and raucous approval of the other animals.

Suddenly the Marquesa stood majestically and announced the time had come for the "lord" to choose his "queen" for the evening, and to no one's surprise he chose the scarlet-haired Madonna Maddalena d'Oggione.

It now became clear to the Maestro and Niccolo the ladies had actually been competing for the privilege of winning this "honor" by blatantly displaying their bizarre "penances" and their occasional and "accidental" pawings of poor Johannes. Niccolo, sensing the embarrassment of the Belgian, glanced at the Maestro, but the mask of a fox failed to reveal what Leonardo was thinking.

There were others who seemed apart from the proceedings.

Guglielmo Gaetani was robed in black and wore the headdress of a rhinoceros. He picked at the food, emptied his goblet of wine several times and seemed morose and melancholy.

Suddenly there was an explosion of cannon fire from the tower that shook the great hall. This salute was followed almost immediately by a blare of trumpets.

Niccolo noticed Gaetani was one of the first on his

feet, his gloved hand groping beneath the costumed robe for the hilt of his sword. He whipped away his mask and paled. The Marquesa was in the process of removing her own elaborate domino as a guard ran into the great hall and whispered something to Meneghina. The chamberlain snatched off his beast face and wheeled to face the Marquesa, but his communication came too late.

Striding rapidly into the great hall, in full armor and obviously livid, was the Marquis of Mantua, captain-general of the armies of Venice, Gian Francesco Gonzaga!

The Maestro leaned toward Niccolo and whispered through his mask, "The lord has returned home unexpectedly and found his garrisons drunken and disheveled, with masked courtiers racing down the corridors with half-naked ladies of the court, and the entire place in bedlam." He removed his mask. "He does not appear pleased, does he?"

The tall, bearded lord stood erect, hands on hips. Behind him servants and soldiers carrying torches and standards blocked the entrance. Niccolo glanced at the pale face of the Marquesa who slowly descended into an extremely low curtsy of welcome and melted with the long and overpowering shadow of her husband towering above her.

The Marquis roared, "Clear this rabble from the hall!"

Soon after the Feast of Fools, some of the resident scholars in the Gonzaga court assured Leonardo and

Niccolo this sudden ending of the event had been "unusual." Everyone suddenly seemed to have played no part in the festivities, and Baldasar Castiglione suggested the proceedings were planned and supervised solely by Ippolito d'Este to break what the cardinal considered "the boredom of Christmastide."

"However," Leonardo told Niccolo later the next day in his workshop, "I believe it is apparent the Marquesa was using the festival for some purpose of her own."

"I don't understand," Niccolo frowned. "What purpose?"

"It was obvious, wasn't it? Two members of the court were especially embarrassed by the rituals!" Leonardo turned to concentrate on his workbooks. "It was certainly clear to me the young Belgian, Vendramm, and the lady he chose to be his queen, Madonna Maddalena, were deliberately singled out by the Marquesa for the ridicule of the court. The cutting of the hair, the wine keg enthronement by the dwarves, these were more than amusing mock rituals. There was malice behind them."

"Why would the Marquesa wish to embarrass Signore Vendramm and Madonna Maddalena?"

"Perhaps like a wind rising before a storm, it was a warning."

"A warning? Of what?"

The Maestro shrugged. "Since you seem to like answering questions with questions, why, pray, do you think our host was so visibly angry?"

"He didn't appreciate the Festival of Fools?"

"Nonsense. His reputation shows him to be a man who is not easily embarrassed by ribald celebrations.

213

No. It was not the decadence of the court which enraged him. It was something which occurred before he even arrived. Something which more than angered him. It is something which *frightened* him."

The return of the Marquis immediately brought changes throughout the court.

The afternoon following the Feast of Fools, Cardinal Ippolito hurriedly left Mantua, claiming his presence was required in Rome for the Jubilee Year celebration.

The same afternoon Leonardo watched from a third-story loggia as Signore Guglielmo Gaetani quickly mounted a black stallion and, leading a mule laden with his possessions, departed to the east.

The following day Maestro Andrea Mantegna, 68, the official court painter, was forced to abandon his frescoes in the Ermitani in Padua and summoned to Mantua. This provided a welcome change for Leonardo who was now able to spend some time with the artist discussing such things as the rising cost of lapis lazuli and the mathematical basis for forced perspective.

For an entire week, there was little sign of merriment or mischief in the corridors or the garrison of the palazzo. Lizette, when she could slip away to visit with Niccolo, reported the Marquis dined alone with the Marquesa for the first few days following their reunion, and there were repeated sounds of loud quarreling from behind the doors to the lady's chambers.

"What does all this mean?" Niccolo asked the

214

Maestro as he watched Leonardo preparing a clay head of the Marquesa from his chalk sketches so the lady did not have to sacrifice much of her time in posing.

The Maestro studied his work, then stepped back, stretched and replied, "It means, my young novice, the winds of politics have shifted again, possibly due to Cesare Borgia's victories in Forli." He pressed the thumb and forefinger of his left hand against the bridge of the clay nose. "Apparently it is the Borgias' day in the sun. It has now become expedient for the Marquis to more closely realign himself and his court with the Vatican family. Gaetani who had taken refuge from the Borgias is suddenly expelled. The cardinal is suddenly recalled to Rome. Apparently the Marquis now feels it is necessary to avoid antagonizing the pope or his children. With Venice now at war with the Turks, and with Cesare obviously intent on taking Ferrara, a province of the d'Este, Gian Francesco has considered it prudent to send poor Gaetani elsewhere. Maestro Mantegna informs me *he* has been suddenly commissioned to rapidly paint a work depicting the triumphal entry of Julius Cesare into Rome after crossing the Rubicon. He assumes it is to be a gift from the Marquis to the Borgian pope for the Jubilee Year celebrations."

"But what prompted this sudden change of attitude?"

"I'm not certain," replied the Maestro as he prodded and smoothed the clay head, "but when the winds suddenly shift direction, it would be prudent to seek shelter."

*

It was nearly a week after the return of the Marquis to court before the customary celebratory dinner was held in the great hall to honor his return. Everyone, obviously much subdued, dined on gold plates laden lavishly and well, feasting on the best roasted meat, the freshest fish and seafood and delicious fruit imported from the south and east. The bottles of most cherished wines were located, dust blown away, and brought out for the head table. Formal toasts were raised to the Marquis and to the two recent victories over the Turks.

No one mentioned the major defeat of the Venetian ships at sea.

Niccolo noticed the Marquis seemed grim and reserved while the Marquesa wore a forced smile. She was robed in an exquisite gown of velvet and loops of gold woven into the pile. The usual symphony of conversation became a muted lullaby.

It was not a happy occasion.

Encouraged by the warmth of the southern winds and eager to escape from the winter-imposed imprisonment in the palazzo, Gian Francesco announced to the court he would have to return to his duties and resume the war against the Turks. In the meantime he intended to enjoy his overlord privileges while he could. There was to be a great hunting and hawking party, and most of the court was expected to

216

participate. Horses from the Mantuan stables would be assigned everyone, and the kitchen staff would travel in four great wagons to provide a mid-hunt luncheon of roasted pig, sauces, fresh bread and scented butter and – of course – the best of the Marquis' wines.

Niccolo was excused, because there were only enough small ponies to accommodate Nanino and the dwarves.

Leonardo did not enjoy such bloody amusements as hawking and hunting, although he had occasionally joined the entourage of Il Moro to sketch the birds in flight or to study the effect of light and shade on distant mountains; but now, with the rest of the court, he went gladly into the open air and out of the confines of the palazzo.

Later he failed to mention anything which occurred at the hunt except to observe in his notebooks "every opaque body can be located between two pyramids, one dark and the other light, one seen and the other not, and this only happens when the light enters through a window."

Later Niccolo learned the Maestro had underlined "one dark and one light" and had scribbled next to it a single word: "Assassins."

The young man also learned there had been a mix-up of the horses assigned to each rider. Someone had listed Leonardo for Pazzo whose name in Italian is "mad" or "crazy," and aptly so. He was a fine stallion, only four years old but huge, nearly seventeen hands.

The Marquis acquired the stallion from an Arab trader who offered the animal at a ridiculously low price, because the animal had been mistreated. It had been confined to a small pasture where malicious youths tormented it, throwing rocks at the unfortunate beast and poking at it with long pointed sticks. Consequently the beast had to be trained anew: a long, long process.

However, the Marquis' trainers were noted as among the best in Italy, and Gino, the best of the best, had been working with the animal daily over a year's time, attempting to dispel the animal's fears and reassure it humans could be friends and benefactors. The animal was now kept in a separate stall enabling it to move about with some freedom and lie down if it wished. This stall opened into a narrow corridor which could be closed off on both ends. Here Pazzo could be cross-tied, groomed, and shod when necessary. The corridor led into the small indoor arena where Gino usually waited with lunge line and whip. The line was played out and the stallion was urged, at first, to run in circles, changing lead on the trainer's command. If he did well, he was rewarded with fruit and carrots. If he disobeyed, or was distracted, Gino would snap the whip to get his attention and begin the lesson again.

When the Marquis reviewed the listing, he immediately crossed out Pazzo and assigned the Maestro to a much older and gentler animal.

Signore Johannes was assigned Zanzara, a playful but mischievous mare who acquired the name of "Mosquito," because she was given to swiftly darting away unless the rider maintained firm control by rein and leg. The mare had originally been assigned to

Madonna Maddalena, but the lady asked for Starlight, a beautiful chestnut gelding, because "she liked his dark brown eyes."

The Marquis had smiled and changed the list passing Zanzara to Johannes.

*

Later Niccolo was to learn the hunting party had encircled a large wild boar in a wooden expanse, and while the dogs and their handlers went about their work of flushing the beast from the thick underbrush. The Belgian had been amusing his lady with stories of the mercantile world of Antwerp and Brussels when suddenly the massive boar, red-eyed and snorting in rage and frustration, broke loose of the entangling ferns and the heavy underbrush and started to dart back and forth across the clearing, slashing right and left with his great curved tusks.

Startled, Zanzara reared and bolted.

Johannes struggled to bring the mare under control, but it was useless, because the horse had taken the bit and was hurtling across the clearing and plummeting down the steep incline leading to the river. The Belgian's saddle had fallen away leaving him on the earth but entangled by the right stirrup. He was dragged for some distance before he managed to slip from his boot and lay moaning on the river's edge.

Still later the stable master told Niccolo the cinch of Johannes' saddle appeared to have been "worn" half-through. The rearing of the animal applied the necessary pressure to complete the severing, and that was why the rider was unhorsed.

Maestro Bernardo assured the Marquis the Belgian was strong and would recover.

That same afternoon, Leonardo and Niccolo were surprised by the sudden appearance of Johannes Vendramm and Madonna Maddalena in the workshop. The Belgian, now in the customary velvet tunic and hose of the court and with his face half shadowed by a large-brimmed hat, bowed to the Maestro as Niccolo escorted the lady to the most comfortable chair in the workroom. Madonna Maddalena's glorious red hair was gathered and braided and woven around her ears and temples like a turban and then covered with a thin veil held in place by a jeweled comb, but her beauty was marred by an obvious air of anxiety.

"Forgive me for appearing without an invitation," the handsome young Belgian pleaded, "but I did not wish everyone in court to know I wanted to meet with you."

"You are welcome of course," said Leonardo. "You need no invitation. You know my friend and associate, Signore Niccolo da Pavia?" The couple glanced in Niccolo's general direction, but it was clear their attention was focused upon Leonardo. "Your hair, it is returning?"

"Yes," said Johannes. It was evident he did not wish to discuss his humiliation as the Lord of the Revels. "I wondered," he whispered, "has anything – well – anything unusual happened to you since your arrival at court, Maestro?"

"Unusual?"

"Have your rooms been searched? Have you been followed?"

Leonardo and Niccolo exchanged quick glances, and Niccolo climbed up and perched on a stool beside the young woman whose attention remained focused on the Maestro.

"I was not aware of being followed," Leonardo replied. "Why do you ask?"

"Because we have both sensed someone was watching us."

"Yesterday," the lady said softly, "I distinctly heard something in the garden bushes, and when Johannes went to investigate, he found this." She held a small, torn scrap of material toward Leonard, but Niccolo reached and examined it.

"A torn scrap of gold braid with a button attached to it," the young courtier commented. He looked at the Maestro and passed it to him. "From a uniform perhaps?"

"Perhaps," nodded Leonardo as he returned it to Niccolo and turned his attention to Vendramm. "Can you advance any reason for someone from the garrison to follow you?"

"None."

"I cannot imagine why someone of the court would steal from another. Do you possess anything of value?"

"Nothing," replied the Belgian. "I brought with me only copies of trade agreements for the Marquis' signature, and several other official documents, but nothing of value. And I recently inventoried the papers, and nothing is missing."

"Trade agreements and other documents?" Niccolo frowned. "What other documents?"

"A projection of the value of salt now since Il Moro's monopoly has been broken. A report Vasco de Gama has sailed again, this time to establish trading posts at Hormuz and on the Malabar Coast. A copy of the Dutch assessment of the Marquesa's jewels ... !"

Niccolo was instantly alert. "The Marquesa's jewels? An assessment of the Marquesa's jewels?"

"Yes," said Johannes. "For some reason it became necessary some time ago to have a courier assess some of her jewels and their value authenticated."

"And ... ?"

"What did the assessment say? Were the Tears – well - were they validated?"

"Absolutely." Johannes shrugged. "They were judged priceless. I cannot tell you their exact value, because such matters are confidential, but I can say with confidence the courier's analysis of the diamonds in the Marquesa's Tears are genuine. That agreed with a previous assessment by another agency."

"Really?" Leonardo said softly. "And how was *that* determined?"

"The usual method, I presume," the Belgian replied, "they cut glass. You see, a diamond is the hardest substance which ..."

"Yes!" Leonardo stopped him. He noticed the discussion was causing Madonna Maddalena some dismay although she struggled to hide it, her small hands clenched defiantly in her lap. "I know the qualities of a diamond, and the test of cutting glass is a valid method of assessment."

"You say this assessment was a copy of another?" Niccolo asked.

"Yes," Johannes replied, puzzled by this sudden inquisition, "but there was some – discrepancy – and the Cambio asked me – while I am in the court – to examine the *original* assessment made some years ago. Over the last ten years, my uncle, a past master of the Hanseatic Guild, has had several dealings with the courts of Ferrara and Mantua. Delegations of three to five persons at a time passed back and forth between Brussels and the Este and Gonzaga courts carrying agreements of trade, monopolies on certain commodities controlled by the Duke and the Marquis, appraisers and lawyers and traders. As I said: business arrangements."

"Yes," Leonardo repeated softly. "I understand. Business arrangements." He paused and asked, "And did these arrangements include perhaps a quantity of diamante?"

Johannes paled. "Diamante? What do you know of diamante, Maestro?"

"Only it is a by-product of your principal Belgian industry, and it was recently proven to be a saleable commodity. For years it was simply thrown away. Now it has become of some value."

The Belgian licked his lips and then said softly. "Yes. It has."

Leonardo smiled as if his inquiry satisfied him. "So you are here, because your uncle feels there is something to be learned from the original assessment." The Maestro turned to face Madonna

Maddalena. "And you, Madonna? May I ask how you came to be in Mantua?"

"Me?" She seemed startled by the question. "Well - my reasons for being here are similar to those of Signore Johannes," the red-haired woman replied softly. "I am Venetian, from Murano. My father, apart from his profession, is an advisor to the doge, and the Marquis was kind enough to offer me an education and a period as lady-in-waiting to the Marquesa."

"I see," said Leonardo quietly. "You are here to be educated, and Signore Johannes is here to be, what was the term? Polished?" He again turned his attention to the Belgian. "And have you been sufficiently polished, signore?"

The Belgian shrugged. "Well," he said, "I have been humiliated and embarrassed, mocked and mutilated, and now I believe I am being followed, so I suppose I have a better understanding of how matters are conducted in Italian courts. It is rather like being inducted into a guild where naked applicants are shoved up chimneys, thrown on the cold waters of a river, or paraded around the piazzi while straddling a barrel. If you survive, you are considered strong enough to conduct business matters."

Niccolo was surprised to hear the Maestro actually laugh.

The tall, bearded man placed one of his heavy hands on the young man's shoulder and mock-whispered, "These are arenas where unscrupulous and ruthless lords of war deal with honest nobility in games affecting the entire world." He stood erect again. "That's why the playing fields are called 'courts'."

"What do you suggest, Maestro."

Leonardo fingered his beard again. "It is always wise to seek shelter from a storm."

After the couple had departed, Niccolo fingered the piece of material and said quietly. "This button – you noticed? It is heavy and shaped like a coin."

"Yes."

"And it is engraved with the Gonzaga G."

"Yes."

When Leonardo offered no further comment, Niccolo shrugged, slipped the material and the button into the pocket of his tunic and asked, "Do you think those two are actually being followed?"

"Quite possibly."

"Why? Does someone suspect Signore Johannes of something?"

The Maestro peered at his young friend for a moment from under his thick eyebrows and said softly, "Why do you assume it is Signore Johannes who is being shadowed? Why not the lady? They are usually together."

"What could the lady have done to warrant being spied upon?"

"Ah!" Leonardo smiled. "Open *that* door, Niccolo, and you may have the answer to a number of interesting questions!"

Within a week Signore Johannes and Madonna Maddalena both "disappeared" from the court.

Some said the young Belgian had received a summons from his uncle to return to Antwerp immediately and secretly. Others said the "warnings" of the search of their chambers, the humiliations of The Feast of Fools and the "accident" on the hawking diversion convinced the young man his life – and possibly the life of Madonna Maddalena – were in danger.

Everyone agreed the sudden departures were an ominous sign, all was not well in the Mantuan court. For the next few days there were tides of couriers surging between Mantua and Venice, between Mantua and Milan and Verona and Ferrara, Padua and Florence.

Northern Italy was in turmoil.

Two days later Niccolo was pleased to welcome Lizette to the workrooms. Elegantly-gowned and smiling, she scolded him for "ignoring me for nearly two weeks." He apologized and suggested he and the Maestro had been involved in "a grim business."

He showed her the sketch Leonardo had made of the reconstructed face.

"Do you recognize the man?"

The little women studied the sketch and said, "No. I don't think so. He's handsome, isn't he? Am I supposed to recognize him?"

A little annoyed at the reference to the man's "handsomeness," he replied, "Well, I suppose he's not especially hideous, but the point is moot, because the gentleman is dead, and his head was buried in the Marquis' garden."

"Well, I don't know him," said Lizette. "He does resemble a man who appeared at the court sometime last autumn, but it is difficult to say for certain, because I cannot judge the color of his hair or his eyes, and I usually notice those things – although his height may have been too tall for me to judge for certain. The gentleman I am referring to was not introduced to us. I seem to remember he stayed only a day or two and did not take part in our amusements or festivities."

"Well, he was a courier from the Cambio, the bank of Venice, and the fact his head was buried in the Marquis' garden links this court to his murder."

Lizette frowned and fanned herself vigorously as if annoyed with the judgment.

"Well," she said shrilly, "I prefer not to hear anymore. Politics bores me, but if such matters interest you, I have something to share." She lowered her voice to a whisper. "I overheard Meneghina inform the Marquis there has been an uprising in Milan. They rose against the French who threw down their arms, and most of the Gascon and Swiss mercenaries did the same thing. Duke Ludovico has returned from exile to cheers and huzzahs from the people."

She paused.

"Il Moro rules again in Milan."

＊

That afternoon the Maestro was again working on the clay model of the Marquesa's head when suddenly the doors were flung open, and the Marquis strode into the workroom unannounced. He was accompanied by Meneghina and two young officers with breastplates embossed with the Venetian lion. The Marquis, elegant and erect and every inch a condottiere, briefly examined the room, the view from the windows, the chalk study of the Madonna and Saint Anne with the Christ child which the Maestro had mounted, unframed, on an easel, the initial charcoal sketches Leonardo had prepared for the Marquesa's portrait, and the clay bust of the lady.

"I regret I was not here to welcome you formally upon your arrival," the Marquis said to Leonardo without smile or frown as he completed his examination. "Are you comfortable?"

"Yes. Thank you, Excellency."

"I tried to be here, but Venice is in turmoil."

"Indeed?"

The Marquis pretended to be interested in some texts, but it was apparent he wanted to introduce a topic for discussion. "Are you acquainted with Venice, Maestro?"

"I was there once, Excellency," Leonardo replied. "Briefly. In the company of the Duke of Milan."

The mention of Il Moro creased the Marquis' forehead. "Are you aware how difficult it would be to defend it? Especially from the north?"

"No," the Maestro replied softly.

"Look you!" Gian Francesco snapped as he looked

around, quickly seized a page of blank parchment, dipped the quill in the ink pod and began to sketch rapidly. "The republic is like, well, a sliver of land reaching beyond the Largo di Garda to the eastern borders with Milan. To the south Venice shares a common border with my own Marquisate and the duchy of Ferrara, and then it dips into the Adriatic. On the western shore of the Adriatic the republic controls the access to the sea, separating the kingdom of Hungary and the Ottoman Empire from this waterway until it reaches as far south as the republic of Ragusa." He stepped back to permit Leonardo to examine the drawing. "The city of Venice itself," the Marquis then continued, again sketching along the edges of the parchment, "is little more than a collection of islands reaching into the lagoon and joined to the mainland by boat and a single bridge. You can walk from one end of the city to the other in an hour. The grand Canal divides the city's heart into two sections."

He made a quick, reversed "s" across one block of the drawing.

Leonardo nodded as he studied the sketch.

"But the mountains, the Alps, the Dolomites here, and the lake areas at Trentino, these are natural defense barriers to the north, aren't they? The few passes could easily be defended. They are like great doors opened to admit invaders and then closed behind them to trap them."

"Yes," nodded the Marquis, "but once forced open, invaders could cut directly south to the Adriatic, hardly more than a day's ride, and follow the Adige all the way from Verona to the mouth of the Po, attacking the city from the north."

Leonardo ran his fingers through his thick beard and frowned at the sketch. "But why look to the land? Venice is a city of water. In a sense, the Adriatic is only a Venetian lake, since Venice controls both banks. If you were to develop a plan whereby you could flood the Isonzo plain here, below Gorzia, you could prevent any attack from the north." He jabbed a finger at a point on the map.

The Marquis watched intently. "Flood the plain?"

"Surely you have seen the results of water suddenly released," Leonardo continued. "The full force of the flood assaults and demolishes even the most heavily fortified areas. Villas, country residences, all must submit to the percussive force of a flood. Horses cannot stand against the striking power of water. Knights are thrown and drown in the weight of their own armor. Archers, lancers, nothing stands against the full impact of the force of water."

The Marquis smiled. "Yes. I see." Suddenly he stood erect and turned to face Leonardo. "Maestro," he said, "I hereby commission you to prepare sketches and perhaps a model of how and where retaining walls might be built to control the flooding of the Isonzo plain! I would need this model and a detailed design soon, before my return to Venice! And you must come with me! I am certain the doge and the Council of Ten will reward you generously for this service. Will you accept?"

Niccolo could see the Maestro was both intrigued and disturbed by the proposal, but the young man knew it would be a project involving his two loves:

engineering and mathematics.

"Well, Excellency," he began, "I *would* probably have to visit the site, and then there is the pressing matter of the portrait for the Marquesa !"

"The damned portrait can wait!"

The Marquis lowered his voice as if in strict confidence. "Our world is about to undergo incredible changes, Maestro Leonardo. Doors to new worlds are being opened. A Genoese trader has established an overland route to the eastern shore of India, Ceylon, Sumatra and the Maldives. A navigator, Vasco de Gama, has organized a Portugese base at the port city of Calicut, and Lodovico di Varthema, who recently returned from there, reports pepper, for example, can be purchased for as little as three ducats per hundredweight! Imagine! Three ducats a hundredweight! While in Venice the same amount sells for over *eighty* ducats!"

His voice became a little louder, more emphatic.

"Well, you can see how this will affect trade! Everything points to new routes, both by land and sea, to the spices and wonders of the east. This means Venice, once the center of all trade with the east, could possibly lose its position of importance and become more vulnerable. It is vital we maintain the appearance of stability, impregnability and prosperity."

The Maestro did not respond immediately. He seemed to be pondering the proposal, and he repeated, "The *appearance* of stability and prosperity?"

The Marquis took the repetition for a form of acceptance, and smiled at Leonardo. "You can be of great assistance to the republic in this matter,

Maestro."

Leonardo nodded. "Then – yes. I think I *will* go with you to Venice."

The news concerning the return of Duke Ludovico Sforza to Milan and that he was welcomed by the people who just six months earlier cheered the French, Swiss and Venetians as "liberators," caused more than a ripple in the Gonzaga court. The distress, especially for the Marquesa, was intensified when Gian Francesco announced he would return to Venice almost at once, and Leonardo would accompany him. Isabella's pleas that the Maestro was essential to the success of her spring festival was met with disdain by her husband.

"War is more important than mobs of self-serving adolescents cavorting through the *camera degli sposi* half-dressed and pretending to be garden nymphs," snapped the Marquis. "The Maestro has devised a way for Venice to defend itself should the Moor muster enough men and money to move against the city."

"But this is intolerable! Really, Gian Francesco, you ask too much! I need the Maestro to finish my portrait and to design for the feasting of our anniversary."

"I leave you his apprentices and young Niccolo. The young man is a genius in his own right. Perhaps he may prove valuable to you, but Maestro Leonardo *must* come with me. He has to see the situation for himself and present his plans to the doge and the Council of Ten. Throughout Italy he is acknowledged as a master engineer as well as an artist. I have even received a request from the Duke of Valentinois as to the possibility of the Maestro being loaned to him for the designing of war machines."

"I hope you refused."

"I replied this is not the time to discuss the possibility, because Venice is a priority. I suggested it may be possible after he attends to the new defenses of the city."

"I hardly think it will pacify the Borgian bastard."

"I think it will suffice. Cesare will have his hands full attempting to retake Milan."

The loss of Leonardo before the portrait was finished only added another brand to the flames raging inside the Marquesa. Her tirades fell not only on Meneghina but also on her favorite, Nanino, who in turn made life miserable for the other dwarves. She railed at her ladies-in-waiting, certain they knew in advance of the flight of Madonna Maddalena from the court. She shrieked and ordered punishments for the guards who had not prevented Johannes and the lady from departing without permission. She threw a chamber pot at the captain of the garrison mercenaries for not going after the couple. For days the food was too salty or too sweet or not roasted thoroughly and the wine was rancid. Shoes, comfortable only a week earlier, were now too tight. Elaborate gowns had been shrunken or been ripped or were suddenly dirty. Nothing was right. Everything was too big, too little, too slow, too fast, too disgusting.

She had one consolation. Niccolo da Pavia would remain in the court, and as long as the young man was here, Maestro Leonardo would surely return. She resurrected a previous plot: if the emperor were to be presented with the incriminating evidence of the corruption and intrigues of the Milanese court, he may join with her husband's Venetian and Borgian forces. He may throw the might of his own army and artillery against the Moor, and drive him again from his position of power, across the Bridge of Sighs and into the doge's dungeons from which no one has ever escaped. Perhaps this would be the opportunity she hoped for, a chance to more thoroughly search the workrooms for the incriminating red book.

"Perhaps," she said to Meneghina, "I have not devoted enough time to our guests. Request the Maestro's dwarf - what's his name again?"

"Niccolo da Pavia."

"Yes. Of course. Well, request his presence at an informal mid-day meal in my apartments tomorrow afternoon."

"To what purpose, Excellency?"

"I understand he assisted the Maestro in treating the late Signore Ottaviano during his illness. Say I am concerned my courtier may have died from some contagion. Tell him the meeting is in regard to the general health of the court."

The chancellor issued the invitation and the reason behind it using the Marquesa's exact words to which Niccolo - recognizing the implied threat – replied. "I will be happy to attend."

"Very wise of you," sniffed Meneghina.

Niccolo knew what really disturbed the lady more than anything else was the fact her hated brother-in-law, the man she accused of being responsible for the death of her beloved sister Beatrice, was now back on the ducal throne of Milan and more firmly entrenched. She could easily deny knowing anything about the discovery of the skull, and since Lucrezia had been seen with the Tears, the Marquesa could shift the bankers' wrath to her Borgian rival. Certainly it was clear, she would argue, Cesare had the courier killed and hired someone to "plant" the incriminating head in the Mantua shrubbery. He then, obviously, gave the recovered Tears to his sister.

"I had requested you accompany me to Venice," the Maestro said when they were alone and Leonardo was packing what he considered he would need. "But the Marquis, partly to pacify his wife, refused me."

"Why 'partly'?"

"Because she also realizes I must return if you are here. Her portrait remains unfinished, and she sees the possibility I might simply return to Florence after I have done what is required of me in Venice. She does not know I have entrusted you with the red book. She believes I must carry it with me, because she has had our quarters and the workrooms searched, and it has not been found. By keeping you and Francesco and Salai here, she feels I am compelled to return, and bring the book back with me. She needs it now more than ever. No, my young friend, be on your guard. Her determination is formidable, but her plan is transparent."

235

"Fine," said Niccolo, "now I know why you will *return*, but tell me – why are you going in the first place?"

"The Marquis requested me."

"And - ?"

"It has been a long time since I last visited Venice."

"And - ?"

The Maestro shook his head, smiled, and replied softly, "Because the answer to all questions are there. How many Tears are there, and why are there so many? Who has the authentic necklace?" He paused. "And why did Johannes flee the court?"

"Johannes? He was humiliated and nearly killed. He was probably afraid for his life."

"He had every right to be, but why? Who would want him dead? And why?"

"So many questions!"

"And the answers, I think, are in Venice."

The following afternoon, Niccolo honored the "invitation."

The Marquesa sat enthroned in an ornate, high-backed chair at one end of the chamber. Behind her chair stood an attendant in the Gonzaga livery and Meneghina, looking both sinister and distracted. Before Isabella was a table laden with roasted meats and fresh vegetables, pastries, and a cut-glass decanter trimmed with silver and containing a ruby-red wine. She gestured Niccolo to the chair opposite hers, and the young man saluted her with a bow and took the designated seat.

"I regret I have paid too little attention to you these days, but the court is temporarily in the throes of anxiety over the news from Milan."

She indicated he should proceed with the meal, and he was pleased to do just that, pouring himself some wine and transferring a slab of roast pork onto his silver plate.

"I trust you and Maestro Leonardo are well and have been made comfortable."

"Yes. Thank you."

"How is the work on my portrait advancing?"

"Very well," said Niccolo as he cut into the meat. "The Maestro has completed the cartoon, the primary sketch, in both chalk and charcoal and is even now in the process of transferring the image to canvas. He presumes you would prefer canvas which is not as heavy as the customary wooden base and more easily hung."

"Canvas will be fine. I understand you have made the acquaintance of our dwarves and have become – a special friend – to our Madonna Lizette."

Suddenly Niccolo became alert. He took a long swallow of the wine and wiped his lips with the linen napkin before replying. "The young lady is very intelligent. We have had many enlightening discussions."

"Yes. I am sure. And I am very proud of their leader - my little monkey." She paused. "What do you talk about with Madonna Lizette?"

"Everything."

The Marquesa gestured, and the attendant who had

been standing behind her, stepped forward, poured some wine into the lady's crystal goblet and arranged some of the food upon her plate.

"I understand a human skull was discovered in our gardens. I presumed you have passed it to church authority for Christian burial."

"We have, Excellency."

"I must admit I am a little disappointed Maestro Leonardo is leaving with my husband for Venice. I had so planned on his remarkable talents to enliven our spring festival."

Niccolo again patted his lips with the napkin. "To that end, Excellency, may *I* make a suggestion?"

"By all means."

"I have received word a traveling company specializing in the new *commedia dell'arte* is in the north again. In the winters they play Sorrento and Naples, and in the spring and summer they come north. They are masters of improvised comedy, working only from a *sogetto*, a short outline of a plot, and they are quite, quite popular. They would enliven your festivities. They could play once or twice in the court and a few more times in the piazzi for your people."

"What in the world is *commedia dell'arte*?"

"Peoples' theatre," Niccolo said excitedly. "A theatre of professionals specializing in comedy and farce. It is very amusing, a little ribald at times, but very, very popular with the people. Although they have a number of these short plots in their repertory, each time they perform them, they change them a little. They play to each audience's preferences and customs. If they play in Naples for example, they may mock Rome or Florence. In Florence, they may make fun of the customs of the Sicilians. They also alter the sketches according to the amount of laughter. If the absurdity of the story and the jests do not seem to invoke as much laughter as they wish, they resort to some standardized physical humor: comic falls or tricks with props."

The Marquesa did not seem enthusiastic. She sighed and murmured, "It hardly sounds appropriate for ..."

"They were quite successful when they performed in Milan."

The Marquesa paused with her goblet to her lips. The smile returned and she slowly placed the goblet back on the table. "Milan? They played the Moor's court?"

"Yes. Just before the invasion. They were in residence for some time. They weren't able to – well - to leave – until after Duke Ludovico fled and the siege was lifted."

Suddenly the Marquesa smiled, took a deep swallow of the wine, wiped her mouth and sat back in her chair. "Indeed," she said softly. "Well, my young friend, they may be the very thing we need. I will dispatch an invitation. Where are they and how are they addressed?"

Niccolo grinned. "They are called *I Comici Buffoni*, Excellency, and I believe they are now in Verona."

"Good," said the Marquesa who gestured to Meneghina. "See to it."

The chancellor inscribed the name and place on his

waxed tablet.

CHAPTER SEVEN

CANALS AND CARNIVALS

The Maestro and the Marquis departed for Venice two days later.

Leonardo was permitted to ride in the light coach-and-four while Gian Francesco and his four major officers rode before him on horseback and in gleaming armor. Before them rode a single equestrian bearing the Gonzaga coat-of-arms. Behind the coach rode eight armed mercenaries in metal helmets and hauberks of mail with shields bearing the winged lion crest of Venice.

Niccolo and Meneghina saluted the party as they passed by and through the great archway.

The Marquesa watched from the windows of Paradise but did not wave or salute her departing husband. Instead, as soon as the party disappeared under the portcullis, she turned to the dwarf sitting on her bed and said, "Now, little monkey, we have the time and the means."

*

The party traveled by a northeastern route which took them first to Verona.

Here the Maestro had the opportunity of presenting Simone, leader of *I Comici Buffoni*, with the invitation to perform at the spring festival in Mantua.

"Thank you, Maestro," said the troupe's Arlecchino. "How is our young apprentice? Has he mastered the stilts?"

"I'm afraid he has had little time to practice," replied Leonardo, "but when you are in residence perhaps you can renew your instruction."

Simone smiled and said quietly, "I'll prepare Rubino."

*

After Verona, the Maestro spent most of his time exploring a text on the history of the papacy which he had uncovered in the Gonzaga library. As they passed over the Adige River at the Ponte Pietra, the Marquis tied his horse to the back of the coach, crawled in beside Leonardo and proceeded to draw the Maestro's attention to the banners and crests on the building displaying the ladder symbol of the della Scala family.

"Verona is Venetian territory," explained Gian Francesco, "and under the protection of the doge, but the della Scala administers it for him."

He pointed out the ruins of the ancient Roman arena, and he ordered the party to pause long enough to purchase fresh fruit from the vendors whose enormous rectangular umbrellas filled the Piazza della Erbe. He then ordered the caravan to slowly pass the opulent Palazzo della Ragione so the Maestro could be given ample time to sketch the medieval tower and the graceful arches of the Loggia del Consiglio bending like marble rainbows the entire length of the covered walkway. The guns of the della Scala saluted them as they passed by the fortress-palazzo, and the townspeople paused in their daily activities to gape at the coach and the armed military. They moved on, past the Gothic church of Sant' Anastasia, and the Maestro requested they pause for a moment at the church of San Zena Maggiore, a charming building set down between two medieval bell towers, because "I would like to see again Mantegna's great altar piece."

The Marquis was annoyed at the delay but reasoned it might be appropriate to view the work of his Mantuan court painter, and this may be as good place as any to water the horses and to permit the mercenaries to relieve themselves.

The delay grew a little longer as Leonardo drew the parish priest into a conversation, and the Marquis noticed a brooding figure watching the two men. His hooded robe stretched from the top of his head to mid-calf, and his face was shadowed. But he was plainly no religious. The scabbard of a sword jutted out from under the robe like the tail of a duck and there was a familiar mark on the gauntlet of the right hand.

But Gian Francesco said nothing, and eventually the caravan moved on.

*

Anxious to make up the time he considered wasted in Verona, the Marquis rushed everyone through Vicenza. They galloped past a succession of palaces and churches and through the Piazza dei Signori. Their haste was also necessary, because Leonardo had to hold a handkerchief to his nose and mouth to get some relief from the great cloud of dust over the city where construction of villas and apartments was in progress.

The party slowed at Padua, because the Marquis deliberately paraded through the Corso del Popolo, across the Bacchiglione river, past the Cappella Scrovegni and through the busy marketplace of the Piazza della Regione. To Leonardo he expressed a wish to remind the administrators of the city of the authority of Venice over them. He was also hungry, and he knew of a comfortable inn near the basilica of Sant'Antonio and in the shadow of the huge equestrian statue of Gattamelata.

The sight of the bronze masterpiece only reminded Leonardo of the larger clay model of the Sforza overlord which he had prepared and displayed only later to have to watch the invaders destroy it.

But the inn proved to be as good as the Marquis remembered, and over an excellent meal of veal and ham, fish in aspic and a fine minestra of vegetables, the nobleman cautioned Leonardo concerning "inns" on the way to Venice. "Some are merely licensed brothels posing as taverns, and good food and drink are not their principal offerings."

"Licensed brothels?" Leonardo asked. "Who licenses them?"

"The doge," replied Gian Francesco over the mulled wine. "It is a lucrative business and a political asset. Emissaries, especially the Germans, expect some carnal amusement when they come to Venice, and the doge sees to it they have it. He provides his visitors with a catalog of available prostitutes who are guaranteed to be beautiful and amusing and free of venereal disease. He provides addresses and the amount expected for their services, ranging from two ducats for the conventional puttana to ten or twelve ecus for the more famous courtesans." He smiled and announced, "Why do you think they call it The Most Serene Republic?"

"I find such moral laxity surprising," said Leonardo not joining with the laughter at the table, "considering it was only three years ago the doge's censors prevented a publication of Ovid's *Metamorphoses* because of illustrations which depicted naked men and women."

"It is a disciplined business you understand," explained the Marquis. "Venetian whores must wear special red caps as a mark of their profession and soliciting from gondolas is strictly forbidden. They must also never wear mens' clothes; but all in all, it is highly regulated business, distinguishing for example between the *cortegiane* – independent courtesans who own their own apartments – and *meretrici* who are attached to houses. The profits from such business are substantial, which is probably why the Church elbowed into it."

"The Church licenses brothels?!"

"Why not? More than one cardinal has publicly

expressed the opinion sexual activity enhances the good, the honor and the piety of the country! The licensed institutions cut the rate of illegitimacy and prevent the transmission of disease, because the ladies are subject to medical inspections by licensed midwives,"

Leonardo suddenly remembered hearing the Marquis himself was being treated for syphilis.

"You must understand, my friend," the Marquis continued between swallows of the heavy scarlet wine, "Venice also has a disproportionate number of influential and unmarried men. Some put the figure as high as fifty percent."

"Why?"

"Because by not marrying, they protect their family fortunes," replied the Marquis, "but they are normal, healthy men with desires and appetites which must be satisfied. Furthermore Venice is visited by people from both the far west and the distant east. Their sexual preferences may range from the conservative to the bizarre and should be respected." He paused and smiled. "Besides," he added softly, "the licensing of brothels keeps the prices manageable and diverts young men from homosexual alliances."

Knowing the reference is to the accusations of sodomy directed earlier at himself, Leonardo simply nodded and focused his attention on the soup.

The remainder of the meal was spent in silence and quiet reflection.

Will I never escape those accusations? Leonardo asked himself.

The caravan arrived in the Most Serene Republic

very late the following afternoon.

The sight of the city built on water first impressed Leonardo when he visited it with the Moor's court years ago, and he was still amazed at the magnificent buildings lining the Grand Canal and reflected in the water. The brooding twilight sky was an immense canopy stretching from horizon to horizon, and the image of it bouncing back from the canals gave the impression the entire city floated on clouds. He remembered it as an "intimate" city: crowded and criss-crossed by bridges leading to narrow walkways and making it nearly impossible to go through the city without meeting an acquaintance. The Maestro felt this lack of privacy accounted for what he remembered as the Venetian attitude: gossipy, nit-picking, opinionated and conservative. He remembered they seemed to prefer Latin to the "vulgar" tongue and among themselves they spoke a fractured Italian which both surprised and confused visitors. Still he remembered the Venetian people to be generous and fun-loving, tolerant to the point of licentiousness, because – as the Marquis pointed out - "it's good business," and Venice, more than any other city in Italy, existed for business. It was the financial and mercantile center where Europe met and traded with the Ottoman Empire.

It was also, he quietly believed, the one place where he could sort out the mysteries surrounding the Tears of the Madonna, and *that* – more than the development of city's defenses – was why he so readily agreed to accompany the Marquis here.

They had arrived to the bells of the campanile in the Piazza San Marco proclaiming the beginning of a

special *carnivale*, the feast of the Beggar Lords, a time
of grotesque masks and elaborate costumes, of music
and merry-making. Consequently their passage
through the Cannaregio district was slowed and
frequently halted by enormous masses of humanity
decked in fantastic uniforms ranging from the bizarre
to the nearly-naked. They snaked through the streets,
parading nowhere, singing and dancing to drums and
flutes, of pipes and tambourines and hurling small
eggs of perfume and balls which erupted with a loud
explosion and rained paper streamers. It became so
bad, the Marquis again tied his horse to the rear of the
coach and climbed in beside Leonardo.

"I did not remember we would come at the time of
the Beggar Lords," he said as a false egg thrown by a
laughing reveler smashed against the glass of the coach
door and burst, leaving both a blurred mess and the
almost overpowering scent of roses. "It will be
madness!"

"I do not mind," said Leonardo.

No, he thought, *crowded streets and the confusion of
the revelry will serve my purposes perfectly.*

"It is an innovation which began in Rome and
spread everywhere like a plague," the Marquis
informed him. "During the four days of the Beggar
Lords the street will be thronged with revelers
carrying placards depicting a giant crescent moon
overwhelming a miniature earth, the world turned
upside-down. There will be days intended to permit the
poor and the drudge to acquire enough happy
memories to carry them through the dreary days. Even
the most dedicated young men and women, future

priests and nuns, will join with cut-purses, thieves, whores and beggars. They will barge into even the most lavish and spatial palazzi without being stopped. The generational wealthy, the overlords of title and trade, are forbidden to bar their doors, and for the entire days of the Beggar Lords, the revelers in their grotesque masks which makes identification impossible will gleefully and arrogantly re-arrange the furniture, snatch food and drink from the tables prepared for them and then invade the cellars for the best wines which had been hidden away. They will mock the frescoes and the tapestries and perhaps add a few obscene and pornographic art to the walls. They will make communal love in the downy softness of the owners' bed chambers, and sometimes, mind you, they will be happily joined by the mistress of the house or her daughters and sons. It will be chaos."

Leonardo glanced through the coach window at the brazen women laughing and flirting with the *bravi* in the street, and he leaned back against the cushions and thought: *Spectatum veniunt, veniunt spectentur ut ipsae.*

Niccolo would be so proud of my Latin.

The small delegation crossed the western bridge over the Grand Canal and threaded its way through the district of San Paulo. Here the Marquis decided the coach would have to be abandoned if they were to make any progress.

"The streets beyond this Franciscan church and the *Scula di San Rocco* become more narrow and winding," he explained.

One of the officers delivered his mount to Leonardo

which was less a sacrifice than an excuse to meld with the revelers and perhaps have a little merriment.

The horsemen worked their way through the Campo San Paulo, and Leonardo noticed a young boy playing with a toy on the balcony as they passed. It appeared to be a weighted box suspended from a corkscrew-shaped wing. When the boy dropped the box, the wing caught the air and spun in such a way the toy was kept aloft for some time.

If a man replaced the weights, wondered Leonardo, *and the wing was spun by a series of gears and pedals, why couldn't the entire thing rise and fly?*

He decided to sketch the possibility in his workbook when given the opportunity.

The prossession wound its way through the revelers to the Rialto and crossed the bridge spanning the Grand Canal. Drunken men and women passed bottles of wine between two parallel gondolas as they drifted beneath the bridge. On the opposite bank they were in the San Marco district and the horses cantered down the streets named for beans and wine because those were the products hawked by the vendors who lined them.

When the riders entered the Piazza San Marco, a winding ensemble of masked and costumed men and women snake-danced and sent the pigeons flying.

They paused before the basilica known as the "temple of thieves," because Venetian seamen sent by the doge were rumored to have stolen the body of St. Mark the Evangelist from the Islamic warriors guarding it and smuggled it to Venice under a cargo of pickled pork. After the fall of Constantinople the doge's admirals also sailed away with the four bronze-gilded horses and rare marbles now on display in the piazza and with ikons heavy with jewels presently resting inside the cathedral.

They moved slowly toward the doge's palazzo, a fantasy of white and pink marble, and which Leonardo felt was constructed upside-down, because the heavy rooms of the upper floor rested only on thin colonnades. They were permitted through the Gate of the Card, because the guards recognized the Marquis and they were expected. The Mantuans dismounted as a covey of servants rapidly descended the Staircase of the Giants to take the reins of their horses. Leonardo glanced at the huge statues of Mars and Neptune which flanked the staircase and wondered what Fra Savonarola would think of these pagan gods placed to welcome visitors. He lifted the model and the plans he had attached behind his saddle, refused assistance and carried them up the steps.

Guards snapped to attention as the Marquis led Leonardo and his officers through the maze of corridors, up several stairs and directly into the Great Council Hall. Leonardo found himself marveling at the richly-carved ceiling, the abundance of natural light pouring through the huge windows and the frieze of past doges around the upper part of the walls.

He was pleased he could read the Latin beneath the portrait of Doge Martin Faller which informed everyone this man had been convicted and executed 150 years earlier. He was surprised the traitor should still have his image displayed in the great hall, but decided it was typically Venetian.

251

They throw nothing away.

The present doge, as was the custom, was an old man, a scarecrow robed in bulky scarlet and ermine and bent under the weight of several massive gold medallions of authority. Leonardo knew it was a Venetian custom to elect an old man to the highest office so he would never have the time to make any truly damaging edicts.

The Council of Ten were also men of advanced age, robed exquisitely, and assembled in two tiers of high-backed chairs on either side of the doge.

The Marquis bowed and announced "Magnificence and most illustrious lords, may I have the honor to present to you Maestro Leonardo di Piero da Vinci: the famed and noteworthy painter, sculptor, engineer and architect of Florence and late of the courts of Milan and Mantua."

"You are welcome," snapped the doge impatiently. "Now what have you to show us? Our time is limited."

Leonardo bowed, looked at the pale and wrinkled faces before him, and thought: *Indeed it is.*

He removed the model from its container and placed it on the table before the nobles. He unlatched the leather case, extracted the rolled plans and began his instruction. His explanation of how to flood the plains to defend Venice were aided by his model and Jacopo de Barbari's "birds'-eye" map of Venice. He demonstrated his theory of erecting restraining walls, and only then did the doge say, "It is very interesting, Maestro, but we are also concerned about a possible Turkish attack on Cyprus. It could endanger our Famagusta. Are you aware of the problem?"

"The Marquis mentioned it in passing, Excellency, and I suggested the best solution might be to construct special instruments to keep the battlements free of ladders and grappling arms."

"It is a very long wall."

"I know," responded the Maestro. "What I had in mind was a battery of giant forks, each with seven tines. These are attached to winches turned by oxen in underground compartments."

He could instantly sense the suggestion stunned the authorities.

"Giant – forks?" The doge murmured.

"As the basic unit is maneuvered along the base of the wall, it would sweep away invading ladders."

There was a long period of silence before one of the Council of Ten leaned forward and slowly repeated, "Giant forks?"

Leonardo nodded, but it was obvious the suggestion was regarded as ridiculous and absurd. Almost immediately there was muffled exchange of opinions among the Council members and the doge. There was even a little hand-waving and gasping for breath, but to the credit of the authorities, no one laughed.

The Maestro was quickly thanked for his plan and his dedication to the welfare of the Most Serene Republic, given a medallion of merit and informed an armed escort would be assembled to escort Leonardo back to Mantua. He pleaded to be allowed two more days "in your magnificent city to visit the churches, enjoy the frescoes, and converse with your artists."

The suggestion was met with an icy stare from both the Marquis and the Council of Ten, but the doge, considering the request a compliment, smiled and proclaimed accommodations would then be arranged for two more days in order for the Maestro to "visit our cathedrals."

Leonardo returned the smile and attempted a low bow of respect as he mentally compiled his itinerary.

He was not interested in the cathedrals but the house of the Cambio, the island of Murano, and the Campo Sant'Angelo which fed, he knew, into the Street of the Assassins.

The courtyard of the palazzo rang with the heralding of trumpets, pipes and tambourines as Leonardo's apprentices and Niccolo watched the arrival of *I Comici Buffoni* from the workroom windows. They laughed and cheered as Rubini walked on his hands before the first wagon, performed a series of cartwheels and danced like a mad Pan leading his followers to the Bacchanal. Piero Tebaldeo with a pillowed belly and the red half-mask of the Capitano strutted ceremoniously beside the first wagon, waving his ridiculously lengthy sword and shouting of his conquests in every corner of the world. In the wagon seat sat Marco in the dark robes and soft cap as Dottore Graziano of Bologna or Palermo or Padua or anywhere there was a major university to be ridiculed. On the open wagon, Francesco and Isabella sang romantic ballads to one another and appeared utterly devoted to one another.

Beside the second wagon Simone Corio in the diamond suit of Arlecchino danced as he juggled six

254

colored balls, and perched on the seat of the driver was Turio of Verona, the youngest member of the troupe, in the hook-nosed, pale-green half-mask of Pantalone. Appropriately he appeared to be approximately six times his actual age, wheezing and coughing as he flicked the reins. In the second wagon, waving and flirting with the palazzo guards as they passed, Prudenza and Anna Ponti as Colombina and Lesbina, rustled their skirts and tugged the collars of their blouses down enough to arouse even the dead. Now and again they would break into an entirely different song from the ballads being caroled by Francesco and Isabella.

"Wine and wit and women and war. / Apart from these there is nothing more / which tightens the throat and enlightens the heart, / save the welcome explosive relief of a fart!"

Well, Niccolo thought to himself, *at least they haven't changed.*

The Marquesa watched the arrival with Nanino from the windows of her bedchamber. She then turned away, resumed her seat before her mirror and brushed her hair, attacking the knots as if they were mortal enemies being forced into compliance. The dwarf made a sound like a runting pig, deposited himself in a comfortable chair, draped his legs over an arm, speared an apple with his miniature dagger and said, "They seem harmless enough."

"Niccolo will find his time taken up in preparing the company for the festival," said the Marquesa. "This will

255

be the perfect opportunity to have our men search every inch of the Maestro's workrooms and bedchamber for the red book."

"Suppose someone sees us."

"Make certain they don't."

Early the next morning as Leonardo awoke in his lavish apartments, he was greeted by a gaggle of servant women who brought him nourishment, prepared a bath, and laid out his freshly-laundered clothing.

As he nibbled at the prugnoli mushrooms and sampled the thick broth with a silver spoon etched with the first few words of the *Benedicte*, he was surprised by the arrival of a young man who introduced himself as Signore Giacomo Grottino and announced he had "been commissioned" to serve as the Maestro's "guide." He would, he said, "see to it you are not annoyed or embarrassed by the revelers during the days of the Beggar Lords." He went on to explain "during this time of frolic and unusual freedoms, there are some who may exceed the bounds of good taste, become insulting and even intimidating."

Leonardo smiled and nodded and finished his broth as he thought, *the authorities do not want me rambling around their city, probing into dark corners and asking too many questions – which is precisely what I intend to do.*

"Where would you like to go first?" Giacomo asked.

"A costumer's," replied Leonardo. "We may as well

join in the revelry, eh?"

The announcement seemed to stun Giacomo, but soon the two men worked their way through the throngs to a small shop on the Calle Boteghe.

The proprietor, a fat, red-bearded man approached at the first jingle of the bell mounted above the door.

"What is your most popular costume?" Leonardo asked.

"Why, most certainly the Moon God," replied the proprietor, and in a moment he displayed a long silver robe with huge sleeves reaching almost the length of the robe itself, padded shoulders and a high collar. "It comes with a wig of platinum ringlets and that huge Moon God mask depicting the moon surrounded by twenty stars mounted on short flexible wires."

"I'll take it," Leonardo said quickly.

"I only have the one remaining," said the proprietor.

"It's alright," said Giacomo. "Just give me anything."

In a moment he was enrobed in the black costume of a necromancer with a pointed hat flecked with stars. He passed the proprietor some florins and signed an agreement to return the costumes in two days or forfeit all of the rental fee.

The two men no sooner stepped into the Campo Santa Margherita when they were swept along with a flood revelers including at least four "Moon Gods." Confused, Giacomo singled out the one he believed to be the Maestro and followed the moon across the Accademia Bridge.

Leonardo, freed of the doge's spy, abruptly turned in the opposite direction and headed for a five-story building set in the heart of the shopping district. A tug of the bell cord beside the heavy bronzed door, and he stepped into the world of Venetian bankers.

The Cambio attendant met Leonardo just inside the reception hall, asked his name and the name of the person he had come to see, and "requested" he wait. Occasionally stiff-backed young men of obvious prosperity would rush by in their long robes lined in fur, their golden medallions of authority swinging from their shoulders and laden with documents in their hands. They never paused, but made rapid studies of the new arrival, quickly decided he was of no importance and scurried away. Some smiled or muffled laughter, and Leonardo realized he was still wearing the large moon mask, so he removed it, tied it by ribbons at his waist and tried to suggest he was not a reveler come to mock or destroy the banking house.

Finally the attendant returned and was visibly pleased there was a gray-bearded gentleman behind the eclipsed moon. He bowed his head politely and "requested" Leonardo to follow him.

The pair journeyed through two long corridors, up two staircases and along a colonnaded arcade. The door at the end of this walkway was of dark wood and stretched from floor to ceiling. As if by magic, they swung open precisely as the attendant and the Maestro approached.

The room was surprisingly small despite the impressive doors, containing only a dark mahogany desk, one chair behind it and another before it. A smaller desk was at any angle to the larger one and was covered with neat piles of documents. The floor was carpeted and there was one large window bordered by heavy draperies. The walls were bare, no frescoes or tapestries, but a long mirror was mounted on the wall opposite the window which bounced the light back into the room.

Signore Agnolo Marinoni quickly rose from behind the desk, rushed around it and abruptly approached Leonardo who was, at first, fearful he was about to be embraced, but the banker merely came within a yard or two and bowed from the waist. He was encased in a long gold-and-scarlet robe, bound at the waist by a thick leather belt studded with small jewels from which hung the mark of his profession: a heavy leather purse. A scarlet skull cap clung to the back of his head.

"Maestro Leonardo," he bellowed as if announcing the identity of the visitor to everyone in the piazza outside, "I am honored! Honored!" He took a step back and examined the moon robe and the mask now attached to Leonardo's waist. "You are here for the Beggar Lords?" He gestured Leonardo to the chair facing the desk, and as the Maestro obligingly sat down.

"No," Leonardo replied. "The costume was for self-protection."

He was about to explain further when Agnolo erupted with a hearty, "And how is your small companion, Signore Niccolo?"

"I would think you are in a better position to judge that, signore," said Leonardo, "since he has been in your employ for the past few months."

Accustomed to conducting business matters in secrecy, Agnolo flushed. "I assure you our correspondence has been minimal of late! Minimal!

Have you brought a message for me?

"I think you know more about the situation than Niccolo does," the Maestro said softly. "I am certain he told you there seems to be more than one Tears of the Madonna. The Marquesa apparently has one, and so too does Madonnas Lucrezia Borgia and Caterina Sforza."

"Yes, yes, yes," the banker waved a hand as if dismissing the announcement. "We know of the replicas. Our interest is only in the genuine Tears, the necklace carried by our courier. There are some here who even now insist he took the authentic Tears and ran off."

Leonardo opened two or three buttons on his moon robe, reached inside and extracted a folded parchment. He said nothing but passed it over the desk to the banker who unrolled it and gasped. "Why – why it's Cecco! You made a portrait of him! But how? Why? When did he pose for you?"

"He didn't. I made the sketch from a reconstruction of a skull buried in the Gonzaga gardens."

"He's – he's really dead then?" He dropped the scroll on his desk and buried his head in his hands. "Our poor courier! I knew he wasn't a thief! I knew it!"

"Well, I required a verification of my theory. This sketch is truly of your courier?"

Agnolo sighed, dropped his hands to his desk top and sighed. "Yes. It's Cecco." He suddenly glared at Leonardo. "You say his head was discovered buried in the gardens of the Marquis! That means he was assassinated by someone employed by the Gonzaga!"

"I believe he was murdered," said the Maestro

quietly, "by a Venetian assassin known to Captain d'Angeness and Signor Ottaviano Cristani who were in the service of the Marquesa Isabella d'Este."

"Then the Marquesa has both the authentic Tears and one of the replicas!"

"No. I believe for reasons of his own, the mercenary Captain kept the necklace taken from your courier. I believe he – like the noble placed in command of the theft - was of the Janus school here in Venice." He leaned toward the desk. "You know the Janus?"

Agnolo frowned. "Of course I know the Janus! Everybody in Europe knows of the Janus School of Assassins, but no one ever speaks of it. To know too much of the Janus is to court your own destruction. As bankers, of course, we may know a little more than most, because – well – because they need our services."

Leonardo smiled. "That is what I thought, and I need more information. You know their symbol, the small tattoo usually between the thumb and first finger of the left hand?"

"Of course. The two faces of the Roman god turned from each other and separated by a stiletto shaped like a cross. One face smiles. The other doesn't."

"Tell me of the school. Where is it?"

"I don't know precisely," said the banker again leaning back in his chair. "I doubt if anyone knows precisely. Some say it is on the northern coast of Burano. That is an area with only a few houses of the lace-makers and some fishermen's shacks. Some say it is an even smaller island further out in the lagoon. No one ever goes there save for the students who are trained in – well – in a certain special form of assassination."

"Form?"

"As I understand it, a Janus assassin will kill, but it must never look like a killing. It should appear as something accidental. A man run down by a horse. A tragic fall from a window. Someone with too much to drink who falls in a river and drowns. Something which never points to an actual murder, and most certainly never to the assassin himself."

"Where do they get their – students?"

"Orphanages usually. Boys and girls without parents or relatives who are left at convents or abbeys. When they are about ten or twelve, someone appears and after some interrogation and evaluation, they offer to 'adopt' the child. They are whisked away to the island."

"You say they never leave?"

"Oh, they do when they are employed."

"Employed?"

"It is how the school is maintained. Someone needs someone - removed, they go to a certain shop on the Street of the Assassins near the Armory. There is a tavern there with the Janus symbol carved on the lintel above the door. You order a draught of a certain wine which does not exist. You place a purse with gold on the counter and you sit and wait."

"Wait?"

"The gold is counted, and someone is dispatched to the island. There someone is chosen who may specialize in the type of killing required, or it may be a new graduate who has to be tested. A great deal depends on the amount offered. The chosen assassin is then brought back to the tavern, introduced to the purchaser and they leave. When the assignment is completed, they return to the island – unless, of course, they become sponsored."

"Sponsored?"

"In some cases, the assassin becomes 'sponsored.' It means he – or she – there are female assassins – enters the service of the purchaser. With the nobility he – or she – becomes a member of the sponsor's court and may never return to the island. The sponsor not only becomes responsible for the assassin's livelihood, they must also pay a monthly stipend – again in gold – to the Janus. If that payment is not made – or even late – the Janus agent may be turned on the sponsor."

"Ah!" Leonardo sat back in the chair and adjusted the moon mask which had become entangle with the arm. "I assumed the Captain kept the necklace and passed it to Ottaviano, because he was offended by the way the Marquesa interfered with the planned attack on your courier. I thought it was due to his sense of pride, but it may well be the Gonzaga were late or had stopped paying the Janus, so he was given permission to punish his sponsors."

"It is a possibility," nodded Agnolo. "I assume this Ottaviano was sponsored by the Marquesa and not her husband. I mentioned before, the treasuries of the nobility suffer from wars and their refusal to be more prudent about their expenditures. In the confusion of war they cannot collect taxes, and yet they do not budget themselves. They build palazzi and make generous contributions to Rome in the name of the Church. They support armies and legions of courtiers who do nothing and live as if they deserve everything."

"Then," said Leonardo as he combed his beard with one hand, "I think we can assume with some certainty at least, Ottaviano was also a Janus assassin."

"Perhaps," shrugged the banker. "If he was a member of the Gonzaga court, it is possible. Usually the identity of the assassin remains a strict secret known only to the sponsor. The Borgias, however, do not mind identifying their principal assassin from the Janus. It is Michelotto, in service to Duke Cesare. They make certain everyone knows who Michelotto serves and what he does. The fear serves the family well."

"Then," the banker mused, "I think we can assume Ottaviano, either for pride or because he was permitted by the Janus, must have recovered it from him! It belongs to us!"

"He, too, is dead. I believe he was systematically poisoned."

"Why?!"

"Because the Marquesa found out he had kept the necklace. She could not have him tortured without the Janus finding out and sending another of their brotherhood to avenge the school. Knowing the Marquesa would have him watched and generally make life intolerable for him, he learned earlier he had already been poisoned and, considering himself a proud member of the society, hid the necklace and informed the school. When he died, the Janus sent representatives to bring his body back to the island."

"Then the Marquesa is most certainly doomed. The Janus will be avenged! Unless of course - ."

"What?"

"There is another assassin, another Janus graduate in the Gonzaga court who is *not* sponsored, someone planted in the inner circle of the nobility and whom the Janus would maintain, one who is not merely an assassin but also a source of information, and in such circles, information is worth more than gold. The Janus could use such information to bring about the collapse of the entire court and profit by selling the information to the enemies of the Gonzaga."

"I don't understand."

"It is not uncommon. The nobility sponsors a Janus assassin who becomes a sort of court killer. This is the one the nobility must support and for whom they pay the monthly stipend to the school. But there may be another, perhaps secured independently, whom the court may maintain but are not required to pay the Janus. That one is actually a Janus spy and may not even be known to the sponsored assassin as from the same school. He – or she – is there especially to provide the Janus with information of the court. If it also involves a little murder, so be it."

Leonardo shook his head. "This is becoming more complicated. I had hoped you could provide some enlightenment to the matter, but all I have learned is Ottaviano *was* a Janus assassin, and he probably kept the authentic Tears. My question now concerns these replicas of which apparently the Cambio was always aware. Would you please enlighten me as to their history? Who made them and why?"

"I don't know," said the banker. "We only know there were three replicas made, because from time to time, over the years, they have been used for collateral, but they were proven copies, because they do not conform to the proper weight and light-reflection of genuine diamonds."

"But they cut glass."

"They do."

"How?"

"We have no idea."

Leonardo suddenly stood and said, "I think I do, but I will not take up any more of your time, Signore Agnolo. You have clarified a number of things for me, and I am grateful."

Agnolo was instantly on his own feet. "But wait! Wait! Please, Maestro, where is the genuine necklace? How can we recover it?"

Leonardo sighed, unfastened the mask of the moon god from his waist and started toward the door. "I'm not certain," he said. "But if it is where I suspect, you may never see it again."

"But - !

The banker surged from around the desk, but Leonardo nodded a farewell salute, opened the door and put on the mask again as he strode down the walkway.

The banker stopped, mouth open, and only repeated, "But - ?!"

When Leonardo stepped back into the street, he was swept along by the revelers heading toward the Street of the Spice Dealers. They surged across the Academia Bridge and into the San Marco district. Surprising himself, the Maestro was able to squeeze through and dodge a mob until he found himself where he wished to be: at the Fondamente Nuove. Here a line of boats waited to transport passengers anywhere they wished to go without having to wait for the "water buses." Suddenly something struck him in the back of the head and he was drenched in perfume! He wheeled to face a young, masked woman, naked to the waist and draped in paper streamers. She laughed at him from her perch on the pedestal of an equestrian statue and yelled, "Ho, Man-in-the-Moon! Are you looking for me?"

He shook his head, and he was immediately pushed aside by a young man dressed as Satan with two curved horns attached to his half-mask and a short scarlet cape fluttering behind him. The girl laughed again and leaped into the devil's arms. As the laughing couple permitted themselves to be swept along by the tide of revelers, Leonardo turned and caught a glimpse of himself in the glass window of a shop.

For a moment he studied the bizarre image of a pale moon with bouncing stars, sighed and said quietly.

I'm too old for carnivale.

N iccolo was reunited with the commedia players and exchanged pleasantries. After hearty embraces and compliments on how well everyone looked, the young courtier managed to warn the company against "stealing the silverware as you did in Milan." He advised them the Marquesa would not be as indulgent as the Moor who had been preoccupied with fleeing the city when the light-fingered players "acquired a few souvenirs."

"The Marquesa will pay you well," Niccolo lectured, "so at least try not to make off with anything of exceptional value."

"Well," Prudenza snorted, "it is a matter of tradition, a cherished habit of centuries, but I suppose we can indulge you – especially since you may become our Giangurcolo someday."

"But first you have to grow a little more," smiled Simone.

When the troupe met formally with the Marquesa in the *camera degli sposi*, the players were appropriately awed by the painted courtiers who seemed to have dimension and substance and who smiled or glared at them from all four walls and from the ceiling.

"Do you realize," Simone whispered to Francesco, "if we could make a curtain like this, we could carry an appreciative audience with us!"

Isabella was radiant, and projected the image of a cultivated woman of culture, refinement and wealth. On either side of her chair of authority, Nanino and Lizette stood like miniature royalty, Nanino in his repaired gold uniform and Lizette in an elaborate silk gown with puffed sleeves, an overskirt lined with brocade and a velvet petticoat after the French style. On her head of curls she wore a velvet coif and fall edged with pearls.

Niccolo was fascinated.

"What will you play?" Isabella asked.

"I don't know yet, Excellency," said Simone.

Niccolo felt the need to explain. "You see, Excellency, the *commedians* do not work from a set manuscript. It is not like a play by the mummers or the guilders who usually perform scenes taken from the Bible. The gift of these players is their ability to perform *ex tempore* an entire entertainment based on a single sentence."

The Marquesa frowned. "But how, then, can we be certain the amusement will not be – well – inappropriate for the court?"

"We will submit the *soggeto*, the outline on which we will improvise, well in advance, Excellency," said Simone. "If you find it – offensive – then we will consider something else."

The Marquesa forced a smile to her face and said, "Fine."

Later, when the troupe was sequestered in a large salon, Niccolo suggested the amusement be based on the theme of 'a false diamond'.

"What?" Turio frowned.

"For example," Niccolo explained, "let us suppose Pantalone's daughter, Isabella, is about to be married to Francesco, the son of the Capitano, but the groom's father insists on an appropriate dowry. Pantalone's prized possession is a fabulous jewel, perhaps a diamond, and the Capitano insists it should be given over to him before he will permit the wedding. The old miser is, of course, reluctant to part with it, so he has a copy made of crystal. Just prior to the ceremony, however, Dottore Graziano discovers the fake and is

269

about to reveal the truth to the Capitano when Arlecchino, Scapino, Prudenza and Lesbina – who want the marriage to commence – perform some comic maneuvers which so confuses both Pantalone and Dottore they cannot tell the jewels apart. They give the genuine to Capitano, the marriage is made, and only then does poor Pantalone discover he is left with the fake!"

There is a long moment of silence as the company stares at the young courtier.

"Amusing," Simone finally says, "but strange."

"Very strange," mutters Anna.

"Extremely," Rubini growls.

"I don't get it," frowns Francesco.

Prudenza slaps her thigh and roars. "Where do you get such weird ideas, Niccolo?"

Niccolo smiles and performs a mock bow to the troupe. "From my mother wit."

Dottore shakes his head. "She should let me examine her."

Only four of the seven passengers embarked on the landing at Murano, and only two of these were costumed and masked. Leonardo had abandoned his personna as the Moon God, and was now more comfortably embedded in his customary black robe under a long hooded cloak and his favorite felt cap which squatted on his graying hair like a floppy cushion.

He had successfully lost his shadowy "guide" who had been ordered by the doge to stay with the Maestro while in Venice, and Leonardo imagined he was even now standing before the old ruler and his Council of Ten, and attempting to explain there were too many revelers costumed the same identical way, and he followed the wrong one.

On this, the island of the glass-makers, the celebration was more subdued and restricted to a few of the larger Piazzi. Leonardo was able to ask directions of a fisherman perched on the edge of the wharf, and soon made his way through a tangle of narrow passages to his destination.

A tug on the bell cord was answered almost at once by a young man who performed the same function as the attendant at the Cambio. He inquired of the Maestro's name and who he had come to see, but Leonardo refused to divulge his purpose in being here and simply said, "It is a matter of some urgency."

The young man walked away, and very soon returned with another man: tall, muscular with a tangle of red hair only now beginning to fade into earth-brown. He wore a white smock and gloves which he removed as he extended a hand to the Maestro.

"Maestro da Vinci! What a surprise! What an honor! Come in! Come in!"

He gestured the Maestro to accompany him, and the three quickly passed through a small corridor and into a large room filled with masterworks of colored glass delicately nested on shelves which lined two of the four walls. There was a comfortable couch before a low table, two other larger chairs and a huge window which looked out on an inner courtyard.

The muscular man turned to the young attendant

and commanded, "Refreshments! Bring some refreshments! And the best wine! This is exceptional! It is an honor to have such a guest!"

The attendant left and his host beckoned Leonardo to sit with him on the couch.

"Forgive me for not introducing myself! I am so pleased to meet you! My niece has told me so much about you and how kind you were to her in Mantua! I am Giovanni d'Oggione, grand master of the glaziers' guild, and of course I am familiar with your work and your reputation."

"Your name and work are familiar to me as well," said Leonardo. "I have seen some of your masterpieces in both the Sforza and the Gonzaga courts, and naturally in many fine homes in Florence."

"You honor me," smiled the glazier.

"Not at all," the Maestro replied. "And how is your niece, Madonna Maddalena?"

"She is betrothed! To a young Belgian guildsman with a small fortune and a promising future."

"Signore Johannes?"

"Yes! You know him? Oh, of course you do! She told me how you befriended them both in Mantua."

"Did she tell you why she left the Mantuan court?"

"Yes," Giovanni frowned. "Nasty business. She sent me a letter saying she was actually in fear of her life! That's when her father and the young Johannes' father put their heads together, and the couple were smuggled away before the Marquesa even knew they were gone!" He sighed. "Frankly, Maestro, we were very worried when her father sent her to be educated with the Gonzaga. We thought she might take into her head to marry one of those prancing dandies whose only worth is a centuries-old name and a decaying castle in some God-forgotten part of the world where the cold winds whip off the North Sea or somewhere. But now she is in Brussels with her father and the young son of a diplomat of the Hanseatic League negotiating for her marriage."

He suddenly erupted with a hearty laugh.

"Wouldn't you like to hear that? Such haggling, eh? Imagine! An Italian and a Belgian! In the end it will be the Belgian way of course, because they deal in diamonds and we only in glass."

"It was glass which brought me here," said Leonardo quietly. "Was Madonna Maddalena a frequent visitor to your studios?"

Suddenly there was a shift in Giovanni's attitude. The laugh disintegrated into a faint smile. "Why do you ask?"

"Because I think her knowledge of glass and how it is made may have something to do with the 'nasty business' in Mantua. I think she and Signore Johannes both knew something which put them in danger, something which encouraged the Marquesa to humiliate and threaten them to a degree where they would want to abandon the court. And yes, I think if they hadn't left, they both would have been murdered."

Giovanni stared at the Maestro for a long time, and then they were interrupted by the arrival of three young women bearing trays of cold meats and bread, jellies and pastries and large crystal flagons of deep-ruby wine. They placed the platter, the dishes, napkins and utensils on the table, curtsied to Leonardo and were gone.

Giovanni did not move to enjoy the food and drink, but he gestured Leonardo to do so, and the Maestro – who suddenly realized he was famished having spent the better part of the day in the Cambio and on the boat to Murano – quickly made some choices, filled one of the crystal glasses with some of the wine and began to eat.

"I – understand," the glazier said softly. "I think I know what you are after, and yes, Maddalena was often here watching us work. After all, Maestro, her father and four of her uncles were master glaziers! We all live here on Murano. That is a strict provision of our guild. Each of us and our families must live on this island to maintain our secrets. It is our own little world. Supplies of soda and lime are barged here twice a month."

He reached and took a small sliver of ham and dropped it into his mouth.

After a moment he continued. "You understand how glass is made? Of course you do! A man of your knowledge and curiosity! We take soda, lime and sand; heat them in our furnaces to a high temperature until they are like gelatin, dip our rods into it and blow until the glob begins to harden. We turn and twist and shape the glowing mass until we achieve what we want, and then we – snap! Break off the globe, quickly rasp down the rough edges and set it to cool. It is a process which requires years of training, concentration and secrecy."

Leonardo wiped his lips with the linen napkin embossed with the sign of the glaziers' guild.

"It is your secrets which intrigue me. Would young Maddalena know for example how you work with diamonte."

The statement obviously took the glazier by surprise. "Diamonte? What do you know of diamonte?"

"It seems I am always asked that question when I inquire about anything," said Leonardo. "It seemed to shock Signore Johannes too." He placed the crystal glass on the table and said quickly, "I am not interested in the material itself. I know of the diamond dust, the residue after master Belgian jewelers cut the facets and polish diamonds. I only want to know if you – your guild that is – have actually mastered the process of bonding the dust to glass."

"What will you do with the information?"

"Nothing," says Leonardo quickly. "Believe me. I simply have to know with some degree of certainty you and your guildsmen have mastered the process."

Again there was a long moment of silence before Giovanni replied softly. "Yes."

"And," said Leonardo with what he hoped was a reassuring smile, "and you have used this process at certain times and upon specific instances to produce false crystals which can actually cut glass."

"Yes."

The Maestro emitted a long sigh of relief.

"I know you are cautious, Maestro Giovanni, but I promise you, nothing you tell me today will ever be repeated to anyone other than my friend and associate, Signore Niccolo da Pavia, and only to him, because he is involved with the 'nasty business' at the Mantuan court, and it may be something which can save our lives."

The master glazier sighed, studied Leonardo and

finally nodded. "I trust you."

"Thank you, Maestro," said Leonardo. "And now what I have to ask you is something even more delicate, something more – dangerous – if you will. It must come from the records of your guild which I understand are highly secret; but I promise you again, what you tell me I will take to my grave. It is something I vitally need."

Giovanni nodded again and asked softly, "For what purpose, Maestro?"

Leonardo studied the man, this master artist whose entire world was based on the secret processes and the materials used to make – not just glass – but colorful wonders of rainbowed crystal in a thousand different shapes.

He said softly, "For enlightenment."

CHAPTER EIGHT

REVELATIONS AND RESCUES

Leonardo was welcomed back to the Gonzaga court by the Marquesa and Meneghina, both of whom were surprised when the coach and the armed escort arrived in the courtyard to find the Maestro had returned alone.

"His excellency regrets," explained the Maestro, "he is needed in Venice. The doge has mobilized reinforcements, and the Marquis is again in command. You have heard, of course, the French and their allies have recaptured Milan, and the Venetians are coming to reinforce the city."

"No," said the chancellor softly. "We – we were not informed."

"Yes," said the Maestro as the three entered the palazzo together. "Il Moro, I am informed, was taken captive at Novara and immediately sent to prison in France." His voice softened. "And all the projects for which he contracted me are destroyed – or unfinished."

The Marquesa stopped abruptly, turned to face the Maestro, and smiled. "You're certain the bastard is imprisoned?"

"In France," said Leonardo. "He has lost his state and

277

his property forever, and as I understand it, the Contessa Caterina is in another French prison."

Impulsively, shockingly, Isabella shrieked, "Good! Good! At last there is an end to the Sforza power in Italy! Good! Good!" She reached and clutched the Maestro's gloved hand. "Thank you! Thank you for bringing such welcome news!"

Just as suddenly, the mood shifted to one of contemplation.

"I only wish Gian Francesco were here to share the moment, but I understand his obligations to the doge. I have continually postponed the spring festival hoping he could attend, but now the people will have an additional reason to celebrate."

When Leonardo and Niccolò had an opportunity to be alone, the young man described how the days were spent during the Maestro's absence. He skirted anything involved with his deepening relationship with Lizette, detailed a recent exchange of insults with Nanino and told Leonardo of the arrival and the coming performance of *I Comici Buffoni*.

"I do not think the Marquesa will be thrilled with the theme," he said, "but I believe the court will find it amusing. At least I hope so."

Leonardo described the doge's disdain for his plans to flood the Venetian plains and erecting a machine of tined arms to clear battlements of ladders and grappling hooks. He spoke of the madness of the Beggar Lords and his encounter with the young woman who bombarded him with an egg filled with perfume. He mentioned the fall of the Moor from the ducal throne of Milan and expressed his remorse at never having completed any of the wonderful plans they imagined together. He brooded again over the destruction of his model city and the huge clay model of the equestrian statue to honor the Moor's father.

"Has the Marquesa complained I have not completed her portrait?"

"She does not seem disturbed by it," Niccolo replied. "Her principal mood has been one of anger. She shrieked at the guards who permitted Signore Johannes and Madonna Maddalena to leave the court without her permission."

"A performance," said Leonardo. "Actually she was trying to force the two young people away before they might accidentally reveal something about the Tears of the Madonna – or at least the origin of the three replicas of the necklace."

"There are three replicas?"

"Yes."

It was apparent the young courtier wanted to know more, but Leonardo suddenly shifted the conversation away from the Tears.

"The red book. You still have it?"

"Yes."

"May I see it? Where have you hidden it?"

Niccolo smiled.

"In plain view."

He crossed to a work table where three books were nested between the clay bust of the Marquesa and two of the Maestro's note books. He brought the three to

Leonardo and handed them to him one by one.

"Book one: Epictetus."

Leonardo took the book, opened it, nodded and closed it.

"Book two: *The Meditations of Marcus Aurelius.*"

Again the Maestro took the book, repeated the process and placed it aside.

"Now," said Niccolo, "book three: the mathematical principles of Euclid."

Leonardo opened the book, frowned at it, flipped quickly through the pages and then looked at Niccolo.

"It's the red book!"

"Of course," said Niccolo with an obvious display of pride. "I waited until our rooms had been searched, and then I removed the binding of the Euclid and placed the red book in it. I knew the searchers had gone through these texts before and were not about to examine them again. Further, any other curious person is not about to investigate a book on mathematical formulae."

Leonardo frowned. "And the actual Euclid text?"

"Oh, it isn't harmed. I have it wrapped in a blouse in my room."

Suddenly Leonardo tore the binding from the pages, crossed to where a slow fire was burning in the open hearth, and one-by-one he ripped the pages and fed them to the flames.

Niccolo quickly crossed to him. *"What are you doing?!"*

"The Moor is imprisoned, and this time it will mean his death."

The Maestro dropped the rest of the pages into the

fire.

"The red book no longer has any value to anyone."

*

In her bedchamber the Marquesa sipped a pale-yellow wine from a silver goblet and breathed a heavy sigh.

"Did you find it?"

The dwarf prostrate on Isabella's bed, said, "No. We went through everything in the workrooms and the Maestro's bedchamber while he was gone. Nothing. Perhaps he carried it with him."

The Marquesa took another sip of the wine and placed the goblet on her dressing table. She studied her face in the mirror for a moment, picked at a blemish on her face and then, realizing the flaw was in the mirror, leaned forward and removed the small piece of soot.

"Well," she sighed, "it is really of no consequence anymore. With the Sforza family tucked finally and forever in French prisons, the red book has no value."

Suddenly the dwarf sat upright on the bed. "That means - !"

"Yes," Isabella said quietly. "The captain of the escort tells me Maestro Leonardo 'disappeared' for one day while they were in Venice. I suspect he may have visited the Cambio, and I am afraid he may have learned a little something about the Tears. Something which could affect the value of my necklace and embarrass me before the courts of Europe." She looked at the dwarf in the mirror. "With the red book of no further value, I see no reason I should not – remove the threat - while the Maestro and his pet buffoon are so conveniently in residence, eh?"

The dwarf smiled and said excitedly. "An accident?!"

The Marquesa took one final check of her appearance, picked up the wine goblet and stood, turned and smiled.

"Such unfortunate things do happen," she said.

"When?"

"When I say they will."

That night Leonardo and Niccolo dined with the court on a lavish meal ordered by the Marquesa to honor "the return of Maestro Leonardo to our court." She informed the company much of the meal had arrived in kegs of ice from her husband in Venice and labeled "gifts of the Adriatic."

In keeping with his custom, the Maestro picked at the salmon both baked and smoked, roasted whale tongue smothered in an orange sauce, cakes made from the meat of both oysters and crab, the crayfish, brill and herring which were half fresh and half salted, the fillets of carp and the lobsters broiled scarlet and tucked among a sea of steamed mussels. He served himself more abundantly with the artichoke hearts, the sweetbreads and frogs' legs, the prugnoli mushrooms and the soup of pigeons and almond paste.

In homage to the Maestro, the *commedia* troupe seated at a separate table devoured everything placed before them and whatever else they could pilfer from the platters as the servants marched past. In the style of the best magicians, they made the stuffed Lombard geese, the songbirds roasted on spits and the pasties of pheasants totally disappear

Unhappily, Niccolo watched as they performed the same trick with a gold salt holder, several forks and two crystal carafes.

That night, the two friends had the first opportunity to sit before the warming fire in Leonardo's bedchamber and discuss what he had learned in Venice.

"To begin at the beginning," said the Maestro quietly, "the Cambio courier was killed by the Venetian as ordered by Signore Ottaviano. The signore was himself a trained and disciplined assassin from the Janus school in Venice. The courier had received the authentic Tears from the Marquesa, made certain it was authentic, because he *weighed* it and did not rely on the customary short method of simply using it to cut glass."

"You keep referring to it as the authentic Tears," frowned Niccolo. "Then there are copies?"

"Three."

"How did that happen? Who made them?"

"The master glaziers of Murano – under orders," said Leonardo. "The original necklace was made in Brussels by the diamond masters for a special client." He smiled at Niccolo. "Let's test that fabled memory of yours. According to what the Contessa Bergamini and Signore Agnolo told you, where did the Tears of the Madonna first appear?"

283

"It was a possession of a Spanish grandee, Juan Domingo de Borja"

"Good! He is the one who had the necklace made in Brussels. And then - ?"

"It was brought from Spain by the man's son, Alonzo de Borja, who was then bishop of Valencia and who later was elected Pope Calixtus the Third."

"Very good," Leonardo grinned as he ran his fingers through his beard. "Your ability to recall conversations or anything you read is nothing short of phenomenal. I suspect it has something to do with your ancestry or the way your brain is constructed."

Niccolo returned the smile. "Well, if I die before you, you may dissect it and find the answer, but until then, just let the process continue without bloodletting."

Leonardo actually laughed. Only the second time Niccolo had ever evidenced this miracle. "I promise," he said finally. "Now. What do you know of Calixtus the Third?"

"Nothing."

"Well, I do. While we traveled I read a history of the papacy, and it seems Calixtus was the pope who took a solemn oath on the occasion of his elevation to the papacy. An oath he personally would fund the crusades to save Christendom from the threat of Islam. He saw this as a divine mission, but unfortunately he didn't have enough money. He ordered all the gold and silver bindings in the Vatican library melted down. He sold Vatican art works and even silver salt cellars and gold plate from the papal table. When a great marble sarcophagus was discovered under the floor of Santa Petronilla he ordered it opened and discovered two coffins lined with silver and two bodies wrapped in gold brocade with solid gold ornaments around them. He immediately demanded all the gold and silver melted down to fund the cause."

"And - ?"

"It wasn't enough. Armies are expensive."

"So what did he do?"

"He sent solicitors to all the courts of Europe threatening ecclesiastical penalties if the wealthy families did not contribute to the crusades what he considered a fair amount. It still wasn't sufficient, so he took one more step. Do you remember where the Tears next appeared?"

"In the possession of King Alfonso of Naples."

"Bravo! Well done! Yes!"

"So Calixtus sold the Tears to King Alfonso."

"I didn't say that."

"What?"

"In deference to fact, I believe you were told the Tears were 'listed among the jewels sold to Alfonso'."

"Don't play games with me, Maestro," Niccolo snapped. "Did the pope sell the Tears to Alfonso or didn't he?!"

"Now we must deal with some probabilities," replied Leonardo softly. "You see, Calixtus had a nephew whom he had elevated to the Cardinalate, a man of cunning and deception: He was Rodrigo who changed the last name of the family to 'Borgia' when he too became the present pope."

"So what role did *he* play in all this?"

"That's what I meant when I said we must deal with some probabilities. I find it difficult to believe Calixtus

285

conceived the plan. He was dedicated to the *concept* of the crusades. He made personal sacrifices for the cause but I cannot believe he was the originator of the plan. I think it must have been Rodrigo."

Niccolo's exasperation was becoming evident in his tone and volume. *"What plan?!"*

Leonardo ignored the impatience. He deliberately slowed his narrative as if to indicate such matters of judgment should not be rushed. "It was simplicity itself. Alfonso offered a large amount for the Tears. Suppose the necklace could bring *equal contributions* from the leading families of Italy, families like the Sforza and the Gonzaga!"

"Do you mean - ?"

"Precisely. Rodrigo went to Venice, to the master glaziers of Murano, whose secrets included the art of melding glass to diamante, the diamond dust produced when cutters shape and facet their jewels in the diamond centers of Europe. He came with the authority of the pope and offered a small price but full plenary indulgences for the workers and their families, indulgences which could be passed down through the generations along with the family treasures. I learned this from the records of the glaziers guild."

"Then he - ?!"

"Had three replicas of the Tears made."

"But – why three?"

"Because there were three specific families the pope intended to honor with the Tears, for a sizeable contribution to the crusades."

He smiled.

"Besides, the Church thinks in threes: its theology

centers around a trinity, three distinct personalities in one divinity. The papal crown has three tiers. Christ was in the tomb three days. The *'mea culpa'* is pronounced three times in the liturgy of the Mass, and the breast is struck three times. There were twelve apostles, a number divisible by three. There are three strands of diamonds in the Tears."

"Number games!"

"They can be significant. Don't be so quick to condemn mathematical solutions, my young friend. I told you truth is always in the mathematics."

Leonardo sighed and gazed into the fire for a long moment.

"The point is: evidence from the records of the glazier's guild indicates Rodrigo ordered three replicas made. The Murano glaziers christened them the Father, the Son and the Holy Spirit. The replicas were sold for a large sum of money to three wealthy families, demanding of course the sale should never be made public, because there could be a schism if the faithful realized their pontiff was selling Church property. Remember Calixtus' oath was: he would finance the crusades from his own pocket."

"Then Calixtus sold a replica to King Alfonso."

"Of course not. Calixtus may have *agreed* to the plan, because he thoroughly believed in the crusades, but it was not in his nature to sell anything but the genuine necklace. No. It was Rodrigo who sold the replicas to the other families. Calixtus sold Alfonso the *genuine* Tears!"

"How do you know that?"

"Because the Tears which the Marquesa gave the

courier *were* genuine. The courier tested them by weight and light refraction as he was instructed by the Cambio, because over the years the bankers discovered there were replicas, and they insisted on the *real* Tears."

"But – how did the Marquesa get the authentic Tears?"

"The Contessa told you. You remember? How did she describe Isabella d'Este?"

Niccolo paused a moment and then said, "She told me the Marquesa was – let me think – yes. She said the Marquesa was 'a legitimate daughter of a prince, Duke Ercole of Ferrara.'"

"And her other?

"Eleanora – of – of *Aragon!*"

"Excellent! Yes. Calixtus sold the *genuine* tears to King Alfonso of Aragon who passed them to his daughter, Eleanora, who in turn passed them to *her* daughter, - Isabella."

Niccolo frowned again. "But – wait! The contessa said King Alfonso gave the Tears to his wife, Ippolita Sforza, on the occasion of their marriage, and that is how – no! Wait! She said *'supposedly'!*"

"There must have been some confusion about the Tears even then," said Leonardo. "According to what I have uncovered, Rodrigo sold replicas to the Sforza, the Gonzaga and the Riario, and they found their way through other courts. Naturally the families would insist on their Tears being authenticated, so they were given the universal test: *they cut glass*! What they did *not* know is that the replicas were treated with *diamante* – diamond dust. They would cut glass, but the authentic Tears were the only ones which would register the proper *weight.* So the Marquesa found herself with one genuine necklace and one replica. The *real* Tears had to be handed over from the Marquesa to the Cambio courier. He tested them by both weight and cut glass, and informed the banking house by pigeon he had the genuine necklace and was returning with it."

"Leaving the Marquesa with only the family replica."

"Yes," Leonardo nodded. "And this is where we must deal with more probabilities. Surely the Marquesa wanted to recover the *authentic* Tears. So we know now the courier was murdered by the Venetian who was sent by Ottaviano to recover the genuine Tears and make it appear the courier had simply run off with them. But now there is a problem. The original plan was for the Venetian - a trained assassin from the Janus school and sponsored by the Gonzaga - to do the job *alone;* but for some reason the Marquesa was given some cause not to trust her assassin. That possibly came from her favorite, Nanino, and the Toad took authority and sent mercenaries with instructions to join the Venetian. The trained assassin considered this insulting, but he was in no position to countermand the Marquesa's orders, so he accepted the new instructions and had to carry out the assignment with mercenaries." He paused and seemed to be putting his thoughts together in an orderly progression. "I believe he and his captain of mercenaries were first to enter the room. They killed the courier and the Venetian found the necklace and hid it in his cloak. The Captain

289

saw it, and they agreed on a plan. They would say the courier must have hidden the necklace, and they ordered the others to search the room for it. When they completed their destruction and found nothing, the Captain ordered them to take the body, decapitate it so it could not be identified, and he took the head back to Mantua and buried it in the garden. Then he reported to Ottaviano who – in turn - reported to the Marquesa the courier had *not* been carrying the necklace. She was suspicious, but what could she do? She quietly had the rooms of the Captain and Ottaviano searched, but she could not find the genuine Tears, because suddenly things went wrong. A young officer present at the murder had a spell of conscience, began to drink, and was taken to the dungeons and tortured. He said the Captain and Ottaviano had the Tears. Ottaviano, seeing the truth coming out, killed the Captain to cover his tracks, buried the Tears in a requiem candle, and they were taken to a local church."

"Then what happened to the diamonds?"

"Be patient. By now the Marquesa was convinced Ottaviano and the Captain had lied to her. So she simply set out to eliminate anyone who could associate her with the murder and theft, and Ottaviano was routinely being poisoned! Ottaviano learned about it too late, and quietly accepted the inevitable, but he did manage to get a message to the Janus where the real diamonds could be found. He felt he had completed his mission in the traditions of the school, and he was satisfied."

"So the authentic diamonds went to the Janus."

Leonardo shook his head. "No. That is the irony of it

all. Remember Ottaviano said some of the Lenten Gifts were too valuable to remain in the abbeys or the small convents? Well, that is precisely what happened. The candles were intercepted by the bishop who sent them – of course – to Rome."

"To Rome?!"

"Yes, and so the *genuine* Tears of the Madonna are back where they began their journey: among the Vatican treasures. And I suspect that is where they will remain for centuries - along with *two* of the replicas: the one which found its way to Caterina of Imola – let's call it The Son - and surrendered to Cesare Borgia, and the replica – the Holy Spirit - which had already been passed down through the Vatican treasury – the ones Lucrezia wore for the Holy Year. The Marquesa was left with The Father."

Niccolo erupted with a deep sigh. "What deception! What intrigue!"

"It gets more complicated. To the Mantua court comes Signore Johannes for 'seasoning," but he had another assignment: to test the Marquesa's Tears to see if they were the genuine ones which would mean the Marquesa was responsible for the murder of the courier. He was assisted by Madonna Maddalena who knew from her youth of how diamante could be used to pass a replica as genuine. The Marquesa discovered his real purpose, and first humiliated the young man with the hope he would abandon the court before her necklace could be examined, and then she attempted to have him killed in the hunt. That's when I learned of his real purpose, and I advised him to leave the court at once - which he did."

"I can't wait to tell the Contessa."

"Ah!" Leonardo said again. "That may pose another problem."

The court performance of the *commedians* was scheduled for the Great Hall in the early evening on the second day of June. The troupe had been playing in the Mantuan streets while they waited to be summoned by the Marquesa, and now - an hour before the scheduled performance - Meneghina brought Niccolo a letter, folded and sealed. He did not respond when asked who sent it, and instead informed the young man, "I must make haste. The Marquesa will be expecting me to accompany her in my robe of authority. I will be late!"

And he was gone.

Niccolo broke the seal and was immediately rewarded with the scent of roses. He recognized this as a device often used by lovers to make certain their notes were not intercepted. Once the seal is disturbed, usually by the use of a heated blade inserted beneath the wax so as not to ruin the embedded insignia of the sender, the scent is released. The fact Niccolo could now smell the roses assured him Meneghina or Nanino had not interfered with the document.

He read: "Your life is in danger. The Marquesa is aware of what the Maestro learned in Venice. She is about to set loose her mongrels upon both of you. There is one hope. I have made arrangements which could result in your safe and silent departure this very night. Please – please! Meet with me at the indoor arena of the court stables as soon as the players begin their entertainment. The Marquesa and Nanino will be watching the performance together, so I will not be missed. Come and I can explain what must be done immediately for you and Maestro Leonardo to escape safely. Trust in our friendship, and be very, very careful."

It was signed, "Your Lizette."

The performance began with Pantalone emerging from behind the curtain with an enormous crystal which he cuddled in the warmth of his arms and then held to the light with both hands.

"Oh, my beloved," he cooed. "My dazzler! My snatcher of light! Oh. Friend of my youth and protector in my old age, how I adore you! I worship and honor you and promise we will never, never be parted by anyone or anything! Even should death come for me, I will look to you and tell him, 'Hell no! I won't go!'."

The laughter began.

Niccolo slipped away and quickly dashed down the corridor to the door leading into the courtyard. There was a full moon, and the thought of Lizette risking her life to save his aroused in him something, if not an amatory fire, at least a warm devotion. His walk became a trot as he remembered the days when the pretty dwarf was his only companion, when the

Maestro was gone and they walked and talked together and played teasing games. She knew how to make him laugh which was no small accomplishment. Life with her had been an amusement which, he reasoned, was no small thing.

The trot became a race across the gardens to where the stables welcomed the members of the court to either ride or demonstrate their abilities as friends and guests watched. He spied the light seeping under the service door at the far end of the arena, the iron walkway to the roof where workers serviced the ceiling chandeliers and checked the condition to prevent rain leaking through.

I'm coming!

In the elevated front row of the arena designated for court members to watch the equinary skills of their fellow nobles, Lizette waited patiently for the arrival of her young friend. Her eyes were on the door at the far end of the dirt floor through which she knew he would come to answer her summons. In her gloved hands she held the important white handkerchief. When she dropped it, the groom would open the gate and release Pazzo, the unfortunate stallion who had been teased and tormented by children over his years as a foal. Seeing the diminutive young man, the crazed animal would charge and stomp the young man to death. The door through which Niccolo would enter would be closed and barred from the outside by Lizette's companion and lover, the other principal female dwarf.

"Surprise! Am I late?"

The jubilant voice came from *behind* her which confused and startled her. She dropped the handkerchief over the railing, reached quickly to recover it, but lost her footing, fell over the small railing and tumbled down to the soft sand of the arena at the very moment the groom released Pazzo! The little woman, terrified but alert, instantly started toward the service door, but the crazed horse, seeing another small tormentor, galloped toward and over her, stopped, whinnied defiance and proceeded to bring his hooves down upon the lifeless body again and again.

Niccolo, who had decided to surprise Lizette as they often did to one another, had climbed the roof, opened the trapdoor used by the workers and slipped down onto the elevated back row of the observation area. Now he watched in horror at the raging and shrieking beast prodding Lizette's broken body deeper and deeper into the sand and the wooden floor beneath it!

The groom equally horrified because he understood this was simply to be a demonstration of Pazzo's ability to respond to whip and rod, realized why the animal had reacted so violently and gestured Niccolo, another small man, to stay in the observation deck lest the horse would see him and attempt to leap into the seats. Cooing softly as he approached, the groom gradually calmed the animal, reached and recovered the training bridle and then took the linen from his back pocket and blindfolded the animal. Continuing to whisper into Pazzo's ear, he gently, gently led the horse away and closed the gate behind them, leaving a bloody trail.

Speechless, Niccolo waited until the area was safe,

leaped over the railing and ran to the spot where the broken and shattered dwarf was only a collection of flesh, broken bone and blood obscenely gurgling and forming a scarlet lake.

Only then did he spy the twisted and broken, delicate hand, it's pretty lace torn and ripped away to reveal the small tattoo between the thumb and the first finger.

The mark of the Janus school!

Stunned, he found himself barely breathing as he approached the service door only to find it barred.

"Wait!"

It was a familiar voice.

There was a rattling and clanging, and there was Leonardo in the ridiculous attire of the Moon God! He drew back the panel and said softly but with emphasis, "Hurry! The performance did not exactly please the Marquesa. She did not find a theme of duplicate diamonds amusing and has ordered the players rounded up and sent packing. Her minions are also searching for *us*. If we hurry, we can join the criminals and possibly save ourselves!"

Still stunned, Niccolo muttered, "It was Lizette! She's also of the Janus."

"Yes," the Maestro said calmly. "When I was in Venice I was told the Janus had another agent in the court beside Ottaviano. I wasn't certain who it was, but it is obvious now your Lizette was the Marquesa's agent – and probably the real leader of the dwarves; but we can iron all this out later. We have to run."

Niccolo, still stunned, nodded and murmured, "Again."

*

Hours later, with the dawn beginning to stretch fingers of light above the horizon, the two wagons of the *I Comici Buffoni* raced through the Piazza Sorello and out the city gates. Only when they turned onto a barely recognizable path made by the carts of merchants did they slow, and by this time they were in the grooves of the tracks made over the years and surrounded by trees and heavy shrubbery.

"We can afford to slow now," said Simone to the five performers behind him in the first wagon. "If the Marquesa sends mercenaries after us, they will assume we ran for our lives toward the Alps and sanctuary." He laughed and added, "We were fortunate the guards did not think to ask why our little troupe suddenly included a Moon God."

Behind him, Leonardo stripped away the silver robe and the mask. "It was fortunate I kept the costume, although the doge's spy was probably forced to pay for it when he returned his own robes of a necromancer." He turned to where Prudenza and Anna had removed Niccolo's trousers and were unstrapping the special stilts which had convinced the guards he was of normal height and just another comic member of the troupe. "I am sorry about Lizette. I tried to warn you. I told you what Giovanni told me: sometimes the Janus plants another member of their organization with the family who sponsored their assassin. I doubt if even Ottaviano knew Lizette was of the Janus. His job was to kill. Hers' was to gather information, but when the Marquesa commanded her 'little monkey' to kill you, she had no choice. Remember: by the code it would have to appear an accident."

Niccolo was plainly still in distress. "I – I never thought ...!"

"Of course," said Leonardo as he scratched his beard which had been gathered under his moon mask. "But it should have become obvious when we found poisons among my herbs and potions. Who had access to our workrooms? Not Nanino who came only once, and not Meneghina who came only when summoned. No. It had to be the pretty little dwarf whom you obligingly welcomed there."

The young courtier emitted a low moan.

"Don't be too distressed," the Maestro commanded gently. "She was clever, and your defenses were down with such a friendly and frivolous young woman."

"Speaking of defenses, Maestro," Simone yelled from the drivers' seat. "Where specifically are we to go when we reach the mountains?"

"We are to turn and take another route south, preferably to Florence where I am known and still have a workroom."

"South?" The leader of the troupe shrieked. "Back into the hornet's nest?!"

Leonardo worked his way past his young friend and the two women and came behind Simone. "The hornets will not pursue us," he said softly. "Not if the Marquesa received the message I left on my workroom table for her."

"Message? "Niccolo called. "What message?"

Leonard smiled. "I do not have your remarkable gift of precise memory, Niccolo," he said. "But - briefly –

when I was in Venice I took advantage of the Doge's newly organized service for the transmission of messages between Venice and Brussels. I dispatched to our friend Johannes a complete compilation of what I learned about the Marquesa, the Tears, and her trained assassins. I included my sketch of the courier's reconstructed head, and told Johannes if anything should ever happen to me – or you - within the next few years; if there was any report of either of us, meeting with 'an accident, he was to send the material to the Cambio, and that reputable firm would take instant action against her and the Mantua court for the murder of their courier and demand the return of the Tears."

"But – she doesn't have the Tears," said Niccolo. "All she has is the Father replica. The genuine Tears are, according to you, back in the Vatican treasury."

"And so they are," nodded the Maestro, "and there they will remain. But if the Cambio applies pressure on the Marquis to produce *true* collateral for the Moor's loan - which they will - Gian Francesco will have to dig into his treasury. This would be an absolute disgrace: to have to recompense the Cambio for a loan made to his enemy, but he would be forced to comply, because the bankers now had the evidence his wife caused the death of their courier and the loss of the genuine Tears. If he failed to honor his wife's commitment, every bank in Europe would refuse him funds to conduct his wars, and in *that* instance, I would not be surprised if Gian Francesco would not turn on his wife and use it as an excuse to put his unloved spouse away, possibly to a convent which would be - of course - a home in hell for a woman so used to wealth and power."

Niccolo smiled and leaned back into the plumb arms of Prudenza. "And there," he said, "what will the Madonna do but shed genuine ..."

The passengers voiced the word simultaneously and loudly.

"Tears!"

THANK YOU FOR YOUR REVIEW

I know, unless you are among the relatively small number of readers who "love" to write reviews, it seems like a daunting task.

I feel the same way and yet reviews are the life blood of authors and so I would like to make it easier for you.   Just a few sentences can make a huge difference.

I liked the book because:
I learned something new:
  About Leonardo da Vinci,
  the Renaissance,
  other historical figures not familiar with,
I would recommend it to:
I look forward to the next book:

Thank you for participating in the review process.

GEORGE HERMAN A FUNNY MAN!

George Herman and the Great Depression were born at approximately the same time. The Great Depression was born on Wall Street, and George was born in a small house in Norfolk, Virginia. No one ever convincingly demonstrated a cause and effect. His birth was originally intended for April fool's day, but fate was distracted when ATT shares dropped 100 pints in two minutes.

His mother died soon after his birth and his father's older brother swept the child away to Baltimore, Maryland, thus thoroughly confusing George as to whether he was a Southern Gentleman or a Damned Yankee.

Here he progressed from childhood to permanent adolescence.

George attended the local parochial school where he was awarded 17 holy cards and set a national record for having his hands shredded by five-foot nuns yielding six-foot rulers. Holy cards (for those unacquainted with Catholic ways) were similar to baseball cards; one St. Francis of Assisi was worth

two St. Sebastian's or four Theresa of Avila.
Nevertheless here he had his first play, *A Christmas
Choice*," produced in a classroom. Here, too, he first
appeared on stage in playing the lead role of Beppo in
The Magic Whistle which enjoyed a highly successful
run of 45 minutes.

He spent four years in Mt St. Joseph High
school in Baltimore where he won writing awards and
edited the school newspaper. He also took first prize
in a four-state news-writing competition sponsored
by Temple University by applying the now-
unfashionable method of putting who, what, where,
when and how in the lead paragraph. This was about
the time he looked up from his writing desk and
discovered girls which – as Robert Frost put it –
"made all the difference" for the next few years.

Still too young for the WWII draft, he was
rescued from juvenile delinquency by Jesuits who
offered him a chance at Loyola University. Here he
wrote and directed a musical called *Marelyn* which
was the way everyone pronounced the state's name.
This led to a three-summer theatrical scholarship to
Boston College, so he was able to complete college in
three-and-a-half years with a degree in philosophy.
This prompted his father to ask, "You can make a
living at this?" He couldn't, but the point was moot,
because the United States Army decided it was his
turn.

Using the GI Bill after serving two years he
matriculated at Catholic University. "Matriculated"
refers to attendance and does not necessarily indicate
a transfer of knowledge. Here he won the Hartke

303

Playwrighting Award for his one-act comedy, *The Pygmalion Effect,* and his musical version of Mark twain's *Huckleberry Finn* was produced on the main stage and described by one local critic as "the students prance." In 1954 he wrote and directed a musical production which was performed before President Eisenhower and several drunken celebrants of the Friendly Sons of St. Patrick. A year later he received his master's degree in Fine Arts, again arousing the same question from his father, "you can make a living at this?" Again the answer was obvious, so George spent a year touring with a theatrical company playing Shakespeare and Moliere and seldom winning – even in overtime.

To be continued...

To learn more about George or if you would like to be informed of new books coming out go to:

www.georgeherman.com   and   click   on   the Newsletter tab.

THE NEXT BOOK
ARTISTS AND ASSASSINS

Paintings burned and slashed
Statues pounded to dust
Leonardo fears for his life

*The third adventure of Leonardo da Vinci
and Niccolo da Pavia*

BUT FIRST THERE IS MURDER IN THE VATICAN

"WHERE ARE THE TORCHES?"

Nineteen-year-old Alfonso of Aragon, the flaxen-haired Duke of Bisceglie, posed the question to his two younger pages as they stood together in the black expanse of the Piazza di San Pietro in Rome. The sun had long since descended into the Tiber, and the violent spring cloudburst which had pummeled the streets and alleys in the earlier part of the evening were now rivulets dropping into the cavernous sewers beneath the ancient city. The Duke could see the pitch torches and lanterns which usually spread a carpet of light into the Borgian apartments in the Vatican were unlit, and the nervous wind gave voice to the gloom, whispering soft warnings.

Alfonso considered the possibility the torches had been extinguished by the rain, or had never been ignited. He recalled the *illuminare*, a lazy youth from Lombardi, had failed this simple assignment twice in the past month.

"Sebastiano forgot to light the torches again," he said.

"But the sentries are not posted either, Excellency," whispered Marsilio, the younger page.

The Duke brushed aside a curl of chestnut hair escaping from under his velvet cap. He peered intensely beyond the small circle of light provided by the lamp held aloft by Marsilio, and noted the pontiffs' armed sentries, normally situated every 30 paces around the periphery of the square, were not in their customary stations. This surprised and alarmed the young Duke who sometimes envisioned the papal guards to be carved of marble, supporting the pope, Alexander VI, as the stately columns propped up the crumbling porticos of St. Peter's.

The Duke's yellow-and-scarlet hose and his fashionable doublet trimmed in gold brocade were unable to protect him from the chill, and he trembled under his light cloak. He glanced over his shoulder to see the thick gray haze spreading from the dark surface of the Tiber like an army of vengeful Roman spirits, rising to protest the current demolition of their ancient homes and temples. He deliberately blinked his eyes and pressed two fingers against the bridge of his nose, attempting to dispel the mental fog created by the Muscadine and Pauillac he consumed in the Medici palazzo earlier in the evening. He silently cursed himself for not insisting the Cardinal deposit him at the nearest arch instead of this distant portion of the piazza.

He cursed himself for not having taken the advice of his wife and stayed to home in the first place.

He wondered now if she had anticipated something, and if her suggestion had actually been a veiled warning.

There was a jingle of small bells and the quick shuffling of sandals against the wet cobbles, and the young Duke realized there were others sharing the piazza with them. He placed his gloved hand on the shoulder of his senior page, Gino, to steady himself. He was conscious his medallion of authority and heritage, suspended from his shoulders on the thick gold chain, might afford a glittering target should the invisible others prove hostile, so he momentarily distanced himself a little further from the lamp.

He was about to order Marsilio to extinguish it entirely, when he realized the illumination provided might help him to mark the other shadowed occupants, and, if necessary, to better defend himself against attack.

The Duke held out his gloved right hand, and immediately Gino offered him the *espada ropera*, the swept-hilt rapier. Alfonso was encouraged by the weight and balance of it in his hand, and he whipped at the darkness around his feet, causing the night to shutter.

The red-haired senior page permitted the emptied scabbard to drop to his side as he slipped his stiletto from its sheath. His right arm was stretched before him, slowly moving his blade from side to side as the serpents' way of movement before striking.

There was another sudden jingle of the bells and the slow, sonorous chanting began. The metered phrases echoed from the surrounding walls, a mournful litany endlessly repeated, swelling in intensity with each repetition like muffled thunder announcing the coming of a distant storm.

"Ky-ri-e El-e-i-son"

The invisible chanters maintained the last two syllables until they became a plaintive wail.

"What is it, Excellency?" Marsilio asked, the lantern trembling a little in his hands. "Who are they?"

"I don't know, Marsilio," the Duke replied softly, still struggling to throw off the remnants of the evenings' diversion. He drew his *main gauche*, the left-handed dagger, from its scabbard in the small of his back. He thrust both blades before him, preparing to meet any threat after the Venetian fashion with a weapon in each hand.

"It sounds as though they might be mourners, Excellency," Gino said softly as he slowly swung around behind his master.

"This late at night? And in white?"

As their eyes slowly became accustomed to the dark, the three young men realized they had been completely encircled by figures in long white robes, dimly emerging like ghosts from the tomb, melding with the heavy grave mists rising from the river. Their deep cowls were raised and pushed forward, creating voids were faces should be. Their waists were encircled by thick cord sinctures, but the customary rosaries were not in evidence, and there was neither a cross nor a crucifix suspended from their shoulders.

The Duke studied the encircling band. He realized, with some alarm, they seemed to be slowly but relentlessly spiraling forward, like the pattern created by a whirlpool, chanting as they slowly tightened the ring.

"Ky-ri-e El-e-i-son"

Then, as suddenly as it had begun, the tingling bells and the mournful chanting stopped, and the resulting silence seemed even more ominous and alarming. The Duke was conscious of a dog barking hoarsely somewhere in the distance, and he noticed the river fog was creeping more rapidly over the cobbles toward him and his pages like disembodied fingers in thick, gray gloves.

"Who are you?" The Duke demanded. "What do you want?"

There was no reply.

The unarmed Marsilio stepped between his master and Gino. With his thumb, he turned the large silver ring on his finger, an heirloom from his father; then with both hands he stretched to raise the lantern still higher above the heads of his companions.

Suddenly, as if silently commanded, five or six of the robed men surged forward, and by the flickering light of the lamp, Alfonso caught a glimpse of the up-raised clubs and blades poised to strike.   Trained by masters in the courts of Naples and Aragon, he responded instantly!

Bedlam!

Battle cries and curses thundered through the piazza. Blades flashed like small lightnings in the light of Marsilio's lamp as bodies hurled themselves against one another with muffled groans and grunts.

Men shuttered in sudden pain and open wounds sprayed blood over the attackers and their targets like a baptism of scarlet water!

Alfonso was engulfed in a whirlwind of clubs and flailing arms. He skillfully parried blows from both sides, remembering his training of *repost, thrust, faint, thrust again*. His forward leg advanced with the quick even pace of a dancer, and he felt his rapier's blade strike, bend slightly and then penetrate an opponent.

The wounded man emitted terrifying, guttural roars as he staggered back into the path of those behind him.

The young Duke quickly withdrew his bloodied sword and retreated, wheeled, caught a glimpse of an approaching blade, and feinted, drawing his opponents point away from his body. He lunged, steering his rapier's tip toward the hilt of the assailant sword. The attacker's weapon was wrenched from his hand and sent spiraling into the darkness.

The young noble slowly became conscious of a sharp sting to his right shoulder and another to his right knee. Veils of blood soon clouded his left eye and obscured some of his vision. The weight on his right leg produced stabbing agonies. His entire left arm was dangling and useless.

Still he and Gino continued to thrust, turn and circle, keeping the terrified Marsilio between them, the younger page continually shrieking, "Help! Assassins!"

Engrossed with his defense and in spreading pain, Alfonso was not aware first Gino, and then Marsilio, collapsed in bloodied pools. There was only a moment to glance at the dark scarlet of their blood flowing into the streams of rainwater toward the sewers and the river.

As the younger page fell, his lantern crashed against the stones of the piazza, and the oil spread rapidly over the wet surface. Some of it splashed against the robes of two of the monks who became human torches. Screaming and shrieking in agony, they twisted and pirouetted like crazed puppets desperately dancing at the ends of their strings.

Some of the attackers reached to seize their blazing companions and pulled them down to the wet cobbles.

The fire created the small barrier of bright flame and intense heat which momentarily separated the Duke from his attackers. He saw a path open briefly to his right, toward the steps leading to the second floor arcade. Instantly he pivoted and hobbled across the square, momentarily colliding with two of the robed assassins as he struggled to reach the stone staircase.

He ascended, in short and painful hops, to the narrow passageway and from this elevated position, he became aware of lanterns and torches suddenly blossoming in the darkness below him.

Half-dressed papal guards were pouring from their garrisons on the ground floor. Armed with pikes and swords, they roared the alarm as they sprinted toward the attackers over the broken bodies of the fallen pages

Alfonso could see most of his assailants were now struggling to carry off their wounded and burned comrades. Simultaneously he became aware perhaps three of the more relentless had pursued him up the staircase and were racing toward him the length of the passageway. He felt about to collapse but he realized the narrow confines of the arcade gave him an advantage, so he turned again to face his attackers.

Suddenly there was a tall, black-bearded man at his side, flailing and advancing against the assailants. In a flood of light from somewhere behind him, he saw his savior's familiar double-edged Schiavone blade slice through the assassins.

He recognized his benefactor as the guardian of his wife, the quiet Venetian condottiere known by one name.

Sangreal.

As the two men continued to thrust and parry, the attackers wavered, backed away, and finally fled down the length of the passage, stumbling and falling and rising again as they attempted to support their injured companions.

Alfonso turned to the light pouring from the open door and marking a golden path across the tiled floor of the passageway. Through the cloud of blood and pain he saw the woman silhouetted in the opening. He staggered forward, dropped his rapier, and held his arm out to the lady for support, but the loss of blood siphoned away the last of his strength.

He crumbled at his wife's feet and was wrenched into the dark.

Would you like to be notified when this book becomes available? Copy the link:
https://www.georgeherman.com/subscribe.html

Cover art

BY
Kit Seaton

Kit Seaton is a multi-talented artist I met in Cour d'Alene Idaho when she was designing costumes for one of my plays "Nine Dragons." I was so impressed I asked her to create designs for the book version of the play published by Tuttle. Available in hard cover on Amazon.

Ms. Seaton is now teaching art in Savanah Georgia and has illustrated a children's book "Otto the Odd and the Dragon King.

To Find out more about Ms. Seaton:
http://portfolios.scad.edu/kitseaton
http://kitseaton.com

Printed in Great Britain
by Amazon